LADD
SPRINGS

Dianne Venetta

LADD SPRINGS
Book #1

Ladd Springs Series:

LADD SPRINGS ~ #1
LADD FORTUNE ~ #2
HOTEL LADD ~ #3
LADD HAVEN ~ #4
LOSING LADD ~ #5

Other novels by Dianne Venetta

Romantic Women's Fiction
The Gables Trilogy:
JENNIFER'S GARDEN
LUST ON THE ROCKS
WHISPER PRIVILEGES

Women's Fiction
CONDEMN ME NOT

Ladd Springs
Copyright 2013 by Dianne Venetta
ISBN: 978-0-9884871-1-6
Publisher: BloominThyme Press
Editor: Best Foot Forward
Cover Design: Jaxadora Design

Acknowledgements

They say that in every book you'll find a piece of the author, and Ladd Springs is no different. The eastern Tennessee mountains hold a special place in my heart. The setting is gorgeous, the ambiance serene—the creeks and rivers, hiking trails and fishing holes—it's made for some memorable moments with my family and friends.

Dedication

This book is dedicated to the Good family.

Thanks for the memories!

Meet the cast of characters of Ladd Springs...

Ernie Ladd ~ Owner of Ladd Springs

Albert Ladd ~ Ernie's brother

Susannah Ladd Wilkins~ Ernie's sister (deceased)

Jeremiah Ladd ~ Ernie's son, forsaken from the family

Delaney Wilkins ~ Ernie's niece, daughter to his sister Susannah

Felicity Wilkins ~ Delaney's daughter

Nick Harris ~ Hotel developer interested in buying Ladd Springs

Clem Sweeney ~ Neighbor conning Ernie for title to Ladd Springs

Ashley and Booker Fulmer ~ Susannah's best friend & her husband

Annie and Casey Owens ~ Jeremiah's ex-girlfriend & her daughter

Candi Sweeney ~ Clem's sister, Annie's best friend

Travis and Troy Parker – Neighbors and friends of Felicity

Fran Jones ~ Owner of Fran's Diner, aunt to Annie

Jeb and Willie ~ Cohorts of Clem

Chapter One

Crouched in the Tennessee mountain brush, Delaney Wilkins pushed up from her knees and moved farther into the thicket for a better view. Beneath the canopy of laurel and oaks, the scent of wet earth and decomposing leaves rose thick in the air around her. She craned her head to look between the trees. Some blackened, others gray, trunks stood in varying stages of decay, victims to the slew of storms that ripped through the area several years back. And among them, two strangers. By the outline of their build, the rough jerk to their movements, they appeared to be men. But gender didn't matter. Trespassers were trespassers and they were on *her* land.

Delaney held her breath, suppressing all thought but one. No one was supposed to be in *her* part of the woods. Did they venture too far off the USFS trail and get lost?

Her instincts hummed. The USFS was public land. It was possible. But these two seemed too intent on whatever it was they were doing to be lost hikers. She could hear their voices but was unable to make out the details of their conversation, or what—exactly—they were doing. *Damn it*, she had to get closer.

A quick survey of her surroundings told her the answer wasn't here. Not unless she wanted to take up cliff diving down the slope before her, causing a ruckus that would obviously reveal her presence. Delaney scanned the upper ridge beyond the men. The trail behind her would take her to the top, but it was a twenty minute hike at a good clip. But they could be gone by then. She dropped her focus back to the strangers. There *was* one other way. She spied the narrow trail leading off to her left. It was a footpath she had forged years ago, one created as her secret weapon in games of "hide and seek" played with her cousin, Jeremiah Ladd. At one time, she had used the trail to kick his butt. At the moment, it would serve to get her thirty feet closer. Unfortunately, the pace she'd have to travel to remain undetected would have to be excruciatingly slow.

Delaney considered her options. Her Palomino, Sadie, was tied to a post at the base, the landmark her family had built to mark the opening for this trail. If she had to get anywhere fast, she knew Sadie would take her. Physical confrontation didn't concern her—not with a pistol holstered snug in her boot.

Gravel and sticks crunched behind her. A thunderbolt of fear slammed into her. Shooting hand to boot, she whirled, ready to pounce.

"Hi," came the hushed greeting.

With a sharp intake of breath, Delaney recovered from the initial shock and took in the unexpected sight of Nick Harris, the real estate developer determined to buy her family's property—*but what the hell was he doing here*?

There, in the middle of the path, the six-foot-four man stood like a fool.

"Get down," she hissed, her pulse continuing to hammer as she waved him toward the ground. Surprise swirled around a sudden suspicion teeming in his swarthy black eyes as he spied the hand sliding free from her boot. With a quick check on her quarry, she growled under her breath, "And be quiet!"

Squatting, he glanced in the direction she'd been looking and asked, "What's going on?"

"Nothing," she said, her focus darting between him and the men. "Why are you following me?"

"I saw your horse tied to the post and became concerned."

"Don't be."

Across the woods, the men rose to their full height and it was then Delaney got her first decent look at them. One was tall and bulky, the other was short and wiry. Wearing tattered cowboy hats and dirty T-shirts, they weren't tourists. Were they squatters?

Laughter punctuated the quiet, drawing Nick's quick attention. "Who are they?" he demanded.

"Don't know," she replied, wondering what the men would do next.

"Let's get out of here." He pulled at her arm. "Those men could be trouble."

Delaney shot him a hard glance and jerked away from his grasp. "Those men are trespassing on my land. If anyone needs to get out of here, it's them."

"Don't be ridiculous," he said. "If they're trespassers, you need to call the police."

She scoffed at the notion. Calling the police would not help her discover why they were here. It would only alert the men to the fact that she was onto them. The larger man suddenly slapped the shorter on the back and said something, but not loud enough for her to discern even a word. Within minutes, the strangers collected their belongings and took off in the opposite direction.

Delaney shot to her feet. Where were they going? That trail didn't lead back to the government forest land. *It led straight back to her cabin.*

"I'm getting you out of here," Nick said, his voice closing in on her back.

Delaney wasn't going anywhere, especially with Nick Harris. "I'm going after them," she said. Right after she searched the area below where she'd first seen the men.

"Oh, no you're not." Nick encircled a large, firm palm around her bare bicep.

Hot and unwelcome against her skin, his hand tightened. The hair on the nape of her neck prickled in rebellion. She looked up into his face, noting his thick brow gathered in a storm of its own. "Excuse me?"

"I'm not about to let you run off and chase after strangers. Those men could be up to no good."

"You're damn right they are—and on my property!" Delaney yanked her arm, only to find it immovable. "Let me go," she spat.

"No."

At the force of his objection, she stopped. Glaring at him, Delaney performed a rapid assessment of the situation. While trained in physical defense, taking on the over two-hundred-some pound muscular Mr. Harris was not what she wanted to be doing at the moment. She wanted to get over there and find out what those two men had been doing. She wanted to follow them to see where they were going. She stared up at Nick, her displeasure intensifying as she noted the hint of amusement in his eyes. "Why are you here again?"

"I told you. I saw your horse back there without you on it." He relaxed into a smile. "I became concerned."

Dimples carved into his cheeks on either side of his mouth, compliments to the slight cleft in his chin centered within his angular jaw. Black-brown eyes appeared seamless beneath his heavy brow and deeply tanned skin. With his short, dark hair rich and full, combed away from his face, his appearance was one of rugged masculinity that seemed right at home in these woods. But this was Ladd land. Her land. He had no business interfering.

"My whereabouts and well-being are none of your concern," she said, making no effort to conceal her annoyance at his gallant show of male dominance, "and I hereby officially relieve you of duty. I can take care of myself, thank you."

"I'm not leaving without you."

She grumbled under her breath. She could stay and protest, wasting precious time, or she could feign conciliation and take Sadie after the men. No doubt they were taking the back way out. Nick didn't mention anything about a horse of his own. Delaney savored a private smile, a plan forming in her mind. There was no way he could stop her once on horseback. "Fine," she retorted and headed back toward the trail, taking the incline in three long strides.

Once on the path, she walked as fast as she could, eager to lose him.

Nick caught up with her easily, matching her stride. "Do you have much trouble around here with trespassing?"

"Some." Boots jarred her legs as she navigated the hard-packed, uneven clay, littered with rocks and roots. As they walked side-by-side, Delaney couldn't help but notice her five-foot-five inches and a buck twenty in weight were dwarfed by comparison to Nick.

"How do you handle it?"

Anger rose hot and fast in her breast and she turned on him. "Why? So you can map out a response to silence the trouble, once you swindle the property from my uncle?"

"I'm not trying to swindle the property," he said, his tone measured and even, as though it required effort for him to remain calm.

"Aren't you? Ernie already said *no*. Why are you still here?" she asked, taking him in from the side as she marched down the trail, passing an opening that revealed a cascade of water. It crashed over rocks and gullies and fallen logs, making its way downstream. Flooded with sunshine and white-caps, Zack's Falls was one of Ladd Springs' many assets.

Nick raised his voice over the roar of waterfall. "I'm a patient man, Ms. Wilkins. I understand he needs time to think it over. I'm willing to give it to him."

"You don't know my uncle."

"Why don't you tell me about him?" he asked, his voice drenched in friendship and camaraderie. "I'm not a bad guy. I'll make it a win-win proposition for everyone."

Delaney didn't like the abrupt switch from rawhide to velvet. Nick was trying to con her and she was not a woman easily conned. Well, not anymore anyway. "No sale," she told him.

Nick raised a brow. "Excuse me?"

"You heard me." She flipped her face up to meet him directly. "No sale—in every sense of the words."

Delaney didn't speak for the remaining ten-minute trek to her horse. She had nothing more to say to the man. He was here to get her uncle to sell his property, land that bordered the Tennessee/Carolina state line on one side, the public forest managed by the United States Forest Service on the other, and was chockfull of rivers and creeks, waterfalls and springs. She'd grown up on this land, buried her mother on this land. In her family for over six generations, this property was not only priceless but of sentimental value. None of which Mr. Harris cared about. He wanted to develop it, build some fancy hotel and spa and exploit the natural resources of the property. He didn't care what it meant to her family. But that was neither here nor there. Uncle Ernie would not sell to an outsider. At least they had that much in common, Delaney mused sourly, as she pushed a branch out of her way.

The trail opened to a small patch of grassy field, tall strands of willowy green littered with tiny purple and yellow blossoms, butterflies hanging low and plentiful. Between here and the property, a river flowed, the same one that wound down along the trails from Zack's Falls. Sadie neighed at the sight of her owner and shook her blonde mane in excitement. Heartened by the sight of her mare, Delaney begged off. "Thanks again for your concern, but I'll be okay from here on out."

He eyed her warily. "Where you headed?"

"Back to the cabin." As if it was any of his business. She grabbed the worn leather bridle and unwrapped it from the post. Holding it in her left hand, she seized Sadie's mane and hoisted herself up and on, sliding into a seated position behind the horse's neck. Delaney gently pulled the reins secure and looked down at Nick. It occurred to her that this was a much better view of the man. A handsome man, but a meddling one nonetheless. "See you around."

"Doesn't it hurt to ride without a saddle?"

"Not a bit," she replied. In her book, there was no other way to ride a horse. After a quick rap to her rump, Sadie took off at a gallop, tail waving high and proud.

Nick crossed arms over chest and watched her go. Delaney Wilkins was like poetry in motion. A natural on bareback, she rode with the fluidity gained by a lifetime of experience. Not only did she move as one with her horse, but her skin glowed with the same silky suede coloring of her Palomino, her white blonde hair—a similar glossy mane in both length and style—crashing in waves down her back as she rode. Her light brown tank revealed fit upper arms, small round breasts and a narrow waist. Then there were her jeans. Nick felt a surge in his loins. He'd never met a woman who wore a pair of Levi's like Delaney did—rough, ragged, the ripped edges of white thread shredding around her heavy brown boots—boots that looked to be the one and only pair she owned. Yet somehow he found the shabby attire sexy as hell.

She was sexy as hell. Which would be a bonus if he could convince her to stay on and manage the stables of the hotel he planned to build. *And he would build it.* Ernie Ladd was a tough old goat, he'd give him that. But when it came to negotiating land deals there was no one better to get the job done than he. Patience was a virtue. Setting fire to greed was part of the process. Nick understood that once the kin-folk got wind of the money he was offering, they'd press the old man to sell. Legacy was a powerful driver. But dollars were more powerful.

Nick began the haul back to the main house for another go-round with the old man. He hadn't added a single new property in almost five years, but after the gem he'd opened in the rain forests of Brazil, it was understandable. Visions of a particular brunette slipped into the forefront of his mind, stirring the pot of need. Feisty and fantastic, she had been a great distraction, but so had his attorney. Nick beat the big guys to the punch in securing a property in South Americas' largest growth market. Fueled by the rising domestic traveler in search of eco-luxury, property values had exploded, but so had his headaches as he fought lawsuit after lawsuit. Most were bogus claims stating he didn't receive proper authorization from the Brazilian government, while others were straight-up accusations of corruption. None of which were true. Nick played by the rules, even agreeing to the extortion tactics for financial contributions to the Amazon rain forest preservation fund. As the leader in boutique eco-hotels, he was more than happy to make these financial contributions. It was his business to conserve resources, work his hotels into the environment with minimal impact. He simply didn't like to be forced to contribute or be accused of skirting the law. Mandatory anything rubbed him the wrong way. But then again, he had learned a long time ago, greed usurps all. A concept to which his investors were not immune. The pressure to produce was on. Between expensive litigation and a weak economy, Nick needed to inject new excitement into his hotel chain, and Ladd Springs would do the trick.

Chapter Two

Nick returned to the farmhouse, the main estate on the property—if one could call it that—and found the man in question sitting in one of two threadbare rockers. The woven backs were torn from years of use and neglect, much like the wood-framed home where eaves hung precariously from rusty nails and posts were scarred by chips and nicks. The floor itself was warped and split, as though someone built the house a hundred years ago and hadn't touched it since. It was lived in, but not cared for, much like the owner himself. Nick considered the old man, rocking back and forth in his chair, pipe dangling from the corner of his clenched mouth, and could only imagine what the house looked like on the inside, but he didn't expect an invitation to be forthcoming.

Nick strolled up to the porch. He cleared his throat and donned a friendly tone. "Hello, Mr. Ladd."

Ernie Ladd regarded him with a guarded stare. "What do you want now?" he spat between the hard line of his lips.

The Ladd clan weren't an affable bunch, that was for sure. Even the good-looking ones. "I've come to talk."

"We ain't got nothin' to talk about, I already told you."

Nick pasted a smile on his face, a move handy when met with hostility. "I understand. It's a lot to think about. Have you discussed it with your family?"

"No and I ain't going to. There's nothin' to discuss."

"Who you talkin' to, Ernie?" A younger man walked out of the house, allowing the screen door to slam closed behind him with a loud whack. He was slim, early-thirties, with a scruffy jaw that matched the old man's. The lines in his face were softer, but just as uninviting. Was this Ladd's son?

"This here land-poacher," Ernie griped back.

"Huh?" The younger man's expression zipped closed. "What are you talking about?"

Ernie pulled out his pipe and pointed it at Nick. "This here fella is trying to rob me of my land, that's what I'm talkin' about."

"Whoa..." Nick held up his hands. "I'm not trying to rob anyone of anything. I'm offering to buy the land, for a pretty penny I might add." The last part he directed toward the stranger.

"You call that pretty?" Ernie leaped to his feet with more agility than Nick would have believed him capable. Standing on two legs that looked like sticks with knots for knees stuck into work boots that looked three sizes too big, and with his black belt sash pulled high and tight over a bump of a belly, he glared. Beneath his ball cap, Ernie Ladd's ears poked out and his eyes popped with fury behind large horn-rimmed glasses sitting on the edge of his nose. The man was so bony, so pale, Nick swore his cheeks were about to push clear through his skin. "It's called stealin', is what it is!"

"Calm down, Mr. Ladd, calm down." Last thing Nick needed was for the old man to die of a heart attack. "We can talk price if you want. I'm willing to discuss what you need."

"He don't need nothin' from you," the younger man piped in.

"And you are?"

"The name is Clem. Clem Sweeney and I'm here care-taker of this property and close personal friend of the family."

Caretaker? But he thought Delaney took care of the grounds. The horses, for certain, though he recalled mention of another female tied to the property, a friend or neighbor. Was this Clem related somehow?

"It don't matter," Ernie grumbled. "I'm not sellin' to the likes of him."

"It's not yours to sell." Delaney strolled around the edge of the house and trucked up the side steps. All the men turned to her. In no hurry, she appeared more tired than agitated, her long hair pulled back into a ponytail, accentuating the round of her cheeks, her button of a nose. Other than mascara, she wore no makeup, made no fuss with her appearance. But then again, a woman as beautiful as Delaney Wilkins didn't need the help.

Ernie scowled at her. "Hell it isn't."

"It belongs to Felicity," she said, fatigue escaping in a soft sigh. The rise and fall of her breast became a magnet for his eyes. "Ashley is my witness."

"That woman is crazy. She don't know a thing."

Ashley? Nick turned and caught Clem staring at Delaney, with a flicker of fury. Was there bad blood between them?

"She was my mother's best friend. I'd say she knows a thing or two about the situation." Delaney looked to Nick then, brown eyes flashing like a cat's. "Either way, you're not part of the equation, Mr. Harris. I'd kindly suggest you begin searching for another property."

Sounded like a dismissal to him. Too bad he didn't take hints well. Nick stood firm. "I offered a fair price for the land, Ms. Wilkins. You should talk to your uncle. There would be enough to go around."

"This isn't about money, Mr. Harris. But I imagine that's something you wouldn't understand."

If she was trying to insult him, she was going to have to try harder. "I understand perfectly. But sometimes money supersedes sentimentality." Nick knew for a fact the taxes were due and for the third straight year would go unpaid. "I'd hate to see you lose this property to a stranger."

"You're a stranger."

Touché, he mused. "But I'm offering you a way to stay connected. Or didn't he tell you?"

She tapped her uncle with a healthy dose of suspicion. "Tell me what?"

"He's a liar!" Ernie cried and returned to his seat.

Clem was close at his heel, as though soaking it in like a sponge. Was he concerned about losing his job? Was there a piece in it for him? If so, Nick could use his employment to sweeten the deal. Responding to Delaney, he said, "I offered to split off a hundred acres for the family, land you would keep in the deal."

"Interesting." She arched a brow toward her uncle. "But no deal. This property belongs to my daughter. Period."

"Your daughter?" This was the first he'd heard of a daughter—of Delaney's, or anyone's. When she didn't expound, he turned to the old man for answers. "I thought you and your son owned the property."

"My son doesn't own nothin'. That's my father's name and me." He jabbed a crooked finger to his chest. "He's dead which makes me sole owner. Nobody else."

"I see..."

"This property is my daughter's rightful inheritance," Delaney corrected.

"It ain't."

"It is."

Intrigued by the new twist, Nick asked, "How old is she?"

"Eighteen."

"Should I be having this conversation with her?"

"Not on your life."

He forced himself not to laugh. Mother Bear just swaggered onto the porch, claws drawn. But it was just as well. Nick didn't care who he dealt with when it came to the sale. "Does she plan on keeping the property?"

"None of your business."

Nick took in the lot of them. Opposition to his proposal was the common denominator that bound them together. But with the old man staring down the edge of his life, Nick doubted he was looking to get rich. Not at this point in the game. He'd bet his resistance had to do with maintaining control. Ms. Wilkins, on the other hand, was looking out for her daughter's interests, though he suspected neither had the means to manage or pay for the horses, let alone the taxes and upkeep. One of the little nuggets he discovered from the local town clerk was that Delaney had a good head on her shoulders and a thriving bookkeeping business, but not much in the way of cash in her pocket. Then there was the Sweeney fellow. A man who claimed to be the caretaker, but who Nick's gut told him was anything but. Well, it shouldn't be too hard to uncover his stake in the game. Usually it began and ended with green.

"The offer stands, Mr. Ladd. It's good through the end of the week," Nick added, tweaking the wrench of pressure. Maybe a time table would be the influence they needed. As it stood, they were pretty hard-nosed against it with nothing to do but wait until the tax man cometh! Which could take months, years—precious time Nick didn't have. Not only was he under pressure from his marketing department, but he'd promised investors this project would be started months ago. Nick handed a business card to the younger man, yet settled his gaze upon Delaney, now comfortably leaning against the railing. "If you have any questions, I can be reached at this number. I'm prepared to double my offer."

"Not interested," she said.

Clem Sweeney's small eyes flared as he grabbed the card from Nick.

"I'll be in touch," he said, and walked off the porch and back to his shiny black sports sedan.

Clem removed the laser beam from Nick's back and turned on Ernie. "That man really trying to buy the property?"

"Yep."

"Well, you told him no, didn't you?"

Ernie whipped around like a mad dog and said, "You heard me, didn't you?"

"Well..." Clem fiddled with the buckle on his grimy overalls and muttered, "Yes." He took a step back from the old man. "But did you mean it?"

"Course I did." Ernie shooed him away and shoved the pipe into his mouth. "I always mean what I say."

Delaney caught the stony flick in her direction and couldn't care less. Unlike the rest of the crew, Ernie didn't intimidate her. He infuriated her. "It's not yours to sell, Ernie."

"It's mine, I tell you—it's mine and you can't tell me what to do!"

Ignoring his heated outburst, she shook her head. "This property goes to Felicity." She pushed off from the railing and strode over to him. Delaney bent down so he wouldn't miss a single word. The stench of tobacco rising from him would have made her gag—if she weren't so damn mad. "You made a deathbed promise to my mother that you would give this property to Felicity." Not her. Of course, not her.

"When did you get so greedy?" he asked, the skin of his balding forehead coloring to a mix of crimson and ash. "Your mother wasn't like this."

"My mother kept her word. She expects you to keep yours."

Delaney knew she'd just made a direct hit, deep into his heart. Outside of his own mother, his sister was the only one who ever loved him. She cherished him and had she still been alive, would be caring for him now. From cleaning his house to laundering his clothes and cooking his meals, Susannah Ladd would have done it all with a light spirit and loving heart. That was her way.

She'd still be taking care of him, too, had he seen fit to take care of *her*. If he had paid for her treatment, her mother would have seen a specialist who could have helped her. But he didn't. Instead, he'd raged at the doctors for diagnosing her in the first place and refused to give them a dime more. Ribbons of melancholy wound around Delaney's soul. Her mother died as a result, and it was because of him.

"You gonna let her talk like that to you?" Clem demanded.

"Stay out of this, Clem." Delaney raised a hard finger and pointed it directly into his face. "This is none of your affair."

"Listen here, missy, you don't treat my friends that way," Ernie interjected. "Why, I have a notion to give this property to Clem. The way he's been lookin' after me all these years, he deserves it, unlike the rest of you lazy-good-for-nothings."

Delaney frowned. Though one wouldn't know it to look at him, Ernie Ladd was a wealthy man. Not by his own hand, but by his father's. Grandpa Ladd inherited almost two thousand acres of land—beautiful land—land that became a hot commodity in the world of real estate. One of the most incredible tracts of unspoiled land in eastern Tennessee, it had been in the Ladd family for as long as anyone could remember, giving home to generation after generation. Lush with trees and valleys, creeks and falls and springs, the property became the envy of the state. Everyone had heard of Ladd Springs. Some claimed the springs were akin to the fountain of youth. But with envy came greed. Thirty years back, Grandpa Ladd sold off half of it to a developer. In one day, with the swipe of a pen, mountains and streams that had belonged to her family for over three hundred years were gone. And why?

Because he didn't want to work anymore. Grandpa Ladd wanted to stay home and make moonshine. What a waste. Not only did he sell a section, but he forbade the extended family from setting the first toe on the remainder. It was his, he said, and his alone. When he died, it went to his oldest son, Ernest Lowry Ladd. Grandpa Ladd made sure of it by putting Uncle Ernie's name on the title before he passed. Ernie's brother Albert was a good-for-nothing-loafer and not entitled to a dime, he'd said. And women? Well, according to him, women shouldn't own property. He viewed them as simply another expense in life, a mouth to feed.

So Ernie Ladd became sole owner of Ladd Springs, inheriting the remainder of his father's money as well. Delaney knew for a fact there was almost a quarter of a million dollars left in his account, yet he wasn't paying the taxes. Stubborn fool. Eventually the two issues would cross paths and Ladd Springs would be caught in the middle. "Mom wanted this property to stay in the family and I intend to see that it does."

Ernie stuck out his chest. "I decide what happens from here."

No surprise, Ernie was back in full fighting mode. But the saddest part was that he was dying of cancer. Cancer. The doctors told him he had a few years at best, but instead of enjoying his last days on God's green earth, he chose to fight.

Fight—to his dying day. Ernie would rather jeopardize the Ladd Springs legacy than leave it to her. And now he was threatening to give it to Clem?

Delaney shook her head and walked toward the steps. No way in hell would Clem Sweeney take ownership of her home, but at this point, it was a matter for the courts. If Ernie remained firm in his commitment to deny his son Jeremiah any right of inheritance, then Delaney and Felicity were it as the only other blood relatives,. In Delaney's mind, there was no reason for him to go back on his promise to his sister. Susannah made him swear that the property would stay within the family and that he would take care of Delaney and Felicity—to which Ernie agreed. Wrote it down so Susannah could see it with her own eyes. Albert would be looked after, of course, maintaining his right to live on the property until his dying day. His two sons were another story. One was in jail, the other on the run.

Jeremiah could certainly contest the transfer, but it was unlikely he would. Gone for twenty years now, he wasn't in the picture and no one around here would draw him in. Even his ex-girlfriend, Annie Owens, wouldn't call him, and *she* claimed to be the mother of his child—the same child she was squawking about getting rights to the property for. As if Ernie would ever agree to giving Jeremiah's offspring rights.

As it stood, if Ernie continued to refuse, it would leave Delaney to deal with the probate process. It was a headache she didn't need, one her mother would have never wanted her to endure.

"I'm going home," Delaney announced. She'd get nowhere arguing another second with the man. "I'll have Felicity come by around eight."

Like a pacifier to a babe, it settled the issue as she knew it would. For all her uncle's bluster and blow, he had a soft spot for Felicity. Delaney rounded the railing and caught the intensity in the gaze Clem fastened on her uncle. It struck her as odd, coming from the dullest tool in the shed. She hesitated. Was she missing something?

When Clem realized she was staring at him, he cleared his expression, replacing it with sugar and sunshine. "Have a good evening, Dell."

Chapter Three

Unsettled by Clem's sudden shift, Delaney returned to her hillside cabin. Located behind the main house, her small home was situated on the ridge about twenty yards up, tucked away within a cluster of trees and rocks. It was accessible only by a narrow, winding trail—a steep path which she climbed with ease. Ease, because she'd been hiking it for years. Upon reaching the top, she was only mildly winded and closed the distance to the tidy hideaway that once belonged to her mother.

Built from roughhewn logs secured together by thick swaths of cement, it was square in shape, single story with a tiny loft. It was precariously perched on the mountain's edge, built for her by Uncle Ernie and Albert during high school. They dubbed it her private little corner of heaven, even screened the front porch to keep the bugs away. Tears pricked at the memory. It was her mother's special place, the safe haven she sought when she needed to get away from the stress of life, the demands of family, the gruff presence of her father. Grandpa Ladd was no different from Ernie in that both were thorny by nature, the elder compounding trouble when he drank, swelling his heart with anger and his mouth with obscenity. Delaney remembered bits and pieces of his rage from her own childhood, but it was the tales Uncle Albert told that set her heart on fire. Not only was Grandpa Ladd's heart hard as rock, but his hand was swift with a belt, whipping the boys on a regular basis. Knowing them as she did now, Delaney could understand they might have deserved some of it, at least on occasion. But her mother?

The bastard even took the leather strap to her. Delaney grabbed a sanded smooth railing, kicking her boots hard against the top porch step to remove as much dirt as she could.

Thinking back, Delaney couldn't imagine her mom enduring anything so brutal, yet she never once mentioned it, never once spoke a cross word against her father. Granted her mom didn't speak many kind words either, but from what Delaney had learned, the man deserved a tongue lashing and then some. Checking her boots, she grunted. The stuff stuck like glue, more a mix of wet dirt and heavy clay. Nothing short of scrubbing the boots clean or soaking them in the creek would do the trick, but she kicked off as much as she could.

Whatever. She jogged up the steps. None of it would see the inside of the cabin. Delaney had a rule against shoes in the house, same as her mother before her. Stopping at the engraved glass front door—the glass panel an antique she picked up at a local junkyard—Delaney tugged her boots free and set them alongside the welcome mat. Felicity could sweep the rest of it off the porch this evening, once she returned from her visit with Ernie.

Carrying her gun inside, she indulged in the smooth wood floors beneath her socked feet. Turning on the chandelier, a petite wrought iron piece she'd picked up at an antique store in town, she breathed easy. Coming home was like stepping into another world, a world free of trouble and stress, where she could unplug and get back to the basics of living. Like food. The bag of fresh okra in her refrigerator promised a delicious addition to her fried chicken tonight. Her energy pitched and heaved in a sudden wave of exhaustion, but she had to hurry. Felicity would be home shortly and she needed to get dinner started.

An hour later, Delaney reached into the oven and pulled the tray of cornbread from the oven, the sweet scent of corn billowing in a hot cloud around her face. At the sound of scuffling on the porch deck, she turned to see her daughter's slender figure through the glass.

Within seconds, Felicity let herself in, her pink socks stark against the wood floors as she breezed indoors. "Smells good in here."

"Best air freshener known to man," Delaney replied, bumping the oven door closed with her knee, placing the pan of golden bread loaves on the waiting quilted pad. The fried chicken was cooling on a platter lined with paper towels and covered with foil while the okra continued to sizzle stovetop in a cast iron pan.

"You won't hear any complaints from me." Easing the backpack from her shoulder, Felicity set it down beside the leather sofa and joined her mother in the kitchen. "I'm hungry."

"Good. I made extra. Thought you could take a few with you for Ernie."

She nodded. "He loves your cornbread."

But never said a word to her about it. Not once, not ever, not so much as a thank you. He reserved compliments for one person only. Felicity. Delaney considered her child. From her delicate features and soft-spoken manner to the tender shade of strawberry blonde hair currently pulled back into a ponytail, Felicity reminded Ernie of his sister Susannah. Not only was she the spitting image, she treated him with the same gentle affection, despite his carrying on. Delaney lightly pinched Felicity's chin. "He's lucky to have you."

She waved off the praise. "He's not so bad. And he gives me an opportunity to practice. Let's me play anything I want."

"Because everything you play is beautiful."

She rolled her eyes. "Mom."

It was a ritual Felicity had begun less than a year ago, but one Ernie now lived for. Each and every night, she sat and played her flute for him. Soft and serene, like a beast lulled to submission, he sat and listened to her play. Song after song, she practiced her craft. Fluting was Felicity's passion. One day, she hoped to play professionally as part of an orchestra, but that was only a dream. Her grades were good, earning her a partial scholarship, but it only covered the first year. Delaney's fear was that she wouldn't be able to afford the next three.

"Don't 'mom' me. It's true. You need to further your training, and why he doesn't see that is beyond me. We need title to the property so we can sign on for the logging before they go elsewhere."

Felicity's hazel gaze clouded. "Are you sure that won't ruin the land?"

Delaney wiped her palms against the white cotton apron tied at her waist. "You won't even notice. They want to work the north side of the property. A patch of about a hundred acres. We'll never see them."

Felicity sank to a barstool. "A hundred seems so much..."

"Clearing the forest is good for the land," Delaney told her. "The trees will grow back and we'll have plenty enough money to pay the property taxes *and* your tuition."

"Maybe I shouldn't go to UT. It's causing so much trouble—"

Delaney held up a stiff hand. "I don't ever want to hear those words come out of your mouth again. You're going. That's final."

Felicity's small mouth closed as instructed, but the hint of frown upset Delaney. Her daughter should not feel guilty about getting an education. She shouldn't be dragged into the mess of Ernie's foul disposition, nor should she have to endure threats from a complete stranger. Nick Harris's image formed in her mind. While the man seemed nice enough, looked nice enough—nicer than anyone would ever hear *her* admit to—he did not have her daughter's best interests at heart. He wanted this land for himself, for his hotel. Delaney needed it for her family, her daughter's future. The two were incompatible goals.

Delaney brushed the stressful thoughts from her head, hushed the clamor of her pulse. She didn't want to think about it right now. She wanted to enjoy Felicity. Loosening a mini loaf of cornbread from the black iron bake pan, Delaney slathered it with butter, set it on a plate and slid it toward her daughter. "So how was school?"

"Good." Felicity picked up the yellow bread and held it before her mouth. "The Parker boys asked me to be their date for their graduation party."

Delaney gaped at her. "Both of them?"

Felicity smiled and said, "It's the current running joke between them." She bit off the end of the bread.

Identical twins, they forever teased Felicity. They claimed to have lost their combined heart to her—it was she who had to choose. "And you said?"

"Told them I'd have to think about it." She cast a dramatic gaze toward the ceiling and said, "Because they're *so* different, I'd have to decide what kind of night I want grad night to be—fun or funner." She giggled. "It's such a dilemma!"

"Funner is not a word." Delaney dipped her chin and peered at her daughter. "Please tell me I'm not wasting my money on flute lessons when you should be tutored in grammar."

"JK."

Just joking. Delaney shook her head at the incessant "text turned speech." JK. IDK. LOL. It was like some kind of new language with these kids.

Felicity peeked beneath the foil of fried okra. "Are these from Ashley's garden?"

"They are. Picked them myself." Ashley Fulmer had been her mother's best friend. She was also their local gardener-extraordinaire, with a thumb greener than a meadow in summertime.

"Travis and Troy want to go riding this weekend. Is that okay?"

The mention of riding led Delaney's thoughts back to this afternoon. "Yes. But I don't want you in the woods by yourself."

She furrowed her brow. "Since when?"

Since we have strangers lurking between the trees. "Since today."

"Mom."

It was Felicity's one word rebuttal spoken with emphasis to insist, *I'm an adult now. You can be honest with me.* On one level, that was true. But her daughter was not strong on self-defense. It wasn't in her nature. "There's been some trouble with trespassing," Delaney informed her. "And until we can get a handle on it, I don't want you out there by yourself."

Delaney knew Felicity understood. Ladd Springs adjoined public land—the USFS—and it happened that on occasion people ventured onto private property. That property was Ladd property. But to do so, they had to ignore posted signs against trespassing, which meant anyone on their land were people willing to ignore the rules. Not exactly the nicest slice of population.

"Okay," Felicity agreed. "I'll make the boys stay with me."

"Tough life you have," Delaney teased, breathing a sigh of relief as she tested the temperature of her bread. Her daughter was mature. She knew there was danger out in the world and she was willing to be smart about it. While she refused her mother's offer to teach her how to shoot, Felicity wouldn't purposefully test fate.

After dinner, the tray of cornbread warmed by the oven in one hand, her long, slim, velvet flute case in the other, Felicity traversed the path with ease, careful not to slide on the rocks as she took her shortcut down to Uncle Ernie's house. Leaping over a rock, she hit level ground with a thud, raising both plate and case in sync to keep them level. Crossing the narrow bridge, she took in the thick scent of trees in the air, the moist smell of earth, the constant movement in the creek below. She loved being outdoors. Felicity could almost feel the crisp chill to the water, the slimy texture to the rounded rocks that shifted in color from tans and browns to grays and blacks. The wall of trees surrounding the small clearing was drenched in gold, the sky a gorgeous blend of violet, blue and orange. Early May, days were longer now, leaving plenty enough sunlight to light her way. But later, when the night turned black, her mom would insist on making the return trip with her. It was her prerogative, she'd claimed.

Not that she didn't appreciate her mother's watchful eye, she did. She understood where her mother's overprotectiveness came from and understood it would not change. Ever. Actually, she considered herself fortunate to have a mother who cared so much. So many kids at school didn't. Half their parents were gone, the other half present but checked out. Unlike the Parker boys. Their mom and dad were checked in and totally charged. Actually, their house ran like a zoo, the back door swinging open and closed as kids came and went. Travis and Troy were the youngest of eight, or as Mrs. Parker called them, "momma's little surprise bundle at the end of the litter."

Felicity smiled as she recalled their dual request for her company to the prom. *Felicity, we've wrestled four times and are two for two. Either you choose, or one of us gets hurt.*

I'll go with both of you. She giggled, pleased with herself. She adored the attention, but truth be known, there was only one Parker boy for her. Boots clapping up the steps, Felicity tucked visions of him away and rapped on the wood door. "Uncle Ernie, I'm here!"

Letting herself in, she saw her uncle teetering down the stairs. "Well, you don't have to yell about it."

Felicity's instincts were to rush over and steady him as he made his way down, but the one time she did he got mad at her. "I don't need no help gettin' around my house," he'd hollered. So rather than assist, she patiently waited until he landed on the bottom step, his white knuckle grip locked solid around the wooden post. She held out the tinfoil-covered paper plate. "Mom made cornbread."

He eyed it warily. "It any good?"

Felicity suppressed a smile. Uncle Ernie was so suspicious. He acted like it was tainted with poison! "You know it's the best."

"I don't know any such thing," he grumbled under his breath. "But I'll trust your word."

As expected. Felicity put the bread on the bulky coffee table, the top made from old planks salvaged from the barn that used to sit on the property, the legs knotty sticks made from pine branches. "I learned a new piece this week."

"Alrighty." Ernie ambled over and settled himself in his Lazy-Boy, the seams of which were split open on a top corner. Shifting his weight from side to side, he wedged himself into the seat, his body fitting into the ratty piece of furniture as if he were part of it. "Okay, honey. Play away."

Albert Ladd trudged in from the kitchen. On the heavy side, he moved at the speed of molasses. Dressed in denim coveralls and white T-shirt, Felicity never saw him in anything else, nor did it seem like he ever combed the thin hair that fell from his bald head. Long and stringy, it hung clear down to his shoulders and looked downright un-kept. But that was her great uncle, *bless his heart*.

"Did I hear the princess?" he asked.

She grinned. "Hi, Uncle Albert."

"You gonna play us a song?" he asked, and walked slowly to his chair.

"Yes, and it's a new one." Retrieving the shiny flute from its black velvet case, she pulled a sheet of music from her portfolio, set it on its stand and prepared to play. Shaking the hair from her face, Felicity brought the mouthpiece to her puckered lips and warmed up by blowing a steady stream of air into the instrument.

Hands folded across his small protrusion of a belly, Uncle Ernie laid his head back against the chair and closed his eyes.

Felicity straightened. She pulled her abdomen in, focused on her diaphragm, aligned her fingers on the keys and blew a steady stream of air into the flute as she held it high to her side to her side. Breathing in and out, she played a tune composed by Charles Griffes. The piece reminded her of the ebb and flow of the property's numerous streams and creeks, sweeping rhythm moving high and low, spanning a broad range of timbre. Along the waterways were her favorite spots, the ones she sat by for hours. When she was younger, she used to sit by the water and read. Now, she played the flute. Slow, fast, her fingers danced along its length, hitting keys in rapid succession as she released herself to the power of the music. Swinging and bowing, her head and arms moved in rhythm as she played, dipping and pausing, escalating the pace toward the grand finale.

The door slammed . Felicity cried out, her breath expelled in a rush of fright.

Ernie shot forward in his chair.

Clem Sweeney stood just inside the threshold.

"Damn it, Clem! You nearly gave me a heart attack!"

Tall and lanky, he wore a blue plaid shirt that looked like it hadn't been washed in weeks. "Sounds like an angel is playin' in here," he said, his smile dripping with creep.

Felicity's heart thudded hard against her ribs. She swallowed hard. Clem was not one of her favorite people. He was rude, crude, and took every opportunity to leer at her whenever she was within eyesight. Her mother didn't care for him either. She grew up with the man, so she should know. And if she knew he was here, she'd have a fit.

Drawn to the plate on the table, Clem stepped forward. "Is that cornbread I smell?"

"It's mine," Ernie warned him, "so keep your grubby hands off it."

Albert watched the exchange wordlessly.

"Felicity here make it?" he asked greedily, though the hunger she discerned in his eyes had nothing do with the food.

Felicity stood. "I should go." She glanced between the two men, her mood for music dunked in ice water. She didn't want to be anywhere near this man.

"Sit down—you're not going anywhere," Ernie commanded. "Clem's the one who has to go."

"But we have a meeting," Clem said, his attention jarred free from her, latching on to Ernie. "You scheduled it yourself."

"It can wait."

A meeting? Felicity's mind whirred as she glanced between the two. What could these two possibly have to meet about?

"I ain't waitin' no more. You put me off last night, and now I'm here."

Ernie's eyes practically popped out of his bony skull. "You keep this up, and I'm not givin' you a thing."

The image of her Uncle Ernie frightened her, more skeleton with eyes than old man with a beating heart. But the comment served to silence Clem. Hurriedly, Felicity collected her instrument and music, closed up her case. Tucking the portfolio under an arm, she turned for the door. Through the front windows, she could see the sun had almost set. If she hurried, she could make it before complete dark. "I'll come back tomorrow."

Moving past Clem, she held her breath against the stench of cigarette smoke that clung to him—it was in his clothes, his hair and from experience she knew that if she looked, she'd see nicotine stains on his fingers, too.

Fleeing the cabin, Felicity dashed down the steps and over the creek bridge, her heart pounding. But more than the initial surprise from Clem's arrival, it was nerves that battered at her now. Her mother's warning about trespassers slithered up her spine. The sound of rushing creek and whisper of wind usually appealed to her, but at the moment only served to scare her.

Forcing her legs to keep pace, she trekked up the path to her home. Her mother would not be happy knowing Clem showed up. Nor would she like the fact that her daughter had decided to make the trip back on her own. But taking the time to call for her mother's escort seemed silly and would keep her near the wretched man all the longer.

A branch snapped in the woods below her. Felicity froze at the sound—but only for a second. Was someone there? Her heart kicked into overdrive, adrenaline pummeling her muscles into action. It could be a deer or a rabbit. It could be a bear.

Making it to the porch, she ran up the steps, not pausing until she was at her front door and her mother's figure was in sight through the glass. Felicity breathed in and out, calming her pulse. As she gathered her wits, the door opened in a rush.

"What are you doing here?"

Partly relieved by her mom's aggressive stance, the lamplight washing over her, Felicity lifted her pant legs to remove her boots. "I left early," she said, purposefully vague. Although grateful for the safety of her mother's strength, she didn't want to worry her.

"Why didn't you call me? It's dark outside."

"It wasn't when I left," Felicity said.

Her mother walked inside and closed the door behind her. "You know how I feel about it, Felicity."

The hard edge in her mother's voice demanded explanation. She turned. Met by the expected displeasure circling like wolves, she said, "Clem Sweeney showed up so I left. But, honest, it was still kinda light out. I figured if I hurried, I could make it."

Her mother stilled. "What was Clem doing there?"

Working to smooth out the final bumps in her pulse, Felicity replied, "I don't know. He said something about a meeting."

"A meeting?" She paused. "What does he have to meet with Ernie about?"

Felicity relayed the conversation and her mother frowned. "You stay away from him, you hear me?"

Breathing a sigh of relief, Felicity nodded. There would be no argument on that point.

Chapter Four

Delaney rose early the next morning, intent on searching the spot where she had seen the men the day before. She could hear Felicity's blow-dryer running and knew she'd be out for breakfast soon. Grabbing bread from the cabinet, she pulled out two slices and plopped them into the toaster. The boiled eggs and grits were almost ready. It was a simple meal, but simple usually meant smart. At least in her neck of the woods, it did. Besides, it was the only breakfast she could get her daughter to eat anymore, so it would have to do.

Checking her watch, Delaney mentally sketched out her day. First she had to see to the horses, make sure Sadie had enough feed for the day. The two Appaloosas and Felicity's mare were pigs when it came to sweet hay, and they'd starve Sadie if Delaney let them. At some point she'd have to make a trip downtown to see a client, hit the post office and office supply store. She had a few customers who insisted on paper statements as a backup to her computer records, despite the fact she emailed them a copy to download on their own computer. They were the holdouts, resisting the digital age, though she suspected Mrs. Meyers requested the copies so she could prove it was Delaney cooking her books, should the need ever arise. She shook her head and turned at the toaster ding. That woman barely scratched the surface of her checkbook, let alone a deposit slip! But people were people and they came in all forms.

If Mrs. Meyers wanted paper copies, then paper copies she'd get. Delaney's personal service was her hallmark, garnering her two more clients this week. Which reminded her— she needed to send "thank you" notes for the referrals. Word of mouth was critical to her success, especially in a small town where lips flapped at high speed. When people talked about Delaney Wilkins, she wanted it to be positive.

Draining the water from the pan, she rinsed the eggs in cold tap water, then quickly cracked them open into a bowl, tossing the shells into the sink. Ashley would want those for the garden.

Felicity, dressed in T-shirt and jeans, her waves of strawberry blonde shiny and clean as they flowed about her shoulders, strolled into the kitchen just as the toast popped up in the toaster. "What timing!"

"They call me 'the clock.'"

Felicity screwed her face. "Nobody calls you 'the clock.'"

"Well, they could." Delaney smiled. "Time management is my middle name."

Felicity rolled her eyes, strolled over and plucked the bread free, her freckles brighter after the hot morning shower.

"Here you go," Delaney said and slid the bowl across the counter. "Two perfectly boiled eggs and grits."

Next to her, Felicity poked one with her finger. "They're hot."

"Would you rather they were cold?" Instead of waiting for an answer, Delaney shook her head and mumbled, "Tough crowd, tough crowd..."

As Felicity salted her breakfast, Delaney retreated to her bedroom in search of her cell phone and wallet. Single bed, single dresser, a framed mirror hanging above, it was all the furniture she could fit in the tiny space and still have room for her personal items. Which were few—jeans, boots, tops, underwear, nightshirts. She didn't need much. Hairbrush and mascara were in the bathroom, along with her favorite hoop earrings but nothing more. When she left Jack Foster, she took her daughter and a suitcase and got the hell out. He could have everything else, but he couldn't have her and Felicity. Not after what he did. There were no second chances in her book. Strike one, you're out. Period, exclamation point.

In the beginning, it had been an easier transition. Felicity had been eight and the move held more adventure than sacrifice. But as she grew older, the cramped living arrangement became more noticeable, more trying. Once Felicity hit twelve, the sparks began to fly until Delaney let it slip why they were here. From then on, the girl had been a perfect angel.

Which hurt. Felicity was young when they left and Delaney didn't want her only memory of her father to be an ugly one, but that was his choosing, not hers. If his daughter meant anything to Jack, he would have stayed in town. Stayed in touch, at least. But Jack was a drinker and drink ruled his life.

"Mom, I'm leaving!" Felicity called out from the living room.

Emerging from her bedroom, Delaney was right behind her. "I'll walk you out."

Felicity drove herself to school these days but still had to make the hike down to her car.

"You're gonna be late!" Ernie hollered from down below.

Speak of the devil. Scrambling down the porch steps, Delaney spied the old man through the trees. He was standing by the creek.

"I'm okay, Uncle Ernie!" Felicity called back to him. "It's Wednesday and I don't start class until nine-thirty."

Hands dug into his front pockets, he watched them through the trees as they made their way down the trail. Good grief, Delaney thought, was he looking for something to complain about?

As if he had any clue what the high school schedule entailed. The man barely grazed his senior year before he signed on to work at the mill. Only reason he had a diploma was because his sister encouraged him. Grandma and Grandpa Ladd hadn't been real worried about education. Just wasn't something that seemed to concern them.

When Delaney and Felicity made it down to the open patch of grass by the creek, he confronted them. Big eyes glared at Delaney through smudged lens. "What kind of mother are you, allowin' her to be late to school? Don't you know she needs a degree if she's gonna escape your heavy eye?"

"She's fine," Delaney said, suddenly glad he was here. She wanted a word with him about Clem.

"I don't have any classes first period," Felicity told him, traipsing over to his side of the bridge. "It's okay."

Delaney's boots pounded over the uneven slats of wood, drowning out the gurgle of creek below. The man didn't know a period from a comma. Which was neither here nor there at the moment. She wanted information. "Ernie, what was Clem doing here last night?"

He glowered at her. "None of your business."

"It is when it involves my daughter."

Ernie turned a kind eye toward Felicity. "About that. I wanted to apologize for that hillbilly's poor manners. I'm sorry he disturbed your music last night."

"It's okay."

"It's not okay," he said. "That ruffian should've known better than to barge in like that! If he hears pretty music, he should know it doesn't concern him."

Felicity giggled which drew the light of a smile into his dull gray eyes. "You'll come back again tonight, won't you?"

"I will." She pecked his cheek with a kiss, then her mother's. "See you later!"

Delaney watched her daughter trot off to her car, the used Honda it took three years of savings to buy and a neighbor friend to fix. Ernie didn't help. When Delaney suggested it would make a nice eighteenth birthday present, he'd refused. *She don't need no car. I never had a car at her age.* Delaney had wanted to shout, "Probably because the car wasn't invented yet!" Ernie could have afforded to buy Felicity a new car. He could help pay for her college education. He chose to do neither.

"I'm waiting," Delaney reminded him.

"For what?"

"What business does Clem have with you?"

"That ain't none of your affair!" he cried, and took off for the house.

Delaney followed him. Something was going on. It was the way Clem had been staring at Ernie on the porch yesterday that kept coming back to her. "You're not sharing any private information with him, are you?"

"I don't report to you." Marching as hard and fast as two scrawny legs would let him, Ernie continued his escape.

Now she had a bad feeling. No denial wasn't a good sign when it came to Ernie Ladd. Denial was his answer to everything he didn't refuse flat-out. Hurrying after him, she demanded, "What have you done?"

He stopped and turned on her. "I ain't done nothin' but if I do"—his pasty skin flushed crimson—"it's my business and not yours."

"Clem would like nothing more than to sink his claws into you even more than he has. You already pay him too much to mow the fields. What else are you giving him?"

Delaney leaned forward. She could hear the rasp of Ernie's breath, see the tiny veins etched in his skin. "Clem is the only one who helps me around here," he smacked back. "He's the only one who does a damn thing for me. He deserves this property."

Alarms went off. Her pulse exploded in her chest. "What?"

"You heard me. You can't even keep a man! Why should I trust this property to you?"

"To Felicity. You promised mom you were leaving it to Felicity."

Ernie stabbed a finger toward her face. "Don't you bring her name up to me." Gray eyes turned dark with rage and his voice shook, "Clem should have it. He's the only one who knows how to look after it. You girls would let it rot!"

"You are not giving this property to Clem." Delaney suddenly understood Clem's presence on the porch yesterday, at the house last evening. He was digging in for the kill. He was manipulating her uncle against them with his professed duty and devotion. "He has no right to this land."

"If I give it to him, he does." Ernie stomped off, leaving her dumbfounded. The soft swash of the creek came back to life, the misty chill of morning penetrated her lightweight jersey top.

Could Ernie be serious? Clem Sweeney was a loser. His own family had recognized the fact and kicked him out! Now he lived down the street, holed up in a broken-down trailer on the side of the road, on land bordering the Sweeney-Ladd property line. It was an open wound between the two families. Ernie allowed him to stay, Clem's father wanted him to go. But in the end Clem wasn't worth fighting over, so there he squatted.

Delaney headed for the stables and was at once swallowed up by trees and shade and the dense scent of wet pine. As she arrived at the old horse barn, her mood dipped further. Practically falling apart, it was the original structure, built back in the early forties. Back in the day, these stables housed more than a dozen horses, both work horses and pleasure ponies. The Ladd family had been avid horsemen, but now the tin roof was rusting, the panels bent and caving in at points. The walls, no longer brown, were gray and rotten. Iron posts, propped up on either end of the entrance, had been rigged to keep the roof from falling in. Weeds climbed up the corners. The sad sight brought Ernie's admonition home to roost. *You girls would let it rot.*

Delaney prided herself on being independent and self-reliant, but fixing this old barn was out of her realm. Nails she could hammer and floors she could sweep—and had done so often enough—but these stables needed complete overhaul. The worst part was knowing the decline meant dangerous conditions for her horses, but it was all she had. "Sadie!"

she called out, brushing the negative thoughts from her mind. There wasn't anything she could do about it now.

The Palomino came running from behind the barn.

Delaney rubbed the spot between Sadie's eyes and looked around for sign of the other horses. "How ya doing? Hungry?"

The horse made a low nicker, a rumbling sound deep within her throat.

Through the back window, Delaney saw the Appaloosa but none of the others. "Are the boys out for a stroll?" she asked Sadie, breathing in the scent of her. Which, combined with the smell of sweet feed and damp earth and the faint aroma of manure, made up one of her favorite scents in the whole world. If she could bottle them up and take them with her, she would. Met by a gentle bump from her mare's nose, Delaney said, "Time for feed, but not for you. I'll mix yours when we get back."

Filling the bins with food, Delaney pushed back against a more forceful nudge from her mare. Sadie wasn't giving her any room, probably wondering why she wasn't getting hers. "Sorry, babe," Delaney said and unhooked bridle from its spot by the open entryway. "You and I are going for a ride first."

The horse shook her mane, giving no resistance as the bit was slipped into her mouth. Delaney patted the mare's wide, flat forehead, then shooed a fly from her lashes. Rustling the coarse, white mane, Delaney scratched behind one ear, then the other. Sadie's favorite spots. The mare responded with a hearty push from her muzzle. "Good girl," Delaney cooed with a soft laugh, then grabbing the base of Sadie's mane, hoisted herself up and over, settling in for the trip.

Not one for saddles, Delaney preferred to ride bare back, making her feel one with her animal. Totally in tune, she and Sadie ran free, swaying together as they galloped through fields, slowed over the trails and creeks, swam across rivers. Saddles made her feel separated, disconnected—neither of which appealed to her. With a click from her mouth, Delaney gave a rapid tug on the reins and the two were off. Today she would find out what those two men found so interesting on her property.

When the trail opened to the field, she cantered across the soft meadow grass, her eye on the trailhead. She never saw Nick Harris pulling into the drive.

Slowing his vehicle, he watched her go. Where was she off to in such a hurry? Keeping the books wasn't accomplished on horseback, and according to the cashier at the diner, Delaney was due in town today. He glanced at the digital clock on his dashboard. Mid-morning workout?

Unsettled by the sight of her riding off on her own, Nick pulled farther into the gravelly drive, parking just shy of Ernie Ladd's home. It was time to up the offer. Easing free from the vehicle, he reached for the envelope and tossed the door closed. In the bright sunshine, the dilapidated structure looked all the worse for wear. What a shame. In its day this little cabin was probably quite the showplace. The materials used were solid, the craftsmanship evident. But even the finest built homes needed upkeep through the years.

Nick surveyed the surrounding area, the dense line of trees behind the cabin, the wildflowers poking up here and there between tufts of grass. There was a crudely constructed wishing well, very basic, the wood rotting like everything else. He wondered if it was functional, if it ever had been, or merely there for aesthetics. This was the land of natural springs, after all. Walking toward Ernie's cabin, he could hear the creek, see that it wound around behind the house, snaking along the line of forest that closed into full-wooded wilderness. Farther back, he saw the narrow opening for a trail. Briefly, he wondered where it led. The stables? Another cabin?

There was plenty of room here to locate his gate house. Flat, level, he'd house the office and reservations staff here, then create a winding road back to the main hotel. From the images he'd studied, there was another clearing north of here, about four acres worth, giving him plenty of space for his project. Add the river and he had himself a wonderful *al fresco* dining spot. Thus far he had not been offered a tour of the property. What he did know, he'd learned from satellite images and topography maps. And word of mouth. Nick smiled to himself. One thing he'd say about small towns, they were full of helpful people doling out helpful information.

"Hullo." Nick swung around toward the voice. A large pear-shaped man stood on the porch peering down at him, his body covered by blue jean overalls and dingy white T-shirt. Stringy black hair hung from around a bald spot, while the shadow of a beard colored his jaw. Another friend of the family? "Can I hep ya?" the man asked politely.

Nick cleared his throat. "I'm here to see Ernie Ladd."

"What are you doing back here?" Ernie stepped out the door but held the frame firmly in his hand. It wasn't the stance of a man happy to see him.

"I've come to make you another offer." Nick scaled the four steps effortlessly and stood face to face with Ernie and the other fellow. If you could call it that. Slightly hunched, Ernie Ladd was the size of most women, not men, and his friend was three bodies wider, but not much taller. "You drive a hard bargain, Mr. Ladd. But I respect that in a man. I'm here to up my offer to seven hundred and fifty thousand." He held up the envelope.

Ernie Ladd didn't blink an eye. "No sale."

Nick didn't even discern the slightest hesitation. "You might want to think about it a while."

"There's nothin' to think about."

Nick glanced at the man by Ladd's side. Mute, he wordlessly ambled over to a rocker and gingerly lowered his heavy-set frame to the seat.

"I ain't sellin' to the likes of you."

What did he have against him? People in town called the man ornery, but this was ornery, obstinate *and* unreasonable. "Do you have a better offer?"

Ernie blinked.

Maybe he was getting somewhere... "I'll beat it. Whatever it is, I'll beat it."

The old man's eyes narrowed and filled with venom. "I don't need your money, fancy man." He moved inside. "Now go on and don't come back," he said through the dusty screen door. Nick watched him disappear into a back room in a haze of shadow.

Nick ran a hand through his hair, wanting to pull thick chunks of it out. The man was beginning to grate on him. He had investors breathing down his neck. He'd already been in town for a week. There were other tracts he could use, other locations that would suffice, but none of them were near as sweet as this one. Ladd Springs had a reputation for exactly that—springs. The land was said to be loaded with them and they were the perfect accent to his brand of hotels.

Harris Hotels were noted for their exceptional settings, built into the heart of the natural surroundings, making guests feel at one with their environment. His first success had been a rustic gem in his hometown of Montana. Set against the Rocky Mountains, it was peaceful, rugged, and partially built into the stone wall of a mountainside, a natural waterfall cascading yards away into an open air rock pool. He offered spa services, exercise and yoga, the finest in local dining and personalized attention, down to his guided tours into the heart of the countryside. From there his vision had taken him to the Caribbean, Australia and South America.

Nick's gaze drifted over the man in the rocker, out to the fresh spring palette of flowers and sunshine. This time he'd set his eyes on Tennessee. He'd done rugged, beach, river and rainforest, but nothing spoke to the heart of southern hospitality and natural healing like this property could. Yoga enthusiasts and naturalists from around the globe would seek his springs for rejuvenation. The fields would be colored by wildflowers, punctuated by labyrinths. Paths would trail off and lead to renewal falls. Guests would end their day with a relaxation treatment, followed by a candlelight dinner featuring the culinary specialties of the region. It would be the premier experience in Southern hospitality, combined with luxury eco-living. People would pay top dollar for the experience.

Nick's thoughts were interrupted by a truck barreling down the road. He turned and saw the man from last night speed off in the direction Delaney had gone, the vehicle bumping and bouncing over the rough terrain. Someone was in a hurry.

The truck stopped, the man jumped out and headed into the woods. The same direction as Delaney. Without a word to the man on the porch, Nick took off after her.

Chapter Five

Delaney slid off Sadie's back and walked her to the tree line. Stopping in the shade beneath a heavy section of branches, she pulled the leather reins over the horse's head and loosely tied them to the post. With a light caress to Sadie's backside, she said, "I won't be long." The Palomino emitted a soft snort and pawed at the ground.

With a determined step, Delaney headed into the forest. The trail that began the width of a car narrowed to accommodate foot traffic only. To her left the land rose sharply and, to her right, fell away to a tiny creek cutting across the forest floor. The light was flat, the air held a slight chill. Beneath her feet, a thick layer of crusted clay and chunks of gravel challenged her stride, but nothing could slow her down. When Delaney Wilkins was on a mission, stand back or get hurt.

She could see a good distance ahead and calculated the trip to the spot in question to take about fifteen minutes. Ten if she hurried. Kicking up her movements, curiosity spun her thoughts into a tangle of suspicion and questions. Those men were up to no good, but what were they after? Over the years the Ladds experienced their share of squatters and vagabonds, petty thieves and lazy drunks. Something told her these two didn't fit into any of the standard categories. They were too intent in their activities.

As she neared the site, Delaney slowed her pace. Scanning deep into the woods, she looked for signs of movement. In some areas the trees were thinned, sunlight casting slim shafts of light through the tree tops, a few patches making it midway down tree trunks. Below her, the brush remained dark and damp, mostly covered by a layer of brown leaves.

But she was going straight in. Delaney purposely wore a long-sleeved jersey to help cut down on scratches from traversing the jagged brush. Expediency was her word for the day. Pushing branches out of her way, she made a beeline for her target, detoured several times by massive tree trunks and insurmountable gray boulders splotched by patches of white fungus. Excitement mounted as she neared. What would she find? Stolen property? Were they using the woods as a hideout?

Inundated by scenario after scenario, Delaney was relieved to finally have the answer at hand. Slightly winded, she reached her destination and with a cursory glance detected nothing sinister. No camping gear left behind, no articles of clothing or personal belongings. If they weren't living here, then what?

Moving in closer, she noted the branches and leaves were matted down in areas—most likely the result of their extended stay from yesterday, she mused. However, the extent of flattening was significant. More than she'd expect from the weight of their boots. She tried to recall if she'd seen them carrying anything. Had they been wearing back-packs? Delaney inspected the ground. Would that have been enough to lay the small greenery in a perma-flat slate?

She shook her head. Hard to say. Nick's unexpected arrival had muddled her ability to remember. Stepping toward the rotting tree trunk, she grabbed a stick and began to poke around.

"Dell!"

Delaney jumped, turning in the direction of the trail. What the hell was he doing here?

"Dell!"

Damn it—was there a bell strapped to her buckle? How did Clem know she was here? And why was he following her? Heart pounding, she squared her shoulders and firmed her spine. First Nick and now Clem. What the hell was going on around here?

One thing for sure, she didn't have to answer him. She and Clem Sweeney shared a long history, none of it pleasant.

"What are you doing?" he called out. Fixing her in his sights, he started to make his way toward her.

She blew out her breath in a ragged stream. "What the hell are you doing here, Clem?" she yelled back. "I didn't invite you."

His tone assumed a friendliness as he replied, "You never were filled with honey, were you, Dell?" Shoving branches out of his way, he practically jogged the distance to her. His fetid stench of smoke and body odor arrived before him, soiling the fresh scent of trees. "Whatcha doin'?" he asked, glancing about.

"None of your business."

His thin lips curled into an ugly smile. Almost forty-years old and practically bald, Clem wasn't the picture of vigor and health. "Aw, Dell, you don't have to be so mean. We're neighbors, practically family. Why can't we get along?"

"We are not family and nowhere close. I didn't ask for company. I want to be alone."

Clem stepped toward her and she tensed. "It ain't safe for girls to be out in the woods alone."

"I'm perfectly capable of taking care of myself."

Shadowed beneath his ratty cowboy hat, his gaze dropped to her boot, then leaped back to her face. His eyes took on a nasty sneer. "That you are, aren't you?"

Years ago, Clem learned the hard way that she carried a pistol in her boot. They were teenagers at the time, she hiking along the south end of the property when Clem snuck up behind her. "Surprised her accidentally" is what he claimed after the fact, but either way it didn't change the outcome. She was alone, and he jumped out from a dense pack of trees. She pulled her gun and shot. The bullet grazed his shoulder and he screamed like a baby. Called her all kind of sordid names, all of which she ignored. Leveling her gun at him, she'd ordered him to get out of her woods. He obliged, but only because he was bleeding and scared senseless his scent would catch the attention of a nearby bear.

Fool. No bear would have anything to do with a rank piece of meat like him. But he had been forewarned from then on. Surprise Delaney Wilkins and you'd better be locked and loaded. She held her leveled gaze. Shooting him now would be too easy and probably ensure Felicity lost any chance to the property. If Uncle Ernie meant what he said about giving the land to Clem, he'd do it just to spite her if she harmed the grease ball. "What do you want, Clem?"

His eyes darted to the area behind her. "Just wanted to come see what you were up to, is all."

She stepped toward a nearby tree, glancing about for signs of the men's earlier presence. "And why do you care?"

His gaze narrowed to a fine point. "Your uncle don't trust you. He's asked me to watch out for you, keep you out of trouble."

She stopped suddenly. "Stay away from Ernie. If you think you're going to con him out of this property, you've got another thought coming. This land belongs to Felicity, and I have lawyers to prove it."

"Who cares what lawyers say when it's *my* name on the title." He tipped his hat back from his forehead and said, "Then it ain't yours to say nothin' about," he jeered.

"It'll never happen."

He chortled, revealing his crooked yellow teeth. "Don't be so sure. Your uncle and I have grown mighty close over the years. I'm the only one he trusts, kinda like father and son."

Which didn't speak highly of Ernie's judgment. Clem was on the outs with his own father. But Delaney understood the connection. Ernie was raised by a hard man to become a hard man. He had no respect for women or what they thought—except in the case of Susannah and Felicity. Those two females alone were held free from contempt. "It's a mis-placed trust that will reveal itself soon enough," she said. Normally, she'd let him simmer and boil in his stupidity, but this time she couldn't. There was more at stake than the old man's feelings and finances. Felicity's future hung in the balance. "I'm putting you on notice, Clem. Back off or I'll make it my personal mission to reveal you for the con artist you are."

"There you go again, callin' names. Why can't we just get along?" he whined.

"I don't want anything to do with you."

A knowing leer snaked through his gaze. "You should've picked me, Dell. I would've treated you better."

Reference to her ex-husband made her skin crawl. "Go on, Clem. Leave me alone before I start to get mad."

He chuckled and reached out for her. "What are you gonna do if I don't?"

Delaney stepped back and Clem lunged for her. "What the—?"

Clem grabbed her arm and propelled his mouth toward hers.

"Delaney!" A male voice powered through the trees.

Clem froze, digging his fingers into her arm.

She slung her free hand into a fist across the side of his head, connecting solidly with his ear. Clem yelped.

Nick Harris charged down through the brush. Branches cracked like twigs as he drilled through them.

Clem released her and immediately reached for the side of his head where she'd slugged him.

Delaney's pulse still ricocheted through her veins, thundered in her chest. "Get away from me!" She shoved Clem hard to the side.

He lost his balance, sending his shoulder into a tree trunk. He cried out in pain.

"Are you okay?" Nick demanded, but quickly turned on Clem, yanking his skinny body to attention like a rag doll.

Delaney savored the plug of fear in Clem's eyes. Served him right for making a stupid move like that—what the hell was he thinking?

"Did he hurt you?"

She shook her head and breathed deeply. Straightening, she replied, "I'm fine." As much as she would enjoy seeing the burly Mr. Harris pulverize the loser, it would cause more trouble than it was worth. Her mind quickly zeroed in on Nick's unannounced arrival. What was it with these men? Was she leaving a trail of blinking lights behind her? Not only did they know where to find her, but why were they interested? Delaney made a hasty mental note. *Next time, cover your tracks.*

Nick glowered at Clem, disgust seething in his dark expression, underscored by the enormity of his physical presence. "If I ever see you touch her again, you're mine. Do you understand?"

Clem's head nodded like a shaken bobble doll.

"Now get out of here." Nick gave him a sharp push. "And don't let me see you again."

Clem scurried away, a scared fawn fleeing an angry bear. Delaney gazed up at Nick. Shoulders the size of boulders, muscles rock solid, eyes volcanic hot, he exuded an ominous strength. She had no doubt this man could kill someone with his bare hands. Finding it an attractive quality, she savored a private smile. "I guess a thank-you is in order."

"You're welcome." After checking Clem's progress, Nick returned his focus to her. His dark gaze smoldered. "Does he do that often?"

"No." She shook her head. "I'm not even sure why he was out here." She paused. Nick's brows furrowed, dark and dangerous. She cupped a hand to her forehead. "I'm not sure why you're out here either."

"I saw you head out here earlier, then I saw him do the same. He seemed in an awful hurry." Nick shrugged. "I figured I'd come and check on things."

"Check on things? What exactly did you expect to find?"

Caught off guard by her insinuation, he chuckled. "Oh, I don't know...that's what I came to find out."

Delaney didn't believe him for a second. Nick Harris had already demonstrated his propensity for rescuing damsels in distress. Did he think she wanted him to hover about her? Though his interference did take the bite out of handling Clem herself. But still...

Delaney glanced about them and wondered why he really came. She was no neophyte when it came to people's true intentions. Rarely were they as they appeared on the surface. No, people usually played one hand above water while the other was dabbling beneath the surface into places it didn't belong. Delaney took one last look around and sighed. No sense in trying to investigate with *him* looking over her shoulder. She'd have to make yet another trip. Delaney grunted and took off for the trail.

"Hey—where are you going?"

"Home."

"On your own?"

"Same way I came in." She pushed wayward branches out of her path and headed for the main trail. "I'm sure you can find your way out."

"What about that fellow, that—"

"Clem?" She continued to press forward, appraising the terrain ahead as she trekked over roots and rocks and leaves. She heard Nick crunching over branches behind her.

"Yes."

"I'm not worried about *him*." She grabbed a nearby branch and hauled herself up a narrow path between rock and tree, but hands at her waist stopped her cold. "Whoa!" she exclaimed, shock shooting through her body. She turned around.

"I just saved your butt back there." A small smile pulled at his mouth, but his eyes held a hint of tease. "Don't you think it would be nice to show me the trail back?"

Face-to-face with a man she hardly knew, Delaney's heart thumped against her ribs. The steel grip on her hips made it impossible to move. The rise of his cologne drifted between them, a gleam built in his eyes. She glanced at the hands on her waist and said, "If you don't mind..."

His grasp loosened, but remained intact. "Well?"

Simultaneously enjoying the feel of his hands but not caring for the ease with which he assumed permission, she hesitated. Delaney hadn't been touched by a man in almost two years, and even though she thought she had moved past the need, his warm touch assured her she had not.

Nick let go, the sudden withdrawal jarring. She felt lighter, emptier. Delaney cleared her throat. "Well, if you can't find your way out, I guess I can lead you to the trailhead."

Nick dished out a salty grin. "Appreciate it."

When he released her, Delaney darted up the trail like a deer before he could stop her.

Doing his level best to keep up, Nick could not maneuver the passageway quite as easily. No longer hiking, they were half-climbing, half-scaling rocks, but he wasn't about to let her get too far ahead of him. She was likely to run off without him. He squeezed himself between branches and trees and bushes and slipped on a moss-covered rock. "Ouch!" A jagged limb stabbed into his side. He looked up, but she was yards ahead of him. Managing the last section as quickly as he could, Nick reached the top, heartened by the sight of her waiting. Winded himself, he was surprised by her lack of fatigue. "You're in good shape."

"When you grow up around here, climbing becomes second nature." She turned, pushed her sleeves up her arms and headed out.

Matching his stride to hers, Nick walked alongside Delaney. Apparently content with their silence, she didn't speak a word. There was nothing but the muted sound of boots hitting clay, the piercing quiet of nature. He'd seen a creek below, but there was no evidence of it up here. Only dirt, air and the occasional stream of sunlight marked their hike. Peering at her from the side, Nick found it odd that neither she nor her uncle welcomed his offer. They weren't even the slightest bit interested, which didn't make sense. Money was money. The taxes were going unpaid. Would they rather lose it at auction than sell it to him? Was it possible Delaney didn't know?

"So you grew up on this land?" he asked, opening conversation in his quest for information.

"I did."

"Lived here your whole life?"

"Pretty much." Delaney kept her line of vision on the ground ahead of them.

"Even when you were married?"

She flicked him a glance lit by annoyance. "I lived on the other side of town back then."

Married her high school sweetheart and from what people around town said, the two seemed like a nice couple. Both families approved. They had a child and then one day Delaney up and left him and he moved out of town. That's where the details became murky. Lips zipped closed and backs turned to business. But a man didn't leave a woman that quick unless he had another bed to sleep in. Did a woman? Glancing sideways at her, she didn't strike him as the type. Needy women cheated, vain women cheated, neither of which Delaney seemed to be. "Was your husband from around here?"

"Yes."

Queen of the short and sweet. He smiled inwardly. "Mind if I ask what happened?"

"I do."

Nick laughed softly and held an overhanging branch out of her way, clearing her path as she passed beneath. "Is it always this difficult to have a conversation with you?"

She looked up at him, but the previous irritation seemed to be gone. "Depends on the subject matter."

"How long have you lived with your uncle?"

"Since Felicity was eight."

"Ten years."

She smirked. "You're good in math."

Nick smiled, unaffected by the remark. He liked looking at her face. Soft and flushed from the hike, her skin was lightly tanned from a life lived outdoors, her eyes brown, yet her brows were dark, almost black. A sharp contrast to her pale blonde hair—a contrast that appealed to him.

But then again, most things female appealed to him. "Why the move? Doesn't appear you and your uncle get along too well."

She lowered her eyes and returned focus to the trail. "Sometimes circumstance dictates the living arrangements."

"Bad divorce?"

"Easy divorce."

"Another woman?"

Delaney replied from the side of her mouth, "Would have been nicer."

Nicer—than another woman? Nick's thoughts circled around what could have caused her to leave. Never married himself, there were few things he could think of worse than infidelity. "Does he keep in touch with Felicity?"

"The occasional phone call, annual birthday card."

"So no infidelity, no custody fight. What kind of man walks away with hardly a glance back?" And leaves a woman as good-looking as you.

As they came up to a waterfall, the cascade of water over rock and cliff quickly overwhelmed the quiet. With his mind divided between the roar of water and the intensity of her gaze, Nick could feel Delaney gauge him, making the mental calculations one would before divulging proprietary information.

She raised her voice over the crash of water and said, "The kind of man where the bottom of the river looks a whole lot different than the surface, Mr. Harris. The deeper you probed, the darker he became. We're almost there," she directed, and continued their hike without another word.

Nick trailed her for a while, his mind streaming with curiosity, his eyes glued to her rear. Delaney Wilkins swaggered more than walked. She was confident in these woods, on her horse, but he detected insecurity with regard to her claim on this land. She had a lot riding on her daughter's inheriting the place it seemed, but something told him she feared it would not happen. Lawyer talk aside, all Ernie had to do was sign it over to someone else and she lost. Did she have a backup plan?

Once reunited with her horse, she wasted no time sliding the reins over the mare's head. She pointed. "The house is that way."

Nick knew the way from here. "Thanks."

The horse blew an exhalation as Delaney prepared to mount. Watching her jump on, he marveled at her agility. Even in jeans, she made the transition with ease. As she smiled down at him, the sun caught the gold strands in her hair. She sat astride the animal, her slender jean-clad legs pushed open wide, shoulders back—in command, comfortable. Sexy. He felt a spark of desire. "Where are you off to now?" he asked, because wherever it was, he wouldn't mind joining her.

"I have to work."

"What kind of work do you do?" he asked innocently.

"Bookkeeping."

"You an accountant?"

"No degree, but I know the ins and outs of finance as well as any certified accountant." She lifted a shoulder and added, "I handle the books for several area businesses."

"Nice."

"It pays the bills."

"Something else you'd rather be doing?"

She laughed, almost despite herself. "I'd rather look after the horses all day than fiddle with numbers, but they don't pay me anything," she said, then seemed to catch herself. The merriment in her face shut down, her expression became guarded.

He chuckled. "No, but they *can* cost a fortune. You have other horses besides this beauty?" he persisted, hoping to re-ignite the joy in her eyes.

Pleased by the compliment to her mare, Delaney replied, "We have a total of six on property. Nobody rides anymore but Felicity and I."

"Why keep them?" Seemed an expensive hobby for a woman on a limited budget.

Delaney looked horrified. "I couldn't get rid of them—they're part of the family."

Nick nodded. People got pretty crazy when it came to their animals. He'd heard stories where people would feed their cat before feeding themselves. It was an alien concept to him. Traveling as much as he did, he didn't have time for a wife, let alone a dog.

"Well, I better get going," she said. "Thanks again for stepping in with Clem. It's good to see him squirm."

The comment drew Nick back to the scene in the woods and his insides hardened. It was an image he'd rather forget but would enjoy finishing if the man ever gave him the chance.

Chapter Six

Nick decided a trip to town was warranted. Time for Plan B. Ernie wasn't paying the taxes. The county would only wait so long before they demanded payment, and that payment could come in the form of tax deed sale. If dealing with the owner regarding the sale wasn't going to work, he'd deal with the local government. They'd want their money, and if he offered a way for them to get it, they'd jump—especially if enough incentive was involved. After all, it was an election year.

Pulling onto Main Street just shy of noon, Nick decided to get a bite to eat first. He'd skipped breakfast due to a conference call, and his stomach was rumbling in protest. The parking lot for Fran's Diner was packed. The square cement building had a curved entrance wall, peeling aqua paint and red neon-lettered sign in an airstream font straight out of the fifties or sixties. It didn't appear Fran had spent a whole lot on either building or décor since the place was built, but that was fine with him. From Montana to Texas, Colorado to New York City, he'd be hard pressed to find a burger better than Fran's. Although he was accustomed to dining at five-star restaurants, there was something to be said for a plain old-fashioned good food. Fat, juicy, served with American cheese, fresh tomato and sweet onion, his last meal at Fran's was memorable. Greasy on the digestion, but memorable on the taste buds.

Nick opened the metal-framed glass door and, suddenly dodging to one side, held it open as a young woman and baby stroller hurtled toward him on her way out. He nodded as she thanked him with a tip of her head and a smile. She looked awfully young to have babies, he mused, his gaze trailing her

narrow backside as she passed. But that was small town living. Kids met and married their high school sweethearts and
never looked back—except for Delaney. For some reason she
ditched hers in fairly short order.

As Nick joined the throng inside, his senses were quickly enveloped in a sensory fest of greasy meat and French-
fried potatoes. Thick layers of it hung in the air, thrust out by
a chaotic kitchen that sizzled with smoke amongst a fury of
activity. Waitresses hurried from red-vinyled booth to red-
vinyled booth, scribbling across notepads in rapid sequence.
As expected, every seat in the house was occupied, plus a
healthy line crowded out from the hostess stand. A tray full of
burgers flew by him and his stomach growled.

Nick moved to the end of the crowd and prepared to settle in for the wait when he caught sight of a familiar face. At
one end of the long counter, a young woman sat alone,
perched on the round red cushion of a metal barstool. Book in
hand, half-eaten burger on the plate in front of her, it was the
strawberry-blonde hair that snared his attention. He'd seen
her before. The red-headed counter waitress walked over and
refilled the girl's iced tea, smiled and said something. The
girl turned to thank the woman and a burst of pleasure erupted inside him. Well, what do you know...? Opportunity truly
came in all forms.

Abandoning his space in line, Nick walked over to the
young woman. After giving her a minute to realize he was
there, he introduced himself. Speaking over shouts from the
kitchen staff, he extended a hand, "I'm Nick Harris. I've been
talking to your uncle about purchasing the property. You're
Delaney Wilkins' daughter, aren't you?"

Felicity flipped her heart-shaped face up to him. "Oh,"
she exclaimed quietly.

Was that surprise he heard, or relief that she recognized
who he was?

She darted a glance around, then reached out to accept
his hand. "Nice to meet you. I'm Felicity."

"Hi, Felicity." The two shook hands and Nick marveled at her fragile grasp. Her fingers were like bones and skin within the meat of his palm, but warm to the touch. Clearly, there was only one bull dog in the Wilkins family. "Taking a break from school?" he prompted, wondering at her midday presence in the restaurant.

"Oh no," she said, mildly flushing at the insinuation. "I'm a senior. Wednesdays are half-days for me."

"Half-days?" Nick chuckled. "Wish there were such a thing as half-days when I was in school." She swallowed her smile and reached for her iced-tea. So she was shy, to boot. *Interesting.* "Has your mother told you about me?"

Felicity nodded.

"Order up!" came the shout from behind the service counter. A waitress quickly responded and yanked the paper ticket from above. She slid the heaping plates from the ledge to her awaiting tray and then hurried off.

Ignoring the eyes beginning to stray toward their conversation, Nick said, "I've been talking to Mr. Ladd about turning the property into a showplace. I want to create the gem of the South—*the* premier resort spa for people to come and enjoy the beauty of Tennessee, become one with the land." He noticed the man seated behind Felicity leaned toward her nonchalantly, as though trying to dial in to their conversation without being detected. "I run a group of eco-friendly spa hotels."

Her eyes widened as curiosity took over. "She didn't tell me that."

He smiled. Of course she didn't. She didn't want Felicity anywhere near a positive opinion of him. But according to Delaney, Nick was looking at the rightful heir of Ladd Springs, and getting this young woman on his side might prove beneficial in his endeavor. "Well, she probably has a lot on her mind," he said genially. "I understand how it may have skipped her thoughts to tell you. May I?"

Felicity looked down at her plate, then up at him. She set her book down on the counter and dabbed at her mouth with a paper napkin. She perked up with a smile. "Sure. Why not?"

Nick went into sales mode and explained his plans for the property. He made certain to hit upon all of the environmentally friendly aspects of the project, the warm and homey feel he wanted to incorporate into the hotel, as well as the luxurious spa amenities. The red-headed counter waitress continually eyed him, while the man seated next to her continued to listen in on their conversation. His split attention became obvious when the waitress addressed him twice with no response.

"I offered to split off enough acreage for you and your family to stay and live on the property," Nick informed her. "Including full lifetime privileges at the hotel and spa, my treat. A job, if you want it." He winked. She laughed gaily at that and he raised a brow. "What? Not interested in work?"

"Oh no," she exclaimed. Her finger shot to her lips. "I didn't mean that!" Her youth shone brightly in her embarrassment, her faintly freckled skin tinged pink as she drew her hand away. "I only meant that I plan to have a career as a flutist, not working at a hotel." She collected herself and added, "But thanks, anyway."

"A flutist?" he asked, thoroughly intrigued.

"Yes." She sat a little straighter and turned more fully to him. "I'm going to college next year at the University of Tennessee. They have a phenomenal program where I intend to further my skill."

"You're a flutist *now*?"

"I am," she said, streaks of pride streaming through her eyes, demure yet vibrant as she discussed her passion.

Nick nodded. He'd found *someone's* hot spot. Setting a hand to the counter, he leaned over, but not too close. In these parts he was liable to get shot by some unseen stranger deciding he'd taken one too many liberties with the fair and impressionable young Wilkins girl. He cast a glance at the onlookers with a cautious eye, then peered down at her and ventured, "College is pretty expensive. You're very fortunate to be able to attend your school of choice."

Felicity's vigor lost its punch. When she didn't respond, he knew his shot in the dark had found its mark. "Your mom must be so proud of you, being accepted, following your dream. That's impressive stuff."

"She is."

"Well, if you'd like a job during your summer break, I'd love to have you at the hotel," Nick promised, speaking as though the matter of title had been decided in his favor. "Having a flutist would be a tremendous asset to the Serenity Spa."

"Serenity Spa?" she asked.

He stood to his full six-foot-four stature. "That's my trade name for the hotel spas. In this case, I'd call it Serenity Springs Spa." He grinned and asked in a near conspiratorial tone, "What do you think?"

"I like it." She smiled, and he noted her previous warmth had returned.

"I'm offering a generous amount for the property. You may want to discuss it with your mother." He lowered his voice so that only she could hear. "The money could ensure you don't have to work during your four years at the university, make sure your mom can take care of those beautiful horses of hers."

"She'd love that!"

He smiled. Hot button, number two. "There'd even be enough left over to build a nice-sized cabin for you both to live in."

Judging by the wistful air that entered her gaze, Nick decided he was right on target. The match was lit. It was time to let the fire build. "Listen," he said and placed a hand over his stomach. "It was nice talking to you, but I need to feed the beast. Maybe I can hear you play one day?"

She met his question with a polite nod. "Maybe." When he took a step toward the hostess booth, she added, "It was nice talking to you, Mr. Harris."

After meeting with her clients, Delaney swung by the post office and grocery, then added a stop at the feed store on her way out of town. It was near three o'clock and she needed to get back. Felicity would be home soon and she would not come home to an empty cabin. Fortunately, the attorney had good news. He had prepared an affidavit for Ashley to sign, stating that she had witnessed the promise made from Ernie to her mother regarding the property. All it needed was a signature. Her attorney had suggested she ask her uncle to create a family trust, or sign over a quit-claim deed if he didn't want to prepare a will, but warned she'd better act soon. According to the county clerk, they were putting together a list of properties in default on their taxes and the letters to delinquent property owners would go out soon.

Delinquent property owners. Ernie was a delinquent all right, and he had no business putting the Ladd property in jeopardy. Delaney flipped on her turn signal, and checking for traffic, pulled onto the road and headed out of town. The truck's gauge for her gas tank dinged. She looked down and grumbled under her breath. Dang thing ran through more gas than a cow on a grassy field. Nearest station was five miles ahead or three blocks back. She grunted. No time like the present. Spinning the wheel in a hard right, she bounced over a dip in the street and accelerated. Next corner, she stopped, looked both ways then jammed her foot to the brake. The truck lurched forward in a hard jerk, but her focus had been pulled in a different direction.

Catty-corner across the road, she spotted Clem Sweeney standing outside a convenience store speaking to two men—a very distinct duo she had seen before. From her vantage point, she couldn't make out their faces but there was no question about their identity. They were her strangers in the woods. Same hats, same build, it was them all right. *And they were talking to Clem.*

Fury permeated every cell of her body. Steam blew out her ears. Leave it to him to be tied up with those no good trespassers. Instinct nearly glued her foot to the accelerator, but good sense intervened. Nothing good would come of confronting Clem—not until she could use it to her advantage, anyway. If those men were up to trouble on Ladd property, Uncle Ernie would not take kindly to learning his darling Clem was mixed up with them. A slow smile tugged at her mouth. And learn he would.

Taking care not to draw attention to herself, Delaney took the turn, easy and slow. Some days, driving a nondescript truck, much the same as half the town drove, had its high points. She wouldn't stand out in a crowd—or turning the corner as she made her way to the gas station.

After filling her tank, Delaney drove home, her thoughts running circles around potential scenarios that involved Clem and the two men. With an elbow out the open window, hair whipping to and fro, she suddenly understood Clem's surprise appearance in the woods. It was no coincidence he'd showed up yesterday at precisely the time she was poking around the spot the men had been the day before. He knew what they were doing there. Hell, he probably put them up to it!

And she would know, too. Soon enough. She had an appointment with the bank in the morning, but after lunch she'd head back into the forest, and this time she'd cover her tracks. No one would be the wiser to her whereabouts—not Clem and not Nick. Though why Nick was so interested in following her continued to elude her. He wasn't from these parts. He didn't know Clem, didn't know her. He didn't know the woods. Didn't he say so himself, asking her to lead him out safely? Why bother to follow her? What was the point?

There was much about Nick Harris she didn't know. For starters, she didn't know why he wanted this property so badly, not when there were plenty of other acres available for sale and for a good price, too. Any number of tracts would be suitable for his hotel project, but he seemed hell bent on getting his hands on this one. Why?

Passing the driveway to her home on her way to Ashley's, Delaney's grip tightened on the wheel. Parked alongside Felicity's red compact was Annie Owen's white two-door sedan. Delaney's heart thumped in defiance. Annie wasn't back at it again, was she?

Instead of heading to Ashley's, she swerved into the yard and sped over the gravel drive, dust billowing up around her truck as she closed in on the house. Slamming boot to brakes, she yanked the gear shift into park and pushed out of the truck, marched over to Ernie's cabin and pounded up the steps. "What the hell are you doing here?"

Chapter Seven

Annie Owens turned to take Delaney head on. She wasn't afraid of her and she would not back down. Her daughter Casey was a direct descendent of Ernie and as such, had every right to stake her claim to the title of Ladd Springs. "I'm here to speak with Ernie." She laced arms across her chest." "If it's any of your business."

Delaney waved an insolent finger through the air and said, "It absolutely is my business when you come here trying to swindle my daughter's property from under her feet."

Annie shook her new page boy cut and laughed derisively. "You can't swindle something from someone who has nothing."

Delaney's brown eyes turned to stone, cold as river rock. "I have a lawyer who says otherwise."

"You're not the only one with a lawyer, Delaney." Annie gave her a once-over. "Casey has rights and I aim to see that she gets what's coming to her."

"Nothing's coming to her, because you're leaving."

Delaney took a step toward her and Annie warned, "Go ahead. I'd love for you to add assault to my lawyer's list of complaints."

Delaney froze.

Heartbeats walloped within her chest wall. "Guess you're smarter than I thought," Annie said. Messing with Delaney Wilkins was not on her list of things to do. She'd hated the woman for as long as she could remember, but taking a tumble with her was not a winning proposition. She was like a cat in heat and would scrap at the slightest provocation. Clem's bullet scar served as a sharp reminder to anyone paying attention.

But Annie was on firm ground in this discussion. Casey was Jeremiah's daughter and despite his refusal to acknowledge the same, the courts would do so for him. That's what the lawyer told her.

"You're wasting your time, Annie."

She gave a terse shake to her head. "Don't think so."

Ernie's chair creaked beneath him as he pitched forward. "You two quit you're squabblin' already, would ya? I done told her I ain't signin' over a thing to that illegitimate brat of hers."

"At least we can agree on something," Delaney said to him.

The words stung, but Annie held her tongue. Beside Ernie, Albert rocked quietly, content to watch the fireworks around him without the slightest interest. Annie wondered if he understood what was going on but decided it was doubtful. The man was as an empty skull atop a listless body. His sons Robby and Billy were no different.

"Go on all you want with your insults, but the fact remains," Annie said, injecting her spine with steel, "Casey is Jeremiah's daughter and blood is thicker than some phony promise you made up to get the property for Felicity."

Delaney's hand flinched at her side and Annie's feelers popped out. She'd best be careful or the witch might just *add* that assault charge, Annie thought. "It's all there." She pointed to an envelope on a small table between Ernie and Albert, but quickly curled her shaky finger into a fist, dropping it by her side. "If you have any questions, you can contact my lawyer." She flashed a heated gaze to Delaney and said, "Come near me, and I'll file an injunction against you."

"Don't worry," Delaney replied. "I won't. And speaking of attorneys," she said, directing her words more to Ernie than Annie. "I've just come from a visit with mine. Ernie, consider yourself officially on notice."

"Notice for what?" he griped, dodging her gaze. Albert turned toward her as though he'd just tuned into the conversation.

"We're going to court."

He pushed back in the rocker and swiped, "I ain't goin' to no court."

"You are, if the judge says you are, or else you'll end up in jail." Albert looked away at the mention of jail. "If you don't stick to your promise, the courts will force your hand."

"What grounds do you have to go to court?" Annie asked, her confidence leaking at the mention of official notification.

"Legal grounds, something you seem to lack."

At the moment, Annie didn't have anything official when it came to paperwork, but she darn sure would tell her lawyer to get her some! A paternity test was her only true path to victory, but without Jeremiah's cooperation, there would be no test. She could ask a court to order him, but court fights were fought dirtier than street fights, and she had no interest in holding herself out for that kind of punishment.

Until now. Casey's inheritance depended upon it. Annie looked down her nose at Ernie. She could get a paternity test based on the grandparent, but that would require yanking a gray hair from that balding head of his—which was tempting in its own right but highly unlikely. For an old man Ernie was surprisingly agile when he wanted to be. She'd seen him take out a snake with his walking stick not two months ago. A shudder ran through her and her thoughts turned to Casey. She deserved to call Ladd Springs her home.

"Well now, who forgot to invite me to the party?"

Annie whirled and her breath caught.

Clem Sweeney smiled oil and vinegar as he ogled Annie's body, his gaze slithering over her scooped-neck blouse, her jean-clad legs, then settling on her breasts. "Mighty nice surprise to see you, Annie."

"Clem." It was all she could spit out, the breath still trapped in her chest. She had not expected to run into *him*.

Delaney looked at him and piped up, "Speak of the devil. Annie here says Casey deserves this property as the rightful heir, on account of Jeremiah and all."

When Clem looked at her, Annie squirmed inside. "Casey is Jeremiah's, you say?"

Delaney nodded. "That's what she says."

Annie didn't like where this was going. "I have to go."

"What's with the sudden rush, Annie?" Delaney asked.

"I've said my piece," she said. "Ernie, the next step is the court."

"I'm tired of all this court talk, now get!" He dismissed her with an aggravated wave.

"Who's talkin' about court?" Clem asked the lot of them.

When no one said a word, Albert pointed at Delaney and Annie. "Them is."

Clem sharpened his gaze on the women.

"You might watch your back around Clem, Annie," Delaney said. "Seems he's after the property, too."

Annie reeled on Clem. "What do you have to do with Ladd Springs?"

Clem ignored her and snarled to Delaney, "You sure are a big talker when your boyfriend ain't around, aren't ya, Dell?"

"I didn't need backup, Clem," Delaney defended. "Never did. I could have handled you fine all by myself."

He snickered. "Maybe I oughta send that city boy a thank-you card."

Annie wondered what they were talking about, but wanted no part. Clem Sweeney was trouble, and it was best she steer clear of the man. Stuffing her curiosity into her back pocket, she headed for her car.

"See you in court, Annie," Delaney called out after her.

Delaney was right behind her, but first she had a few words for her uncle. Strolling near to him, she said, "I've got a sworn affidavit for Ashley to sign stating she witnessed your promise to my mother. We will take it to court if you don't honor your promise to my mother before then."

Her attorney said that if Ernie wanted to change his mind, it was his prerogative, but perhaps the affidavit would convince him otherwise. However, if he died intestate, which meant without a will, then Tennessee law dictated who received what—Jeremiah had first rights, Albert second, and she and Felicity were third in line. Along with Casey, should Annie ever prove her paternity claim. Without Jeremiah in the picture, Delaney knew she would have a better chance in court. Armed with Ernie's deathbed promise to her mother, the lawyer said it would then depend upon whether Uncle Albert fought her for title—something she was certain would not happen—and which judge heard the case. Who sat on the bench was anyone's guess.

Ernie's eyes became beads of hate in his colorless face. He pulled the pipe from his mouth and rubbed the white whiskers of his jaw. "What do you want, Delaney?"

"I want the property."

"Why?"

"She wants money," Clem responded for her.

"It's not the money," she said to Clem, irked by his nosey presence. "But Ernie knows my desire runs deeper. It's about family and tradition. It's about ensuring my daughter has a place to live, a legacy to pass on." She paused, allowing it to sink in. "It's what you were supposed to do, Uncle Ernie. My mother would turn in her grave if she knew you were even considering allowing this property to fall out of family hands."

He didn't reply and Clem became squirrely. "You're as greedy as they come, Dell. He sees right through you, can't you see that?"

"It's up to you, Ernie," she said, without acknowledging Clem. "It's your call. This isn't about me, it's about Felicity. Your *granddaughter*," she emphasized, as though it were a fact that had slipped his mind. "We can play nice, or we can play ugly, but one way or another, Felicity and I will not be kicked off of Ladd Springs."

Without another word, Delaney stomped off to her truck. Boots crunching over gravel, she hoped it sunk in. She hoped Ernie would remember his sister and do what was right. Clem's cozy visits were doing nothing but stir up mud—especially after his stupid stunt in the forest. What the hell possessed him to do such a thing? He'd been after her all through high school, but since she married and divorced Jack, not a peep. She swung open the door to her truck and hopped in. It was strange behavior, even for him.

She'd brought up the part about Jeremiah, because Delaney suspected Clem and Annie had a thing, years back, but it was only speculation. Was Casey Clem's daughter?

She turned the ignition and tore out of the driveway. Sure would make her life easier if she was.

Delaney drove the short distance to Ashley Fulmer's house, a modest log cabin sitting on ten acres of manicured lawn, a backdrop of forest to the rear. Potted plants filled with flowers hung across the front porch, knick knacks of every size and shape littered the walls, hung from shutters, sat perched out by the walkway in welcome. But the eccentric décor was but one facet of the woman inside. After a quick rap on the door, Delaney let herself in and called out for Ashley.

Ashley poked her head out from the kitchen and waved with a toothy grin. "Hey, darlin'!" Dressed in denim skirt and sequin-covered fuchsia blouse, her platinum hair twisted high atop her head, she had more bracelets jangling from her wrist than Delaney had owned in the course of a lifetime. But Ashley was the Queen of Bling around these parts and clogging champ. When she spruced up for a run on the dance floor, watch out—this woman had fire in her boots, glitter in her eyes and a win in her heart. She and her husband Booker were county champs for five years running now. "C'mon in, make yourself comfy. I'm in the middle of supper."

Ashley was her mother's closest friend, closer than any sister could be. She had laughed with her mom during the good times, cried during the bad and held vigil bedside as she fought through the darkest days of her life.

"Smells like someone's making pie."

"You've got a nose like a bloodhound. My blueberries were ready early so I decided to make pie. It's in the oven now."

Delaney laughed softly. "What else would you do with blueberries?"

"Aw, honey, you know they're my weakness."

"And oh-so-delicious in pie form."

Ashley laughed in agreement. "You know life is good when the blueberries are plump on the bush!"

Delaney strolled over, grabbed a big hug from her, and was instantly enveloped in soft motherly comfort and powdery perfume. With her mother gone, Ashley was the next best thing. "How are you?" she asked.

"I'm brighter than a peacock in heat, how 'bout you?"

"Getting by," Delaney replied. Uninterested in dwelling on her troubles, she admired the frilly smock Ashley wore. "I like your apron."

"Isn't it precious?" With floured hands, Ashley held it out for inspection. "One of the girls from church was selling these at the bazaar last week and you know me, I had to have one. Matches my boots," she said in a flirty fashion, outstretching her leg, twisting her boot on its toe.

Bejeweled in a punch of rhinestones, yellow and pink and purple, the apron was trimmed in green lace, a tiny floral pattern running through each swatch of fabric. It had Ashley written all over it. "Bet it was calling out your name."

Ashley laughed, her generous bosom rising and falling with each breath she took. "There were three more like it child, it was all I could do not to grab them, too," she exclaimed and winked. "But it just wouldn't be fair to the others, you know what I'm sayin'?"

"I do," Delaney replied and hated to put a damper on Ashley's good mood, but she was here with a purpose. Best to get to it and get on with it. "I have that paper for you to sign."

Without a second's hesitation, Ashley said, "Whip it out, Delly, and I'll get my pen." Ashley snatched a dishtowel from the counter beside her and wiped the flour from her hands.

"I think you have to go to your bank to sign it. Something about it has to be witnessed."

"Not a problem. I'll put it over here in my 'to do' pile. I'm going to town tomorrow, I'll do it then." Ashley stopped short. With hands to her hips, blue eyes lined in black swamped with concern. "Why so glum, darlin'?"

Delaney shrugged. "Ran into Annie at Ernie's place on the way over here."

"What's that wild cat want with the old coot now?"

Ashley was Annie's godmother and loved her like a daughter, but she called a skunk a skunk and a young woman with a wild streak, exactly that—wild. Delaney sighed. "She's still making noise about getting the property for Casey."

"It'll never happen," Ashley said, all signs of light-hearted fun erased from her tone. That property belongs to you and Felicity. She knows that."

"I don't want it for me, Ashley. It's for Felicity," Delaney defended.

"I know you say you don't, but your momma's spirit lives on that land and you need to be there, to be close." Ashley picked up a raw chicken breast and dredged the prickly pale skin in a pan of flour, speckled with orange and black. Cajun fried chicken was one of her specialties, and Delaney almost wished she could stay for dinner. "It was important to Susannah that you live here 'til your dyin' day. And she would have loved Felicity to do the same."

Delaney's throat closed and she nodded.

"She deserved half that property and she would have passed it on to you—you know as well as I do, it's true."

"But Jeremiah is entitled to his share, isn't he?"

"He was until he ran off with that little vixen and left his father to rot." Ashley patted the flour around the breast, filling in around the rib cage, packing it onto the flaps of hanging skin, mincing no words when it came to family. "Whether Casey is really Jeremiah's offspring or not is irrelevant. As far as I reckon, he surrendered his rights the day he deserted his father—whether the man deserved his devotion or not."

Delaney rubbed a hand over her forehead. As much as she'd like to agree with Ashley, she couldn't. Legally speaking, Jeremiah could contest any will that didn't include him. Stood a better chance should Ernie die without one.

"Don't you fret, Delly. We'll get this done. A deathbed promise will hold up in a court of law. He wrote it down himself and I watched him do it."

And burned it three months later. Grief at losing his sister had overtaken Ernie in the beginning but eventually festered into hatred. He couldn't think straight, he couldn't see straight. He could only feel the loss of his sister—the one person in this world who cared about him had died. Wanting to keep her close, Ernie buried his sister near the slope between his cabin and hers. In his own weird rationale, it was his way of taking care of her, watching over her. He built a wooden cross to mark the spot, even planted flowers. He was pitiful—and over a loss he could have avoided.

After a brief visit with Ashley, Delaney drove home. Predictably, Ashley had invited her to stay, but she needed to get home, to be there for Felicity. Passing the main house, Delaney fumed inwardly at the greedy hands working to massage Ernie their way. Although she felt sorry for Annie and her pathetic past, Casey was an illegitimate heir. Annie and Jeremiah had never married. Hell, they barely had a relationship! He used her for his pleasure. He knew she'd be there any time he snapped his fingers, and he took full advantage. To make matters worse, he ran off to Atlanta with Annie's sister Lacy, leaving Annie pregnant and alone.

But Annie had been fairly loose back in the day. Casey could belong to anyone and without a positive paternity test,

Delaney was not willing to grant her rights to Ladd Springs. As far as Clem went, Delaney would be damned if he got anywhere near the title to the property.

Sure as she was breathing, that man and his cohorts were up to no good in her forest, and she would expose him to be the con artist she knew him to be. But first, she had to secure the proof.

Chapter Eight

After slipping her gun into the loop inside her boot, Delaney pulled her pant leg down and stood. Felicity had already left for the day, getting an early start on her history exam in first period. It was a study ethic to be envied and one that earned her the partial scholarship to UT. But the scholarship didn't cover living expenses. It didn't cover car insurance, gas or clothes, all of which were expensive. Felicity offered to work, bless her heart, but Delaney was against it. She'd have the rest of her life to work. Right now, she needed to focus on her studies and her flute practice, and as her mother it was her job to see that it happened. That it *all* happened.

Skipping breakfast, Delaney headed for the stables. Most of today would be spent working, but this afternoon she was going to learn once and for all what was going on with Clem and his men—right after she retrieved Ashley's signed affidavit and delivered a copy of it to Ernie. If that didn't put a bug in his bottom, nothing would. And if her attorney was right, time was running out. The property would go up for auction to settle the taxes, but she didn't have the cash to bid, though she knew someone who did.

There was no doubt in her mind that Nick Harris had the money and would gladly step in and scoop this property up for pennies on the acre, but he'd have to step over her dead body before he could sign on the dotted line, and even then he'd better be afraid she'd drag him down by the boot strap. This property belonged to Felicity, not some stranger who solely wanted to profit from its riches.

When Delaney finally made it home after her rounds, she turned into the driveway and her heart sank. Nick's car was parked in front of Ernie's. Did the man ever quit?

She had business with Ernie and she could do without the complication of *him*. As she rolled the truck alongside Felicity's red compact, anger detonated in her chest, as over by the wishing well, she saw Nick and Felicity were sitting alone together. *Alone.*

Delaney jammed the brakes, flung the gearshift into park and leaped out of the truck, catching her knee hard against the door frame. Damn! That was going to leave a mark. But despite the throb she stormed over to them, her pulse rampaging through her veins. "What the hell do you think you're doing?"

Felicity jumped to her feet, her eyes clouding with apprehension. "What?" She glanced nervously between Nick and her mother.

Nick rose slowly, his broad chest outlined by a tailored red button-down, his legs long and solid in fitted blue jeans.

Delaney pointed a finger in his face. Heat rose beneath her tank top, the air warm, the sun passing in and out of clouds overhead. "You stay away from my daughter, do you hear me?"

"Whoa," he said, holding palms up between them. His dark eyes took on a cautionary alertness. "We're just talking. I'm not causing any trouble here." He glanced at Felicity. "A friendly conversation, right?"

"Taking advantage of a teenager? Really?" She looked to Felicity. "What's he trying to do—convince you to sell him the property?"

"No, Mom—*honest*." She chanced a timid glance up at him and said, "We were just talking about the University of Tennessee."

"You have nothing more to say to him."

"Why don't you let her decide that? She is eighteen, which makes her an adult in my book."

Delaney grunted. "I want you off my property. *Now.*"

Nick looked to Felicity, as if seeking her opinion, but she would not look at him. "Okay, I'm going. Like I said, I'm not here to cause trouble."

When he didn't budge, Delaney pressed, "Well? What are you waiting for?"

He peered down at her with a quizzical expression. "Do you know the taxes haven't been paid on this property for the last three years?"

She didn't reply.

"And that the clerk is scheduling this land to go up for sale at auction?"

She knew it and didn't need his reminders.

"Are you willing to allow that to happen?" Nick glanced down at Felicity, currently mired in a look of complete and total agony. The poor thing was caught square in the middle and not of her own accord. Delaney knew full well that Felicity would rather walk away from the land than allow it to cause a rift in the family. Nick's voice drew her back to him. Soft, sensible, it pulled at her. "You're willing to jeopardize her rights to ownership, the same ones you claim to be fighting so hard for?"

Hot sun splashed on her head and shoulders, setting fire to her ponytail and flushed skin. Of course not! The last thing she wanted was for anyone to jeopardize her rights, but as it stood, she had none. Knowing he could swoop in and take everything didn't help matters. "I said, 'Get off my property,'" Delaney repeated.

He shook his head. "I think you two need to do some serious talking. I'm offering you a way to keep this land and enough money to secure her education and your future. Why are you so dead set against it?"

She bristled. "Keep this land?" She flung an arm toward the forest. "A measly hundred acres? That's what you're so proud to be offering?"

"Can you afford the over thousand you have?"

Darn right she could, but she wasn't about to let him in on how. Delaney settled hands to her hips and said directly, "I know men like you, Mr. Harris, and you're interested in one thing and one thing only—money. Yours." She whipped a finger toward Felicity. "You don't care about us, and I don't appreciate you pretending otherwise."

Nick eased away from her and drew the sunglasses down from his head. "You must know something I don't know then, because you're not making a whole lot of sense."

"I know about family and tradition and I know about loyalty. Values I imagine may be foreign concepts to you, but around these parts they're worth their weight in gold."

For the first time, he smiled. Arrogant, comfortable with himself. "You don't know the first thing about me, Ms. Wilkins."

"I know enough."

"You don't, but I'll be happy to fill you in any time you'd like. Just say the word and I'll tell you anything you want to know."

The supple, intimate tone rattled her. Under any other circumstance, it was an invitation she might accept, he a man she might like to entertain. But not when he was trying to get her land. She couldn't. "Let's go, Felicity." Delaney reached out and took her daughter by the arm. "If you'll excuse us."

Without waiting for a reply, Delaney steered Felicity's slender figure straight over to Ernie's cabin, her temper clanging between Nick's audacity at approaching her daughter and the extent of his knowledge about the property auction. If she had any reservations about what was at stake, she didn't anymore. Nick Harris had his eye on the tax deed and Ernie was going to hear about it.

"Mom, I'm sorry," Felicity whined at her side. "I didn't know you'd be mad if I talked to him."

"I don't blame you, honey, I blame him." She loosened her grip on Felicity's arm, a sudden stream of guilt washing through her.

"But he seems like a nice guy."

Delaney heard the question unspoken. *Why did you have to be so rude to him?*

Felicity was an innocent. She didn't understand the way people manipulated and twisted. She saw what she wanted to see, what she understood. Her daughter couldn't fathom deceit. She couldn't fathom greed and underhanded dealing. It wasn't in her nature. It wasn't who she was, and Delaney wasn't about to taint her heart with it now. "Mr. Harris wants to buy the property and turn it into a hotel."

"I know. He told me. He wants to make it a hotel and spa, called Serenity Springs, like all the others he owns."

She turned to Felicity, her spine jarred as she stepped on a large rock and stopped. "How long have you two been sitting there?"

"Not long. But he told me most of this yesterday at Fran's."

Panic stabbed her side. "He followed you to Fran's?"

Felicity rolled her eyes. "He didn't *follow* me. I was there eating lunch and so was he. He introduced himself and told me about his plans."

Thank God they were in public, was all Delaney could think. She'd go see Fran tomorrow and get the real deal on what transpired between the two. Fran Jones was more than diner owner. She was the town's source for information and there was no doubt in Delaney's mind that Fran had noticed the tall, dark stranger speaking to Felicity. Nothing got past the woman and she would spill the goods—willingly. "What else did he tell you?"

"That he wants to give us land to live on, and enough money for my college." She hesitated. "That's good, right? Then we wouldn't have to cut all those trees down?"

Delaney's heart split. Felicity was focused on the trees instead of the forest. She was irrationally bound by the image of tree stumps instead of taking in the big picture. Delaney brushed the loose curls from Felicity's eyes and said, "Sweetheart, if we sell to him, we'll have sealed the fate of this land, a fate far worse than a few trees. We'll have lost control of our legacy, our future."

"But we don't need a thousand acres to live on. A hundred is enough, isn't it? You could have your horses, we could still back up to the forest."

Ladd Springs was so much more to Delaney than a place to live. It was home, yes, but it was history. It was her childhood, her mother's childhood and her mother before her. This was Ladd land, her family birthright. But staring into delicate, trusting eyes, she feared her child would not understand. "This property belongs to us, to you. I'm giving Uncle Ernie a chance to do the right thing."

"What if he doesn't?"

"He will." Ernie Ladd was a lot of things, but stupid was not one of them. He wouldn't lose this property to a tax sale. In the end, Delaney believed he'd do what was right by his sister and pass it down the line.

"Delaney!"

She and Felicity turned at the sound of his voice bellowing from the porch.

"Get over here!" he hollered, and like a man expecting to be minded, he sought out the nearest rocker and dropped to a seat.

"Time to pay our respects," she said, a sweep of anticipation zipping through her.

Delaney retrieved Ashley's affidavit from the front seat of her truck and met Felicity on the porch. She intentionally refused to make eye contact with Nick as he passed her en route to his car. She didn't want him to mistake her attention as second thought.

She couldn't afford second thoughts.

Envelope in hand, she hustled up the steps and briefly wondered where Albert was. Usually he was molded into a chair beside his brother. He sure as heck didn't have anything else to do.

"I have the paper from Ashley," Delaney said and handed it over.

"Keep your paper. I've got one for you, instead."

Her surprise was swift. "A paper for me?"

"Here." He shoved it her way with one hand, the other clutching his pipe between bony fingers.

Handing her envelope to Felicity, Delaney reached for his manila file folder and opened it. Scanning the document in short order, she looked at him. "No deal." She slid the piece of paper into the folder and gave it back.

But Ernie wouldn't take it. "You're a fool if you don't."

"I'm no fool, Ernie and neither are you."

He muttered under his breath, but nothing audible. Delaney took her document from Felicity and handed it to Ernie. "Ashley has signed a sworn affidavit that says she saw you write down your promise to my mother about giving this property to Felicity."

Ernie glared at her, bitterness dripping from his gaze. If he'd been an ax murderer, her head would be rolling on the ground.

"Mom wanted this land for me and Felicity and you told her you'd do it. You should be happy that I'm relieving you of the pain of giving anything to me." Delaney gestured toward Felicity, hating that she had to hear any of this ugly business. But to deprive her? It was unthinkable.

"There ain't no such paper," he said to her, sidestepping Felicity's gaze as best he could.

"There was until you destroyed it."

Ernie grew very quiet. He flicked a glinty eye toward Felicity then settled his wrath on Delaney. "You're nothin' but a greedy gold-digger. Ever since you took up with Jack Foster, you showed your true colors."

"Felicity, go on up to the cabin," Delaney directed. "I'll catch up with you."

Felicity didn't hesitate. With a curt nod, she scrambled off the porch and up to their cabin. Her mother's cabin. Susannah's cabin.

Delaney quieted the chaos of emotion churning in her heart. "This isn't about me, Ernie. This is about Felicity."

"I don't believe that for a second." Ernie leaned on the arm of his chair. "You'd steal that sweet girl blind, the minute I signed it over to her. Just like you tried to do to Jack."

Delaney ignored the insult. "You're a miserable old man, hell bent on making everyone around you just as miserable. It makes no sense, Ernie."

A glimmer of satisfaction trickled into his expression. "You ain't denyin' it, are you?"

Jack Foster came from a wealthy family, that much was true. But Delaney had never been interested in him for his money. She had loved him. First love, only love, she had believed in *'til death do you part*. Problem was, it was likely to be *her* death that parted them. But Ernie didn't care about the truth. He only cared about being hurtful. "Do you know this property is scheduled to go up for auction?"

Awareness registered in his gray eyes.

"Are you willing to let a stranger have this property over Felicity?"

"No stranger will take this property." He jabbed a thumb to his chest. "I decide what happens to it."

"I can assume, then, that you'll pay the taxes you've neglected to pay, putting this land at risk in the first place?"

"My financial business ain't none of your affair."

It was mind-boggling. He was incendiary, spiteful, dead set against her getting anywhere near ownership for years, then turns around and offers her ten acres to live on if she released her legal claim to the title. As though she were that stupid. As though she were that easy to placate. "Why are you doing it? Why make Felicity suffer? She spends night after night playing her flute for you, yet you're unwilling to give her a dime towards college. It doesn't make sense."

He lowered his gaze. "I don't answer to you."

"But what about Felicity? Your sister? Do you answer to them?"

Ernie shut down. Jamming the pipe back into his mouth, he sat back in his rocker and closed his eyes, a grim expression carved into his face. He was a bitter man, an unhappy man, and Delaney wondered if he wouldn't fight her to the end just to prove it.

Ernie had lost his will to care about those closest to him. A foreboding settled upon her shoulders. Would he take that despair to the grave and leave them out in the cold?

Delaney returned to her cabin to find Felicity pacing the living room. At her mother's entrance, she blurted, "What happened?"

"Ernie tried to bribe me with ten acres for my release on the rest, plus fifty thousand cash." Delaney closed the door with a smooth thud.

"What did you do?"

"I didn't sign," she said, and pulled the hairband from her ponytail.

"What?" Felicity asked, shocked.

"I didn't sign. I won't."

"But you have to, don't you?"

Delaney glowered and ran her fingers through her hair clear down to the ends. The cool interior of the cabin was a soothing relief. "I don't *have* to do anything."

"Can't Mr. Harris help us?"

"No." She walked past her daughter and into the kitchen.

"But why not? He said he'd give us a lot of money for this property—and we'd get to keep some!"

Delaney understood her concern, but until the title was in their hands, Mr. Harris' offer was meaningless. Ernie was the only one who stood to gain from that deal, and while the fifty thousand dollars he offered her would go a long way toward paying Felicity's college expenses, accepting it and a lousy ten acres in lieu of complete ownership amounted to defeat. She pulled a mason jar from the cabinet and filled it from the tap.

They needed money, yes. Without it, Felicity would struggle through work and class and not have enough time to practice her flute. If the girl had any chance to make the cut for a professional orchestra, she would need hours upon hours of practice—time she couldn't spare, if forced to hold down a job. If her grades dropped, the scholarship would disappear.

"What are we going to do?"

Delaney downed a healthy swallow of water and corrected defiantly, "You mean what is *he* going to do?" They may be in a bind, but she was not willing to concede. Not yet.

"*Mom.*"

Delaney hated the swells of doubt in Felicity's eyes. Her daughter shouldn't be stressing over money and property rights. She should be carefree and excited over the prospect of attending UT next year. She was being pulled into the mix of a family feud and it was inexcusable. But then Ernie always did go for the jugular.

Delaney set her water down and closed the distance between her and Felicity. She pulled her baby into a strong-armed hug and promised, "It'll work out, you'll see."

Chapter Nine

Delaney negotiated the rocky trail with ease, making her way down to the spot in question without issue. Careful not to be followed, she double-backed and triple-backed just to be sure, checking the path ahead and behind her for signs of the men. Running into them would complicate matters.

Working through the brush, she scanned the horizon through the trees. She stood perfectly still, held her breath, and watched for signs of movement, listened for the sound of voices. Nothing. She glanced about. As far as she could tell, she was alone. Breathing in the scent of wet laurel, she forged forward. Overhead, the canopy of trees rustled with the breeze, peppering sunlight in shades of buttery gold. Dusk would be upon the forest soon and her visibility would be reduced to nothing. But she couldn't get away any earlier. One of her clients was being audited and needed his accounting organized for inspection. Fortunately, Felicity and a few girlfriends were with the Parker boys tonight, as they were every Friday night, catching a movie and hanging out at the boys' house afterward. But Felicity would be home by eleven—per *her* strict orders.

Arriving at the area, Delaney noted everything was as it was before. Matted forest floor, nothing left behind in the way of backpacks or camping equipment. No signs of a campfire. She surveyed the trees and rocks but saw nothing out of the ordinary. She looked for broken branches, any clue to their activity from the other day. But she detected nothing. Like before, all looked as expected. What was she missing?

A patter of sound and her heart bolted. She glanced over her shoulder. Was someone there? Maybe an animal, she thought, peering around, seeing no one. Taking a deep breath, she calmed the angst building in her chest. It was nothing. She was alone. Squatting, she sifted through leaves and dead branches on the ground. There had to be something here. Those men were not hanging out in this specific location without purpose. She looked around. Were they hiding something in the bushes? She rummaged through nearby rhododendron and a scraggly bush, one she couldn't identify.

She'd heard tales of hikers through the years, hiding out in the woods, stashing drugs and stolen goods where no one could find them. Maybe that's what they were doing. With hundreds of thousands of acres, she figured the USFS and adjoining properties were as good a hiding place as any. A branch cracked.

Delaney sucked in her breath, ducking instinctively. She gulped, waiting. When no more sounds came, she warily raised her head. Leaves fluttered high above. An animal?

Black bears were a growing population in this area. Her chest tightened. Momma bears were not known for their rosy disposition. Running into one was not on her list of things to do. Delaney swallowed back her fear and suddenly worried about Sadie. Tied to the post, she would be easy prey for any animal with a knack for attack. Should she go back for her?

Delaney glanced around. She wasn't accomplishing anything here. Rising to her feet, she considered her options. It was going to be dark soon. Maybe she should come back tomorrow and resume her search. Setting a hand to the rock beside her, she leaned against it. The stone was cold, damp, mottled with white fungus.

Yes, it might be better to return in the morning. She'd feign business and head out first thing. Felicity would be all right for a few hours without her. Delaney pulled her hand away and noticed a stick poking straight up from the stone behind it. What the—?

That was an odd position for a branch. Inspecting it more closely, she realized the stick was propped up artificially. Excitement surged through her. Could this be a clue?

She moved to the other side of the rock. A large dead branch was lying over top of it. She removed it and looked closer. In the trickle of sunlight, she caught the sparkle of a dusty stone surface. She wiped at it and her breath caught. She rubbed harder and stepped back, stunned. *Oh my...*

Adrenaline liquefied her limbs. She'd heard of this before, but never dreamed it was anything but a tall tale—or a thing of the past. With a shaky hand, Delaney reached out and traced the lines etched in the gray stone. In the faint light, she could see layers of rock separated by a distinct discoloration. Her breathing grew shallow. She might be mistaken—most probably was mistaken—but she would swear she was looking at gold.

In the rough. On Ladd property. Her mind staggered at the implication. Could it be?

Heart beats thumped behind her breast. The narrow threads of yellow were jagged, uneven, and ran the entire width of the stone. Several areas looked as though they'd been chipped away, revealing the vein as it penetrated deep into the boulder. Delaney ran a shaky hand across the section, the surface sharp and irregular beneath her fingertips. Disbelief poured into her skull. Those men had discovered gold. *Gold.*

Immediately she started calculating the significance in dollars and cents. The price of gold was at a record high. Depending on how much there was in this rock, it could mean Ladd Springs was worth millions. *Ladd Springs. Millions.*

The thought made her dizzy. But how to get it out? What to do with it? Who to tell? Delaney bolted upright. *Those men knew there was gold on her property.* Panic sliced her in half. *Clem* knew there was gold on her property. His visits with Ernie, his eagerness to please, mow the lawn, fix the plumbing...

It was no wonder he was working so hard to ingratiate himself with Ernie! He wanted the rights to the gold.

She had to get out of here, had to think. She had to figure out her next step. Ladd Springs had gold. It had to be real.

Those men believed it was real, risking the chance of getting caught in order to loot the land. *Clem* was looting her land.

Ernie had to be told. But just as quickly as the thought occurred, futility settled in. He would not believe her. He would call her a liar, and it might even send him further onto Clem's side. He might sign the property over to Clem just to spite her.

Delaney needed proof. She patted her pockets, but they were empty. She hadn't brought her phone. Damn the luck. Where was it? Home? Truck? Delaney took one more look at the vein etched in the rock before her, the waning light dulling its luster, and a ravenous desire slinked in. *There was gold in Ladd Springs.*

On the ride back to the property, Delaney worked to organize her thoughts. She had to formulate a plan. She had to be sensible, rational. Finding gold on the property incurred an entirely new set of concerns. Once she and Felicity acquired ownership, she'd have to arrange for access to the location. They'd need equipment to get it out. Machinery. Men. But deep in the woods, it wouldn't be easy.

Sadie trotted over the river bridge, her hooves making a hollow echo over the rush of white-capped water beneath them. A quarter mile down was Clem's trailer. It sat off the shoulder, just past the first curve. Delaney imagined him in it, counting the days until he had stolen all the gold for himself. Well, that low life was in for the surprise of his life. When she revealed her find and his connection to the men in question, Ernie would have a fit! He'd renounce him on the spot.

But she couldn't let Clem know she was on to him. She'd heard the stories about how far miners were willing to go to stake out their claims. It seemed nothing was off limits, up to and including murder. The fine hair on the back of her neck stood, as she recalled Clem's sordid actions from the other day. He had surprised her with the move to grope her, but now it served as fair warning. Put nothing past the man. Nothing. She must conceal her knowledge of the gold until she was able to announce it with the confidence that he couldn't steal any more. Was this how lottery winners felt?

Struck by the comparison, Delaney assumed they probably did. Tell no one until you see an attorney and have confidentially arranged to have the winnings transferred to your bank account. Sadie tripped as she side-stepped the gravel in favor of the grass. She shook her mane with a rumbled of snort. Delaney held the reins forward, giving Sadie the room she needed as they neared the dip in the drive. Passing by Ernie's cabin on her way to the stables, she saw Ashley's car parked out front. Delaney suppressed a quick rise of optimism. The cavalry had arrived, and right on time. With a click from her mouth, she hurried Sadie forward. "Get on it, girl. We've got plans to make!"

Inside his cabin, Ernie scowled at Ashley through the dusty haze of light, the room lit by a tiny Tiffany lamp perched on the end table by his chair. The scent of stale tobacco hung in the air. Spiral braided floor rugs were scattered out across wood plank floors, their fabric stained. Dirt and sweat permeated the room. It was a pathetic way to live. Ashley frowned. If Susannah were alive, this dump would be spotless.

"What do you want?" Ernie muttered, not moving his eyes from the television.

Holed up in his recliner, she regarded him with a twinge of pity. "Quit your grumbling, old man. I've come to talk."

"I don't wanna talk to you."

She planted a fist on her hip, pointing the other at him like the barrel of a gun. "I'm here to speak my peace and then I'll leave you to yours." Though she doubted he had any peace to speak of. Since Susannah died, Ernie had hardened his crusty shell until it was downright impenetrable. He wouldn't let anyone in, wouldn't listen to any kind words or offers of support. He wanted only to stew in his grief.

Which gave her pause. It was a grief Ashley understood. When Susannah died, it had felt like her other half died. Susannah was more than a friend to her. She was sister, soul mate, the half to her whole. Without Booker, she would have not survived Susannah's death. Her heart went out to Ernie. She had survived. He hadn't. And now he was staring down the end of his own tunnel. Hopefully the man would finally find peace.

"I'm here to talk about you and Felicity," she said.

"No you ain't. I read the paper." He jabbed the mouthpiece of his pipe toward her and accused, "I know you're in cahoots with Delaney."

"I'm not in any cahoots with anybody. I'm here to talk some sense into you." Without bothering to ask for permission, she lowered her tired old body onto the sofa, the cushion sinking flat beneath her. If you could call it a cushion. Felt more like plywood than pillow. Wouldn't surprise her if it was a throwaway he salvaged from the junk pile out back. Ernie hadn't bought a spec of anything to outfit this place. Everything in it was a remnant from those who roamed these rooms before him. She looked around the cabin. The walls were dank and dirty, the light fixtures coated with a thick layer of dust. Even the antique Queen Anne dining set was suffering under his neglect, its elegant curves chipped and scratched. Everything was old, battered, tattered and stunk to high heaven.

Ernie jammed the pipe back into his mouth and glared at her, his eyes glassy marbles magnified beneath the lens of his black-rimmed glasses.

Pitiful. The man was pitiful. But he was Susannah's brother and Ashley swore to look after him, whether he wanted her to or not. Those baskets of pole beans and okra didn't drop out of the sky. No. She'd been delivering them to Ernie for years, to see that he ate a decent meal, kept his strength about him.

"I know about your illness," she stated quietly.

He swiped his glance away from hers. "Dad-burned whole town knows."

"I know it's gone to your pancreas."

Ernie whirled, animosity splintering his gaze. "How do you know about that?"

"I have my ways." Ashley buried her hands in her lap and asked, "Why aren't you seeing anyone about it?"

"Why should I?" He glanced away. "Ain't nothin' nobody can do."

"Doctors can help you, Ernie. Booker's sister-in-law went through a similar situation. The doctors said she only had months to live, but she proved them wrong."

"I ain't never been so lucky."

It was the first hint of sorrow she detected in the man and her heart pinched. Staring at him, mired in his misery, she shook her head. "Is this how you want to go out?" she asked. "Do you really want to forsake your kin for a silly vendetta?"

Ernie hooked into her with a sharp, "Delaney's a money-grubbing—"

Ashley silenced him with a raised hand. "I'm tired of hearing your excuses. Gerald Foster isn't this issue and neither is his son."

"He's a crook!" Ernie exclaimed, his voice nothing but a ragged croak.

"He's no more crook than you are astronaut." And she wasn't going to stand another word of his trash. Ernie refused any and all reason when it came to Gerald Foster. The minute Delaney started dating his son, Ernie nearly had a stroke—as though she had betrayed him somehow. Ashley pushed her shoulders back, heaving her generous bosom forward as she declared, "Susannah told you there was nothing between them and I can vouch for her. *There was nothing between them.* She only had eyes for Harry."

Ernie hated Gerald because he thought he'd sullied his sister's honor by taking Susannah before she was married. Ernie believed it to be true, because he had watched the two spend hours upon hours together, hiking the trails, taking picnics by the river. But Susannah and Gerald were never more than friends. God knows Ashley had tried to convince Susannah otherwise. Gerald was a good man, a loving man. Unlike Harry Wilkins, he would have devoted his time and attention to her. But Susannah could be stubborn as a goat with a tin can, and when she wanted who she wanted, she was going to have him, whether her best friend and brother approved or not. Susannah and Harry were married on her eighteenth birthday. Gerald went on to marry a pretty society girl from Chattanooga, and the two had four sons, all of them wild and wooly and socially unacceptable, much to their mother's distress.

But Ernie held the grudge to this day. Because Delaney had married a Foster, she was to be forsaken. Muttering incoherently, he chewed on the end of his pipe.

"Delaney hasn't done a thing to you, and it's not right for you to hold your silly feud against her."

"Money. That's what she's after."

"She doesn't want your money," Ashley said heatedly, answering him with a dismissive shake of her head. "This is about doing what's right. You and I both know what happened the night of Susannah's death, there's no denying it. Now I don't know about you, but I believe in the sparkle and glitter of heaven and I have every intention of trotting through those pearly gates in my best boots and rhinestones. Whether you believe the way I do, or simply think you're going to rest in peace once you cross the threshold, either way, you're slapping a lock on those beautiful gates if you go back on your promise to Susannah."

Ernie grimaced.

"Think of Felicity," she implored him. "That girl adores you, Ernie. She's willing to look past your crusty exterior and see the beauty in you. Plays like an angel for you, too."

Anger sparked life into his demeanor. "You leave her out of this."

"I won't. She wants to play in the symphony, but she can't if she can't make it through college." Ashley could see that talk of Felicity softened him, as she knew it would. "She spends night after night playing for you and this is how you pay her back?"

"It's her mother that's the problem," he replied gruffly. "If she made better decisions, she'd be able to pay for Felicity's schoolin' and not put her through hard times."

"Delaney is a fine mother—don't you go disparaging her," Ashley said, pointing a bejeweled finger at him, the ten carat faux diamond sparkling even in this poor excuse for light. "She's even agreed to put the title in Felicity's name to prove it to you."

He glanced away. "Cuz she's manipulatin' the poor child."

"The only one around here doing any *manipulatin*'," she mimicked, "is you. And I'm high tired of it. You're going to do what's right and I'm going to see to it." She thrust a hard eye at him and said, "We *both* made promises to Susannah that night, and I intend to see mine through."

Ashley stood. He acknowledged her movement and she returned a withering gaze. She was finished here. "I have a mind to talk to that sweet child and tell her not to step another foot in this cabin to play her flute for you, the way you're treating her."

"What?" he cried, and shot forward in his chair.

"You heard me." Ashley knew what the evenings meant to him. They were his only reprieve, his only escape from his dreary existence. They allowed him to remember brighter days, days spent with Susannah, when she used to sing to him. By the creek, alone on horseback, when they were young, she would sing him calm like a lullaby-soothed baby. Susannah knew how to keep her brother on the straight and narrow. She kept him in school and kept him from drinking. Like a puppy dog-in-training, Susannah gave Ernie heaps of love, but followed through with a stern command when he strayed off course.

"You can't do that," Ernie rebuked, but his voice cracked.

"I can and I will. You sign on the dotted line or that sweet thing will get an ear-full from me."

Ernie looked like an angry possum, an animal that knew it had been cornered and had only one card left to play. "You're a mean-spirited woman, Ashley Fulmer. You're a selfish, no-good backstabber."

"I'm doing what needs to be done."

"You never did like me," he muttered.

"My feelings for you are irrelevant at the moment. Susannah loved you with all her heart." Ashley's heart squeezed as memory cut deep. "She looked up to you, treated you like you were her savior. The least you could do is act like it."

Tears misted his eyes and he brought a hand to forehead, rubbing the papery, blotchy skin. If she let herself, Ashley could feel sorry for him. But the way he was treating Susannah's daughter and granddaughter prohibited any such compassion. She took a step toward the door, careful not to let her skirt catch on the sofa table. "You let me know when you've come to your senses," she ordered matter-of-fact, indicating the document she'd signed for Delaney. "Tonight's only the beginning of your problems, you keep up this nonsense."

Chapter Ten

Sitting on the edge of her bed, Delaney slipped the small camera into her backpack and zipped it closed, her fingers more jittery than she cared to think about. Pulse running on high speed, she chalked it up to adrenaline rush. She wasn't kidding herself. Gathering photographic evidence could prove risky. But without it her word against Clem's would be tossed aside like a cigarette butt. She needed to stake out a claim of her own—a witness claim.

Rising, she flicked off the lights and headed out. Two water bottles, a granola bar and flashlight—she was prepared to wait the men out, if need be. She had no reason to believe they wouldn't. Delaney's instincts hummed. If she knew Clem, he'd loot that gold as fast as he could.

And she had all day to get her proof. Felicity had stayed over at her girlfriend's last night and planned to spend the day with them, which meant Delaney didn't have to be home until supper time. Slinging the canvas pack over her shoulder, she walked toward her bedroom door and caught a glimpse of her reflection. She stopped, and zeroed in. She looked tense, edgy. The lines around her mouth were set hard, her eyes filled with trepidation. She looked worried. A half laugh escaped her lips and her heart thumped. She looked *scared*, is what she looked.

Kicking her legs into motion, Delaney brushed the thought aside. There was no room for fear. No reason to fear. She knew these woods like the back of her hand, could travel trails and cliffs like a deer, warding off trouble with the barrel of her gun. When she wanted to be, Delaney could be as stealth and lethal as a rattler or as fierce as a mama bear. There was nothing to fear. Besides, she didn't intend for them to see her. This mission was about her seeing them—photographing the men as proof for Ernie. And there was no better proof than a full-color image.

Locking the door behind her, she went in pursuit of her mare.

Sitting in the lobby of the town's premier hotel, the lunch crowd thinning around him, Nick prepared to call his partner. Avoiding it any longer would only strain their relationship and that was a strain he didn't need. Malcolm Ward was an integral part of his empire. Nick would need him to see this project through. An elegantly dressed brunette caught his eye as she walked by, her smile a shade too intimate for strangers. Pushing back against the cushion, he returned the gesture.

Dialing Malcolm's number, Nick ran through his options as he waited through several rings. He could begin the negotiating process for the land south of here, but it lacked the privacy of being bordered by the USFS. It had streams and rivers, but none of the springs. There was another piece up in Carolina he could look into but, although it had waterfalls and forest, it too lacked the added beauty of open meadows and of course, the natural springs.

Serenity Springs was the spa he wanted to create, and that meant he needed Ladd land. According to local lore, the springs on the Ladd property were not only numerous, but said to be speckled with gold flecks. Gold flecks that sparkled in the crystal clear spring water when captured in a glass and held up to the sunlight. He grinned. Whether he believed the legend or not was irrelevant. Transforming the springs into wishing wells and refreshment spots along his Meditation Trail would pay tenfold what any glittery water amusement would do for him. He called them his contemplation spots, where guests could stop and enjoy a spectacular view or immerse themselves in the peace of solitude.

As he was about to hang up the line, a voice shouted, "Nick—where've you been? I've been calling you for two days!"

Pleased to hear the manic voice, he replied smoothly, "I've been scouting for property. What's up?"

"What's up?" came the incredulous reply. "You were supposed to close this deal a week ago, that's what's up. What's the delay?"

"I ran into a couple of obstacles." An ornery old man, a beautiful woman, and a darling young teenager—none of which mattered to Malcolm. His partner wanted results. "But I'm making progress."

"You better be. I've got investors breathing down my neck for information. They're threatening to pull out—"

"What? Why? If it's not this property, it will be another."

"They have other prospects."

Other prospects? As soon as he thought it, Nick realized who he meant. He should have stayed away from Jillian Devane— CEO of Eco-Domani, his fiercest competitor in the eco-resort market and a woman with a vendetta deeper than money. Aggravation stirred in his gut. She was nothing but trouble. "How's she courting them this time?"

"Appalachian Gold."

Nick groaned. "You've got to be kidding me."

"Wish I was, but she thinks she's going to beat you to the punch."

Jillian was more than a beautiful woman. She was a brilliant hotelier, with a chain of hotels that rivaled any in the market—except his. When it came to innovative energy consumption, recycled building materials and straight up creative use of land and space, the designers at Harris Hotels consistently stayed one step ahead of Eco-Domani. They rocked the tourist industry with each and every hotel opening, and Jillian was more than envious. She was vindictive. They had an affair, but she'd wanted to take it one step further and combine their resources for an Eco-Domani/Harris hotel empire, solidifying the deal with marriage. But he'd refused and things got ugly. A rueful smile pulled at his lips. Things didn't get really bad until he walked away from her body as well. A hot-blooded Latina from a wealthy family, nobody walked away from Jillian Devane. Nobody.

"I'll take care of it," Nick said into the phone.

"You better. I hear they're working on a deal in the Smoky Mountains as we speak."

Plagued by the familiar mix of lust-filled admiration for the woman and his own gritty resolve, Nick vowed he would not be beat. Jillian would not lure his investors from this project. She would not open her doors before he did. He'd walked away from the fight once. He wouldn't do so again. "Call Belinda and get her working on those drawings we discussed. Have her call me when she has some sketches. Tell her I'll email some photos this afternoon."

"Will do."

Nick ended the call and wound his brain around the next step. Time for another visit to Ladd Springs.

After securing Sadie at the trailhead, Delaney set out on the trail. It was warmer today, breezy in the field as she rode over, but air flow didn't make it this far in. Here it was quiet, still. Dressed in her customary tank top, jeans and boots, she was comfortable. Her hair was pulled into a tight ponytail, the length of it long and loose down her back. Trees were an assortment of dark trunks, narrow and thick. Leaves floated from branches and hovered high and low, reducing visibility to mountain walls and the expanse of the valley between. Delaney scanned the perimeter of green and brown, the spots dappled with light, but stopped suddenly. Was that a voice she heard?

Standing completely still, she strained to listen. In the distance, she heard the low drum of waterfalls. Faint, but she recognized it. Her breathing grew shallow, her mind laser sharp. Other than that, there was nothing. Satisfied all was well, she slid the pack onto her back and continued forward, forcing herself to lighten her stride. No pounding—no branch breaking—she had to remain undetected. When she neared the location, she paused, and listened. She searched trees and brush for signs of movement. Nothing.

Surveying the area around the trail, she found a winding path that went up a nearby slope. Gauging the angle, she decided it would provide her best vantage point. She'd be able to see them, but they shouldn't be able to see her. Lifting a boot to a jutting rock, she scaled the steep incline and wedged herself between a rock and a tree stump, split in half by either lightning or old age. Settling in, she took out her camera, looped the strap around her neck and prepared to wait.

An hour into her wait, she crumpled the granola wrapper and stuffed it back into her backpack. "Leave no trace behind" was her motto in the forest. Scrolling through the last of her emails, she heard them. Gripping the smartphone, she switched it to vibrate and slipped it into a pocket of her backpack. She held her breath and watched the infamous duo advance. Their voices carried easily in the silence and she heard one tell the other, "I know, I got it." He rummaged through the sack he carried and raised the small tool. It looked to be an axe or blunt-edged hoe of some kind. Anger welled. To steal more gold, no doubt.

Delaney brought the camera to her face and peered through the viewfinder. Standard fare when it came to cameras, it lacked a powerful zoom, but would have to do. She toggled the tab to bring them into view as magnified as possible.

They were plain looking. The big one hadn't shaved, the smaller no need, scraggly tufts of hair clumped about his chin. He wore a hat and a ragged plaid shirt. The other had on a simple red shirt and both wore jeans. She clicked off a few shots, then drew the camera away for a direct look at the men. Lowlifes, to be sure. Neither looked like they had a brain cell to work from or a dime to their name—if the dirty clothes were any clue. Delaney moved position slightly to gain a better view. The thinner man wasted no time in wielding his axe against the rock.

Chling, chling. The high-pitched sound carried through the trees. With each swing, Delaney seethed. How much were they taking? Were they doing so at Clem's orders? Were they giving it to him? Taking it for their own?

So many unanswered questions. So much she had to capture. She raised the camera to her eye. So far away. She snapped a few shots and analyzed them on the tiny screen. Zipping through them, she deemed none were clear enough, specific enough. Delaney looked up.

She had to get closer.

Setting a hand to the tree, she carefully eased her way out of position, one eye on the men as she felt her boots make contact with the ground. Gingerly she moved down the trail on her haunches. Obscured by a cluster of huge trees, their leaves and branches providing adequate coverage, she scoped the area for potential hiding places. The gold was on the opposite side of the rock. If she could make her way over to the far ledge, she might have a chance at getting a picture of them chipping away at the stone. Which is what she needed—proof they were stealing from Ladd property.

Delaney treaded lightly up the trail, her back to the mountain behind her, staying vigilant for signs of detection. Though she was probably being overly cautious. The two fools were more concerned with their theft than getting caught. As she made her way higher, the trail curved downward, and below she noted a ditch of sorts. A ravine. A slow smile pulled at her lips. It would serve as the perfect cover in case of emergency.

"Lookee here," one of the men exclaimed.

Delaney froze and looked to see what he meant.

"That's a big one," replied the other.

The smaller fellow was holding up what she had to assume was a gold nugget. Anger fired in her belly. She lifted camera to her eye and angled her body around the shelter of leaves to capture the best shot. She clicked, but the man leaned down, then stood up again. Peering through her camera lens, she tried to center the moving figure within her sights. *Click, click, click.* She did the best she could to get a good shot of his face.

A branch cracked. Delaney ducked.

Her pulse pounded as she searched the area. Where had the noise come from? Was it the men? The fall of a decayed branch?

Neither of them seemed to pay the noise heed, continuing with their work. Their work! Stealing is what they were doing and she had a mind to stop them right now. Shoot the both of them and ask questions later. Unfortunately, it wouldn't solve her problem. Clem Sweeney had to be stopped—sooner rather than later.

Her only hope was to do so through these two.

Lowering the camera, Delaney moved over a fallen tree trunk, careful not to step on a branch and bring attention to herself. While they hadn't minded the last pop and crash, she didn't want to chance it. Working her way closer until she was about ten yards from the men, she tucked herself away in the ditch, close enough to see their faces. Instinctively, she recorded them to memory. Thin build, pointed nose, jutting chin, jerky movements. Round face, bulbous nose, broad shoulders, curly black hair, definitely the one in charge. Delaney wondered where Clem knew them from, how he signed them on to this scheme of his. Holding the camera steady, the zoom feature maxed out, she snapped photos in rapid succession. The larger man drank from a Thermos. A familiar ringtone rose from her backpack.

His hand froze. Her heart stopped. His head turned in her direction.

As the country music tune continued to blare, Delaney didn't move a muscle. Not her camera, not her hand. To do so would certainly reveal her position.

Partially concealed by brush and trees overhead, she prayed he would not see her. The cell went to voice mail. The forest was quiet once again. But the men were not.

"Did you hear that?"

"Hear what?" asked the other.

"That noise," he said, visibly scanning the ridge where she was hiding.

"Nah, I ain't heard a thing. Now, c'mon. We got to hurry and get this gold out of here 'fore Clem wonders where we are."

"Shhh—" he hushed loudly. "What are you trying to do—tell everyone what we're doing?"

He looked around, dumbfounded. "There ain't no one here, but us Jeb."

The large man clamped a hand to the other's mouth, whispering harshly to him.

Delaney racked her brain for an escape. If she moved, they'd see her. If she stayed and they came looking for her, she'd be cornered. There was only one way out for her. The way she came in.

Now on alert, the two men surveyed the woods. They looked toward the trail, upward of the mountain, checked the area behind them that lead to the USFS. Unsatisfied, the bigger man held a finger to the smaller and said something, directing him to move.

The skinny man began to make his way through the brush.

Delaney's throat closed. Her limbs noodled. *He was coming toward her*.

She slid a hand into her boot, closed it around the gun. If it was clear he was coming toward her, she would use it—in a heartbeat. With bated breath, she watched him push through branches and vine, clod hopping his way toward the narrow ledge where she was hiding. In instant decision, she knew. That's it. Game over. Delaney stood and leveled her gun at him. "Stop right there."

His head yanked up.

"Don't take another step or I'll shoot."

"Well lookee here," he said in a grotesque purr and tipped back his ratty black hat. "We have a girl been watchin' us."

The leader of the two shoved the nugget into his pocket and began to come toward them.

"Stop," she called out sternly. "Stop or I'll shoot."

"Get her!" the big one yelled and pulled a gun.

The fellow hesitated, then lurched forward.

She pulled the trigger, the shot echoing from its chamber, shattering the calm. He staggered back as another shot ricocheted off the tree behind her. Delaney's heart exploded in her chest. She fired another shot, then took off running, wary of the man with the gun.

"Get her!"

"I been shot!" he howled.

"I don't care!" Abandoning his injured cohort, the bulky man chased her, clawing his way through the brush. Her mind raced, her heart thumped. The camera bounced against her chest in sharp jabs. She grabbed it as a second gunshot blasted the mountain beside her. Panic seized her. She couldn't get shot! Couldn't get caught!

Glancing behind, she saw him struggling to negotiate the steep path up to trail level. Fear pushed her to run faster, put distance between them. Boots landing hard, Delaney worried she would trip, her heel catching on an exposed root—but she didn't dare slow down.

She could hear the man grumbling as he chased her.

Camera clenched in her hand, arms swinging, Delaney found her rhythm. Her thoughts swerved toward Sadie. She ducked a branch. Estimated time and distance. She could outrun this man. She could make it to her horse and make her getaway. Her chest grew painfully winded. But if he spotted them, a bullet would easily bring down her mare. The image of Sadie careening to the ground, crying out from a gunshot wound wrenched Delaney's gut. She couldn't put her horse in jeopardy. She needed a shortcut, a different path. A detour.

"You're a dead woman!" the man shouted from behind. He fired off another round from his gun—and it was close. Too close for comfort.

Impossible. He couldn't be that close! Had she made no progress?

Sweat soaked her tank beneath the backpack, her thighs burned. Her cheeks flushed from exertion, her pulse thudded between her ears. Up ahead, she knew the trail curved sharply to the right, then plunged steeply. There was a side trail that stemmed off from there. It was an old path she and Jeremiah used when running late for dinner. She hadn't used it in years and it might be impassable now, but it was all she had.

If she stayed on the trail she'd be wide open and vulnerable.

Anticipating the turn, Delaney released the camera and grabbed the closest limb. With every muscle she had, she swung her body up and off the trail. She grabbed another and another. Her boot caught on a root, branches cut across her skin, but she drove in. Tree, branch, rock—she used whatever she could grab and pulled herself upward into the mountainside.

With the steep hillside cluttered with trees and bush, vines and weeds, negotiating the rugged landscape proved difficult. As she attempted to launch herself deeper into the mountain brush, she reached for the pointed edge of a boulder, the sandy surface digging into her palm.

Seconds later, Delaney heard the man's labored breathing, the patter of his heavy steps as he passed below. But she didn't look down. She didn't check to see if she had been spotted. She'd hear the gunshot if he had.

Delaney continued forward, praying he wouldn't see her. She prayed he would leave Sadie be.

Pulling into the Ladd homestead, Nick slowed his car to a complete stop and tossed the gear into park. With a heavy sigh, he stared at the dilapidated old cabin and wondered why this project had to be so difficult. Most people jumped when you waved hundreds of thousands of dollars at them. Especially poor ones. There were no questions asked, not a care in the world—nothing but an agreement regarding dollars and cents. And time. How soon could they get their money?

It was always the same. But not with the Ladds. They stood to lose a bundle if this property went to auction and for what—a family feud? Bad blood? Short-sightedness?

It didn't make sense. None of it. Not Ernie's refusal and not Delaney's. Nick dropped his head back to the headrest and thought about Jillian Devane. The woman behind Eco-Domani reminded him of a panther, lithe, dangerous curves, jet black hair down to her bottom, dangerous gold eyes that could kill with a single look. She had been memorable in so many ways. Both good and bad, but memorable just the same. Not the kind of woman you wanted to cross, but he had never made any promises to her. Never suggested he was hers for the taking, never offered her more than a good time.

Yet when he left, she had pounced and pounced hard. Her perfect white teeth became fangs out for the kill. She was not happy when he moved on, but moved on is what he did. Jillian was beautiful, he'd give her that. She was a temptress of the highest degree, but she was shifty. Where she intended to pin you down, she refused you the same honor. Where she defied his eye to wander, hers slid around and snared men like the skilled seductress she was. He chuckled softly. And skilled she was.

Movement up the mountain snagged his mind from thoughts of Jillian. Was that a deer? He homed in on the lightly colored animal moving between the trees. He'd always enjoyed stealing a peek at wildlife when the animal was completely unaware of his presence. It spoke to his youth, days in Montana spent chasing rabbits, hunting deer. He'd been drawn to the wild freedom of nature, the independence. The childhood impression had been deep and lasting, one he carried with him through his career as an hotelier.

Nick bolted forward in the seat of his car, his eyes fixed on the figure creeping clear of the forest and down the mountain, her movements tense and cautious. Bewilderment funneled through his mind. That was no animal. That was Delaney!

Chapter Eleven

Delaney carefully traversed the grassy slope, her legs rendered rubbery weak, her knees stressed by the steep angle of descent. Her skin stung from scratches, aggravated by the sheen of sweat on her arms. She was hot and tired but ignored it all. She had made her escape. Now she had to go back for Sadie.

But should she wait? After the man lost her, would he have left the forest? Or gone back to looting Ladd gold? And what of his friend? Would he require stitches? Would they be at the hospital now?

Hitting level terrain, Delaney hurried down the rocky clay trail, dodging stones jutting up from the ground as she practically ran down the hill. She couldn't leave Sadie tied to the post for a second longer than necessary. If anything happened to her mare, Delaney would never forgive herself. She had abandoned her. But she'd done it to spare Sadie the danger, hadn't she?

A tiny voice inside her head that continued to poke at her conscience. Had she endangered her horse by leaving her? Delaney shook the questions from her mind. She took a deep breath and calmed the renewed pounding in her chest. There would be no answers until she made it back to the trailhead.

"Hey!"

Breath slammed free from her lungs.

"What are you doing?"

Delaney whirled and her chest detonated with alarm—relief—*confusion*. Nick Harris stood about fifty feet ahead of her. She had totally missed him.

"Out for a leisure hike?" he called out, but his amusement quickly cooled to concern. He jogged up to her and asked, "Are you all right?"

Her eyes darted back and forth across his. Grateful for the safety he represented, she was also wary of telling the truth. "Nothing."

"Nothing?"

Delaney realized she had mistaken his question. *What did he ask her again*? Didn't matter. She had to get to Sadie.

Nick gently pulled her to a stop. "Slow down," he said, his voice steeped in what sounded like genuine concern. "You don't look so hot."

The retort that normally would have burst from her lips evaporated. She didn't *feel* so hot. She'd nearly been shot!

"What's wrong?" He scanned the ridge above. "What happened? What were you doing up there?" His dark gaze smoldered as it fixed upon hers.

Questions, questions, questions—she needed to get to Sadie! Delaney kicked her legs into action, but Nick's grip steeled as he held her. The move stunned her. He shook her to attention. "Talk to me," he commanded.

"There was a man in the woods, I ditched him, but I have to get back to Sadie." She stumbled over her words, trying not to divulge too much. She peered up into his eyes, which were swimming with temper.

"What man?" he asked, his voice suddenly low and dangerous.

"A man, a stranger—I don't know who he is." Delaney tried to yank free from his grasp, but the effort was useless. Sapped of strength, she posed no opposition to his ironclad hold. "*Please*. I need to get to my horse."

"We need to call the police."

"No!" she cried. "They can't do anything to help," she added breathlessly. "It's a waste of time."

"Of course they can. They can go after this man you're talking about."

And find the gold? Discover she'd shot first? Delaney shook her head adamantly. "No. I can handle it."

Nick scoffed with a biting laugh. "You're in no condition to handle anything. Look at you!"

It was the first time she thought to consider her appearance. Delaney looked down and held up her arms, checked out her clothing. She was covered in orange-black smudges and littered with bruises and scrapes, many bleeding. Her backpack was stuck to her back, the silver camera hung from her neck.

What must he think?

"Where is Sadie?" he asked.

"She's by the trail," Delaney replied automatically.

"Let's go."

"*No*. I can get her myself."

"You're not going anywhere by yourself."

Reflex urged her to refuse, but glancing at the sizeable hands on her arms, Delaney acquiesced. She inhaled deeply. She doubted he'd let go if she didn't give in. She blew out her breath, some of the tension releasing with it. "Fine."

Nick loosened his hold, but didn't fully release her.

Afraid she would escape? Delaney wondered silently, but quickly surrendered to the inevitable and marched down the trail, accompanied by her shadow. She wasn't going anywhere without Prince Harris. She suppressed a swell of pleasure at her nickname and sighed. Maybe it was for the better. If the men saw her, they might think twice about shooting with Nick by her side. She had to admit the man was not only formidable in stature, he exuded an ominous threat as he strode alongside her. There was something about Nick Harris that broadcast strength. Power. It shouted loud and clear that he meant business.

For a moment they walked, no sound but boots on ground. The light breeze cooled her skin, calmed her mind. Blisters were forming on her feet after the impromptu run, one beginning to throb.

Nick broke the silence. "Why did you leave Sadie at the post?"

"Didn't want to spook her," Delaney lied, concentrating on the brown-gray path ahead, careful to avoid the rise of rocks and roots embedded in the ground.

"Spook her?"

"Sadie is very intelligent." Delaney looped her thumbs beneath her shoulder straps. "She'd know if something was up."

"What exactly was up?" he asked, pitching his head down toward hers.

Nick expected her to look him in the eye, but Delaney wasn't that keen on her ability to lie. If she faced him head on, he'd see through her in a second. "Around these parts," she said, maintaining focus on the trail, "we're used to trespassers. When they come around, we handle them."

"Handle them, how?"

Delaney didn't respond. As they passed Ernie's cabin, she peered over at it, wondering if he was staring at them through the window. Not good for him to think she was in cahoots with Mr. Harris.

She accelerated her pace and Nick asked, "Is there something you're not telling me, Ms. Wilkins?"

Tightening her hold on the backpack, she stole a glance to her side and shook her head. Rounding the clearing to the field bordering the forest entrance, her pulse quickened. She could see the whip of a white-blonde tail from here, partially obscured by the line of trees. "There's Sadie." She turned to her side and said to him, "I should be good now." Nick laughed. It was a presumptive sound that irked her. "Thank you for your concern"—she steadied her tone—"but I'm fine. You don't have to continue any farther."

"How about you let me be the judge of that." He waved a hand toward Sadie and with a brief dip, asked, "Shall we?"

"No," she wanted to snip, *we won't*. But if she'd learned one thing about this man, it was that he didn't listen very well. "Really, Mr. Harris. You don't have to bother yourself."

His pleasure widened into a thousand watt smile. "It's no bother, I assure you."

The glint in his eyes sparked her annoyance. Add the subtle smirk dangling on the edge of his lips, and she was downright infuriated. She was *fine*. Now that she was over the initial scare, she was completely capable of handling things from here on out. Ruminating over the unexpected kink he presented, Delaney glanced over her shoulder and asked, "Why did you stop by this afternoon?"

"Same reason as always." He paused, then quipped, "Why the camera around your neck?"

Delaney's gaze dropped briefly to her chest. "Nature photography," she said. Unlooping the camera, she unzipped her backpack and dropped the camera inside. Wordlessly, she closed it and looked at him. "Is Uncle Ernie expecting you?"

"Should he be?"

"Do you always play games, Mr. Harris?"

Nick cocked his brow and set hands to rest along the ridge of his belt. "I'm the one playing games?"

As they idled beneath the canopy of leaves, sunlight filtering in moving spots across the ground around them, a kick of wind released sticky strands of hair from her neck and shoulders as Delaney considered her options. She could allow him to tagalong, or devise some excuse to make him stay back. She stared into what were now becoming familiar brown eyes, and hesitated.

If she had a good excuse, she would have delivered it by now.

He smiled. "Sadie's waiting."

With an audible groan, Delaney surrendered. She lifted her ponytail from its matted position against her neck and backpack and drew it forward, the swatch of tangled hair resting atop her breast. "Fine. But you stay back," she warned as she started walking. "I don't need you spooking Sadie, either."

"Wouldn't think of it."

Trekking along the edge of the forest, Delaney couldn't help but look deeper into the brush for signs of movement. Were the men here? Were they watching them? She had no idea what the man would have done once he lost her. Did he realize she knew exactly what they were doing? Or did he think she was a snooping hiker?

Not with a camera perched on the end of her nose. Unless they were brain dead, they understood exactly what was at stake. The scene unfolded in her mind's eye—the bullets, the face-to-face contact, and a skittish tingle streaked through her chest. Would they tell Clem?

They'd have to, wouldn't they? Jittery angst turned to chilly trepidation. She didn't imagine Clem would confuse the issue, either. Not like there was a surplus of blondes running around Ladd forest.

"Have you thought any more about what I said?"

"What?"

"About our conversation," he prompted.

"What conversation?"

"The taxes, the auction…"

Trampling through knee high grass, Delaney stated in no uncertain terms, "We're not going to lose the property to auction."

"You have the money? Is that your plan to get the property from your uncle?"

"My plan is my business," Delaney said. Sadie whinnied as she neared.

"*Sadie*…" Delaney breathed out, relief swamping her. The horse whinnied again, the bugling cry comforting to Delaney's ears. Next to Felicity, Sadie was the most important living creature in her world.

Delaney strode over and unleashed her horse from the post. A fly buzzed near her face. She waved it off, then rubbed the flat expanse of damp-haired skin between her eyes. "Good girl." She turned to Nick, "Okay, well, thanks, but I'm good." Delaney turned to him, startled by the change in his expression. She followed his line of sight and her heart caught. Farther into the woods, standing center of the trail, was the big man. *The one with the gun.* She clenched the leather bridle in hand. Instinct urged her to run, but she hesitated. Big man was fixated on Nick.

Nick was by her side at once, moving her behind him as he stared the man down. "Is that him?" he asked under his breath.

Delaney spied the gun in his hand. "Yes," she uttered, thighs dissolving into pools at her knees.

"Can I help you?" Nick asked, making it clear courtesy was not his intent.

For a fleeting moment, Delaney thought about reaching for her gun. Nick was unarmed, she needed to do something. But the man stepped toward them, icing any such move. Next to her, Sadie grew still, her ears stiff, twitching. The sun beat down.

Nick angled back and reached a protective arm her way. "I wouldn't take another step if I were you."

The man seemed to find Nick's warning humorous. Delaney's throat went dry as she saw Nick slide a gun from the back of his jeans, allowing hand and gun to linger behind him.

"My problem ain't with you, mister." The stranger flicked a glance her way. "It's the woman I'm interested in."

"She's with me."

Delaney could see the man go through the mental calculation of risk and reward. It was clear he wanted to settle the score with her, clear he knew a lot was riding on her not walking out alive, on her not talking. Fear thundered through her limbs. Would he go through Nick to see that she didn't?

"I'll tell you again," the man said, "I ain't got no trouble with you. She and I have some unfinished business to take care of."

"Not today, you don't."

The man never blinked. He raised his gun.

Nick mirrored the movement, his arm solid and straight. "I wouldn't do that if I were you."

Stunned, the man hesitated. Nick jumped forward. Sadie reared with a frightened squeal.

Delaney closed her eyes, pushed into her horse and braced against the blast. But none came. When her lids popped open, Sadie was prancing restlessly at her shoulder. The man was running away. Fast.

Nick jogged several yards up the trail behind him. With one eye on Nick, Delaney hushed her mare, stroked her neck. "Whoa, Sadie. It's okay."

Nick paused, gun raised, staring after the man. When he seemed satisfied the stranger was in full retreat, he returned to Delaney. "Can I assume that was your trespasser?"

She nodded, tugging back Sadie, anxious to gallop off in the direction of home.

"You need to call the police." Nick stuck the black pistol back into his rear waistband. "When a man levels a gun at you, he means business."

Heart pulsing erratically against her ribs, Delaney tried to make light of the incident. "Seems to me he's the one running scared."

"Not for long."

"Well, I think you did the trick," she said, avoiding Nick's questioning stare. "I don't think calling the police is necessary."

He screwed his expression. "Do you *like* to take chances?"

"What?" With shaky arms, she slid the bridle over Sadie's head and down onto her back. "No, I'm not taking chances, I just—"

"Did you expect him to show up here with a gun?"

She gulped.

Nick took a step closer and demanded, "What happened in there that you're not telling me?"

"Nothing. I told you—I stumbled across them when I was hiking and warned them to get off my property. Guess they didn't listen."

"Them?"

Had she said there was only one? Delaney raced through her story, grasping for details. "I think there was another one," she muttered and tried to leap onto her horse.

But Nick stopped her, pulling her to the ground so hard, her boots hit the dirt with a decisive thud. He spun her around to face him, and her pulse scattered. Sadie's ears pricked forward. Delaney blinked against the bright sun.

"Not so fast," he said. "I just risked my life for you and I want to know why."

"I didn't ask you to risk your life for me," she exclaimed, guilt pouring into her as she acknowledged she might well be dead if he hadn't. Against the glare, she couldn't quite make out the nuance in his expression—and wished there was no need.

"Well...aren't you a sweet one?" Nick took the reins from her and began to lead Sadie back toward the house.

"Hey—" Delaney snapped to attention. "Where are you going with my horse?"

"Back to the house," he replied. "Are you coming?"

Whose house? And why was Sadie following him so easily?

Nearly head and shoulders with her mare, he seemed fully in control of the situation, as though he'd handled more than a few horses in his time. Nick walked without hurry and Sadie jauntily kept pace beside him, her white tail swishing back and forth. Only his crisp white-button down gave him away for a city-boy, showing a wrinkled shirt tail he hadn't bothered to tuck back into his jeans. Her gaze dropped to his long-legged jeans and expensive leather boots that looked right at home amidst the green hills rising around him. A strange longing pulled at her. Nick Harris was a good-looking man, she'd give him that. And today she'd have to add courageous to the column of desirable qualities. He hadn't flinched when that man raised his gun. In fact, he'd been so smooth in securing his own, the man hadn't even see it coming. Then he drew first and Nick ended it. There was no prolonged macho standoff, no haphazard show of force. Nick simply stated his position and then followed through. Now he was following through with another position—*she wasn't making the trip back to the house alone.*

Delaney brushed away strands of hair sticking to her face. She shook her head, gathered her wits and cut her losses. Fighting with the man who had just saved her life was bad form, no matter how you looked at it. She owed him a debt of gratitude, her personal feelings notwithstanding.

But ditched by Sadie? Staring into the buttery cream butt of her horse, Delaney fumed. *Traitor.* She took off after the two, grumbling to herself, "I'm coming, I'm coming."

Once they crossed the bridge and neared the Ernie's cabin, Nick looked around, his mind seeking the most likely direction for the stables.

Delaney reached for the reins. "I'll take those now, thank you."

Ignoring her play, he glanced toward the small clearing just past Ernie's place, the gentle slope leading up into the mountain where he'd spotted Delaney earlier, and a miscellany of openings into the trees surrounding them. But since he had not been offered a tour, he didn't have the first clue. "Where are the stables?"

"Back down that way," she pointed.

Nick saw a trail leading into an arched tunnel of trees and branches. He headed for the opening.

"I can walk Sadie myself, you know."

Nick paused. "I believe you." Irritation flared in her dark eyes, setting them ablaze. He liked spirit in a woman. Liked independence and strength, too. "But I'm not letting you anywhere near those woods, unescorted." Besides, he wanted to reserve the opportunity to enjoy more than simply her temper.

"You're being ridiculous."

"And you're being careless."

"Excuse me?"

"Humor me, will you?"

"I don't need to humor you," Delaney huffed. "This is my land and my horse." But as she tried to yank the reins from his grasp, he lifted them above her head and out of reach. "Sorry." He shrugged, suppressing the pleasure he found in riling her temper. "No can do."

Delaney's black brow furrowed. "Are you always this controlling?"

"Usually no need," he replied. "Most people I deal with have more sense. But you, you're like an angry honey badger running around the desert."

"*A what*?"

Nick grinned. "A honey badger. Craziest animal I ever saw. Chases venomous snakes across the desert floor like nobody's business." He laughed and added, "Though when she's bitten by her prey, she can become downright docile." Nick gently tugged at Sadie's bit and walked off ahead of her. He imagined Delaney to be contemplating an attack of her own at the moment, but it couldn't be helped. She was a stubborn one and required a patient hand, but she could benefit from a strong hand, too. Whether she was willing to admit it or not, Delaney had been spooked by those men and more so than her horse. When he first saw her, Nick recognized the blank look for what it was. Fright. Something happened out there and it scared her, but for some reason she wasn't revealing details. That man clearly believed she had something he wanted. Did she know what it was?

Delaney caught up with him and, with a decidedly calmer tone, asked, "May I walk my own horse, please?"

Nick looked askance. "Oh, I don't know." He stroked the mare's muscular neck. "Sadie seems pretty happy in my hands."

"She's *my* horse," Delaney snarled and yanked at the reins in his hands.

Nick allowed her the small victory. Demoralizing Delaney wasn't the goal. Keeping her safe was.

He followed as Delaney led the way through the woods. Leaves sat suspended from branches overhead, hovering in the air above them as they walked, dense enough to block most of the sunlight. It made this section of the forest quiet, peaceful. Soft pillows of leaves blanketed the forest floor to either side of the trail, punctuated by black logs rotted by years of decay. The faint sound of creek water could be heard down below. To him, it felt like they were strolling through a cavern, the air rich with the musky scent of nature. It would make for a memorable hike for his hotel guests.

With two long strides, Nick caught up with Delaney, Sadie's hooves rhythmic and steady as she walked at Delaney's side, her head bobbing in cadence, with the occasional shake to her mane. It made him miss his horses back in Montana.

"Thank you for saving me back there," Delaney murmured. "I didn't expect him to be waiting at my horse."

"No?" The surprise apology heightened Nick's awareness of Delaney's femininity. Add the close proximity, the privacy of their situation and his impulse was to touch her, to brush the hair from her neck and wrap his arm around her slim shoulders. But he didn't. Not yet. "You seemed pretty concerned about her. Which makes no sense unless you knew that man might turn up."

"I was—and I did," Delaney underscored. "Sadie has been with me since she was a foal. If anything happened to her, I'd die—right after I killed the bastard who hurt her."

Surprised by the degree of vengeance in her voice, Nick merely agreed. "You've raised a beauty," he admired, and patted her rear.

"She is."

Nick wanted to probe. He wanted to know why Delaney had been hiking in the woods with a backpack, why she carried a camera, why she exited the woods on the far side instead of where she hitched her horse. But he didn't ask—there'd be time enough for that later. "Where's Felicity?" he asked, casually changing the subject.

"At a friend's house. Thankfully," Delaney added.

"Good. You expect her home soon?"

She doused him with an eyeful of suspicion. "Why?"

Nick indulged her with a reticent smile. "I'm concerned for her safety. She should know there's the potential for danger in the forest."

"She does," Delaney snapped, then instantly retreated. She heaved a sigh and slowed, tilting her face up to him. Brown eyes softened with motherly concern. "I told her not to go out alone until further notice."

"This isn't the first run-in with these gentlemen, I take it?"

"Second."

Nick approved the contrite tone to her answer. Maybe he could get through to her after all. "Wise of you to counsel her against it."

She flipped him a nod in thanks.

Nick trailed her to the stables and watched as Delaney executed her duties without remark. She handled the horses with gentle authority, cleared the center corridor of horse crap without fuss, the pungent scent permeating his nostrils as she rolled it by in her wheelbarrow. Delaney didn't dawdle, but performed every task with the efficiency of routine. "Finished," she announced. Swiping the back of her hand across her forehead, she slung the backpack over her shoulder and looked to him. "Should I assume you're escorting me back to the house?"

Pleased with her acquiescence, Nick replied, "You should."

"Yay," she mumbled.

As she walked past him on her way out, he detected the sweat and dirt clinging to her person. Drawn to her rear end, he mused with satisfaction. *It only gets better from here, my dear.*

Chapter Twelve

Nick made repeated attempts at conversation on the way back to Ernie's cabin, but Delaney was having none of it. There was no way she was going to reveal her discovery to him. She would handle those men through Clem—once she decided on a strategy for attack. Having Nick Harris poke around her business would be nothing but a nuisance.

"Okay, so thanks again," Delaney said, walking backwards away from him. She offered a meager wave. "Appreciate everything you did, but I've got to get home."

"Your place up there?" he asked, gesturing toward her cabin on the ridge above.

Startled, Delaney almost didn't reply. "Uh, yes. It is."

"Good to know." His posture relaxed as he tucked his hands into the front pockets of his jeans, shirttails still hanging loose around his waist. "I'm going to hang out tonight, keep an eye on things."

She nearly stumbled and stopped suddenly. "What?"

Nick casually perused their surroundings and nodded. "I don't want him coming back and finishing what he started."

Urgency kicked at her. "That won't be necessary, I assure you—"

He silenced her protest with a hand. "I believe it is."

"Mr. Harris, *really*, there's no need."

His expression sobered. All trace of humor vanished. "You had a run in with some pretty unsavory characters, Ms. Wilkins. When a man points a gun at me, I believe he means business. I'm willing to bet that man won't stop until you give him whatever it is he wants."

Delaney's temper re-ignited. *He won't get a thing from me.* "I appreciate your offer, but like I said, it won't be necessary."

Nick crossed arms over his chest and asked, "Do you know what he's after?"

"No," she answered, a tad too quickly. Delaney ran a hand over her head, around the cotton hairband of her ponytail, then dropped it to the strap of her backpack. Catching movement from the corner of her eye, she flashed to Ernie's cabin to see Albert ambling out onto the porch.

Her grip on the flat strap tightened. *Great.* Delaney took a step toward her cabin, but then turned back to Nick. With a tip of her head toward the main house, she said, "I think there are enough people around, the man won't attempt anything here." It was one thing to fire at her in the woods where there wasn't a soul around. It was quite another to do so within range of potential witnesses.

"I think you're underestimating him." Nick's gaze tightened on her. "Why?"

"Why?" She dropped her gaze to the ground beneath him, sidestepping his penetrating glare. "Just a hunch." Besides, she couldn't imagine the man would have the audacity to seek her out at home.

"Women's intuition, huh?"

She lifted her gaze to meet his. "Yeah, something like that."

Nick smiled. "Just the same, I think I'll stay."

"But you have no right!"

"You can always call the police."

The man knew darn well she didn't want the police involved.

When she didn't reply, Nick said, "So it's settled."

"No, it's not *settled*," she snapped. But did she have a choice? Delaney checked the sports watch on her wrist. Four o'clock. Clearly, the events of the day had taken their toll. She was hot, tired. It was getting late. She rolled her eyes toward the open section of sky, the late afternoon sun casting a veneer of yellow-gold over blue. *Gold.*

Delaney heaved a sigh. The prospect was thrilling and complicating at the same time and she needed time to think. She dropped her head back to face Nick, hauled the backpack further up her shoulder and said, "Fine. But will you do me a favor and stay out of sight of my daughter? I don't want her to get the wrong idea, or anything..." The quick warmth to her cheeks bothered her, as did the smile forming on his lips.

He chuckled. "Wouldn't think of it."

Delaney grunted. Trudging off in the direction of her cabin, she focused on the night ahead. The men from the woods didn't know where she lived. They only knew where her horse had been. Would they contact Clem? A sliver of doubt scampered through her. Would he tell them where to find her? Delaney slowly turned her head for a second look at Nick.

Nick acknowledged her with a slight nod of his head, and Delaney turned away. Maybe having him close by wasn't such a bad idea after all.

Climbing up the hill, Delaney plodded in the front door of her cabin. She flicked the lights on and deposited the backpack onto the kitchen counter. Mentally hitting the re-wind button on the day, she recalled how close she came to getting shot. A mild shudder raced up her back. The man had shot at her and his bullet had been close. Too close.

But she hadn't been hit. She was okay. Retrieving the camera from her pack, Delaney leaned her hip against the counter and scrolled through the photos. As she zoomed in on several, the first release from the trauma began to take hold. She could breathe easy. She could relax. She pressed a button and scrutinized an image. She could decipher the man, his build. She could pick him out of a line up, if she had to. The pictures weren't great, but they were good enough for visual ID.

Relief streamed through her. The risk had been worth it.

Delaney laid the camera on to the counter. Looking back, she'd known there was an element of danger involved. But peering down at the tiny screen of her camera, she had also known she would get nowhere without photographic evidence. It was her only chance at stopping them, dead in their tracks. *Dead in their tracks.* The thought hit close to home. Too close.

Suddenly, she remembered the phone call that had sent everything spiraling out of control. She'd never checked her messages. Delaney yanked open the backpack and grabbed the cell phone. A voicemail from Felicity. Her heart leaped. Quickly, she jabbed at images on the screen until she was listening to the message. Delaney closed her eyes. Thank God, it hadn't been an emergency. Felicity wanted to stay the night at her friend's house. Under the circumstances, it was perfect timing. Now there would be no need to explain Nick's presence on the property after dark.

Delaney called her daughter, and after a brief chat, felt almost normal. Only her sweat-stained shirt and filthy jeans remained grim reminders that she needed a hot shower and she needed it now. With only a passing thought to Nick, she strolled into her bedroom, disrobed and stepped into her shower. With warm water streaming over her body, she closed her eyes and breathed in deep and full. Actually, it was kinda nice knowing that Prince Harris was standing guard tonight. Inundated with a spattering of nerves, she grinned. Even if it was a silly, outdated notion, it was nice to know a big strong man was watching out for her.

An hour later, Delaney poured herself a glass of red wine, then walked to the sofa. It was the rare treat she allowed herself when Felicity wasn't home. She drank in private, not because she was ashamed, but because she wanted to set a good example for her daughter. Jack Foster had been a drinker. He'd been a hard drinker, and it had affected his behavior in undesirable ways. Delaney wasn't sure if Felicity remembered those days—those awful, violent days—but she wasn't about to take the chance. There would be no association between her loving mother and her alcoholic father. None.

No sooner had Delaney sat than she abandoned the sofa for the window. She nudged the curtain aside and peered outside. It was dark, a near moonless night. Her porch light was on, cutting her ability to see down the trail to any extent, making for an obscured approach, if one was so inclined. Was Nick there? Did he mean what he said about not leaving her alone?

She closed the curtain. If Clem did have a notion to come after her, she would be ready. Delaney spied the dishcloth, her fully-loaded pistol partially hidden beneath. Inhaling against the sudden fluttering of her heart, she understood that self-preservation came first.

As she idled in the center of the living room, her stomach growled, sharp and lingering. She realized she was famished. When was the last time she ate? Startled by the realization it had been a single granola bar for breakfast, she went straight to the refrigerator.

Outside, Nick Harris walked the perimeter of Ernie's cabin before heading up to Delaney's cabin. A light was on inside, but there was no sound. Was the old man asleep? At nine o'clock, he might be. Didn't appear he had anything else to do. There was no television antennae attached to his roof and he didn't strike Nick as a reader. Ernie Ladd was a smoker and a hothead, with little else going for him. Other than this beautiful property. Nick glanced up at Delaney's cabin. Speaking of beautiful...

Desire stirred in his loins. A beautiful woman was up there alone. Felicity's car wasn't parked out front, which meant she wasn't home. Through the dense cover of trees, Nick could see dots of lights emanating from her cabin. What was she doing? Nick lit the ground with a flashlight he picked up at a hardware store in town and made his way closer. He could hear the creek before he saw it, lifting his light to illuminate the rickety wooden bridge. Wandering over it, fast moving water caught the white beams from his light.

Swiping a quick flash of light around him, he extinguished it. Committing the layout of the terrain to memory, he headed to a large tree—one that marked the way straight up to Delaney's cabin. Leaning into the rough bark, he settled into the night. The rhythmic vibration of katydids pulsated loudly against a steady stream of higher-pitched crickets, with the occasional frog piping in. Other than nature at work, he detected no sounds, no movement. Nothing. It was a lonesome sound, but it was a sound that called to him. No stranger to the night forest, he used to camp for days at a time in the rugged landscape of the Rocky Mountains with his father and knew the sounds of serenity well. He and his dad would hunt by day, drink whiskey by night, share stories around the flames of a campfire.

His father's stories usually centered on his own youth, a litany of his adventures and without fail he wound a history lesson into the mix. Indians, pioneers, trains, industry titans... Pleasure rolled through Nick. Those were good days. Simple joys for a simple time in his life. His horizons didn't expand until after he built his first hotel, one he built outside his hometown.

Nick recalled the days and nights spent designing, building, dreaming up new ways to work his masterpiece into the mountainous land that was a part of him. Living at one with nature had been ingrained in his mindset from the beginning. His mother worked a summer garden every year, and he worked right alongside her. From seed to harvest, he learned every step of the process, could identify plants based on their leaf shape, their smell—even count the days to corn harvest from the first sign of yellow-green silk. His mom used to laugh at him, calling him a perfectionist in the making.

Fond feelings washed through him. She was right. He was a perfectionist. His father taught him a different side of the land. With the right tools and a tree, Nick could craft the finest piece of furniture, throw up a structure from floor to roof, with enough wood left over to make a fire in the hearth. The backyard shed had been his first solo project and the thing stood to this day. Quality came from basic materials and sturdy construction. It was a lesson that stuck with him. Build it right the first time and you won't have to mess with it again. From day one, Nick demanded the finest in materials be used to construct his properties. He expected his staff to deliver top-notch service to his guests. And his women...

He rolled an eye upward through the black of night. He only spent time with the most beautiful, intelligent creatures on the Planet Earth. Made no sense to waste time with anything less. Though "obstinate" was a new trait for his roster. He'd dated headstrong women before, independent thinkers with a definite mind of their own, and he enjoyed them, enjoyed the challenge they presented. But obstinate?

Nick laughed softly. Delaney Wilkins was obstinate to a damn near fault! She was almost foolhardy, the way she dismissed his protection. His senses sharpened. The woman was in danger, there was no mistaking it. Convincing her of the same was proving to be the challenge.

Making his way up the trail toward her cabin, Nick kept his footsteps light. If trouble showed up tonight, he wanted no distance between himself and Delaney. The man on the trail this afternoon had a decidedly determined look in his eye. He wanted something and Nick would bet his life Delaney knew what that something was. She was no innocent in the matter, he was sure of it. And where she seemed to have recovered from her harrowing experience—whatever it might be—she refused to share the cause with him.

But it was exactly that cause which put her life in danger.

Nick hiked the steep path. Emerging from the forest at the top, he paused to catch his breath. One thing about city life, it robbed the body of physical fitness. Venturing out onto the open trail, he assessed Delaney's cabin to be a one-room floor plan, perhaps with the addition of a loft—certainly no bigger than a two-car garage. He marveled at the diminutive size. *The two* of them lived there?

The scent of cornbread tickled his nose. Pleasure coursed through him. *She cooks*. Add another plus for the lady in the knockout jeans. A quick vision of her jean-clad rear end rose sharp in his mind's eye. Low, hip-hugging jeans that hugged her curves, caressed her every movement took center stage in his brain. From what he'd seen, it's all she seemed to wear. But Delaney would receive no complaints from him. He liked her in jeans. He'd like her out of them, too.

A ripple moved through his groin and he chastised himself. This would not do. Lusting after her while on guard would only distract him. His intention was to protect her tonight, not seduce her. Desire coiled around his thoughts. Hopefully there would be a time for that little feat later.

Pleasantly full, Delaney rinsed the last dish and poured herself a half glass of wine. The cornbread and leftover fried chicken had definitely hit the spot. Tilting the bottle away from her, she read the label. She had no idea if it was a good year or not, no idea if it was from a good vintage. She relied on Ashley for that. That woman was the closest thing to a connoisseur Delaney had when it came to wine selection, claiming she drank for her heart, to keep the "pipes" clean. Delaney suspected Ashley enjoyed her wine more than for health reasons, but it wasn't her place to judge.

A loud rap sounded at her door. Panic ripped through her heart. Jerking the wine bottle upright, Delaney snatched her gun. But sizing up the figure through the door glass, she blew out her breath. Large man was fat. Clem and second guy were scrawny. The white shirt cinched it. Pulse pounding, she slid the gun beneath the towel, calming her breath. It was only Nick.

Briefly checking her attire for appropriateness, she decided the loose, heavy weave T-shirt and long cotton pants weren't overly revealing. She was presentable. Her pulse scattered through her veins, as she wondered what he wanted.

Had he seen something? She opened the door quickly. "What's up?" She looked past him, but it was pitch black. She wouldn't be able to see a man if was standing ten feet off the porch. She gazed up at him. "Is someone here?"

Nick smiled, openly giving her the once over. "No." He peered over her head and said, "I smelled cornbread."

Delaney pulled back, her surprise complete. "Cornbread?"

He gave a sheepish nod. "Didn't realize how hungry I was until the air filled with the sweet scent of home cooking. My nose doesn't deceive me, does it? You are baking cornbread, right?"

Cornbread? The man had scared the be-jeepers out of her for cornbread?

"Well, yeah..." she said. "About an *hour* ago."

He waggled his thick brow. "Any left?"

Delaney laughed at the easy sparkle dancing in his black eyes.

"What's so funny?" he asked, feigning offense.

Allowing the humor to loosen the knot in her chest, she shook her head. "My bodyguard is hungry." She looked up at him and saw that he, too, thought it a bit silly. Sharing the absurdity of the moment, she added, "My first Sir Galahad and what do I get?" She rolled her eyes. "I have to feed him."

"If you recall"—he cocked his head toward her, with a slight lift to his brow—"this wasn't a planned assignment."

"And then he blames me for his penchant for damsels in distress. Go figure!"

Amused by her remark, Nick flashed a dimpled smile. Still dressed as she had left him, it appeared he hadn't left since their escapade, and deciding there was no harm, she allowed him in. Felicity wasn't home, and besides, she owed him one. The man with the gun *could* be outside. Delaney stepped aside and swept a hand for him to enter. "Might as well come in."

Nick strolled in, arced a glance around the interior, and she wondered what he thought of the humble abode she called home. Exposed beams, rough-hewn log siding, wide plank floors and only the barest of necessities in furniture, it was all she and Felicity needed. The only thing she had updated since moving in was the floor. Unable to tolerate the natural surface of the wood beneath her feet, Delaney had sanded and refinished them herself. Barefoot living was a must in her world.

"Nice little place you have here." He nodded in approval. "It's rustic."

Delaney closed and locked the door behind him. "Rustic is a kind word, wouldn't you say?"

"It's nice, really."

"Thanks." Delaney walked around him and into the kitchen where she adjusted the dishtowel so it fully concealed her pistol. She didn't need Nick all worked up over the fact she intended to take care of things herself tonight. He'd probably dole out some sort of lecture about how it wasn't safe for a *woman* to handle a weapon.

As if on cue, he asked, "Are you scared?"

Delaney peeled back the foil and plucked one of the mini loaves from the white plate. Conscious of his gaze on her, she set the bread on a napkin. She certainly didn't want to feel scared. "Not really," she replied, and reached for the butter knife.

Storm clouds gathered in his eyes, making them appear both dark and menacing, sending a shiver up her spine. "You need to take that man seriously, you know."

The bread and paper grew moist within her palm. She swiped a hunk of butter from the dish, slathered it over the top of the loaf and handed it over to him. "I get it. A lot of whackos running around..."

"Dangerous whackos," he said, and took the bread from her. "Thanks for this."

"You're welcome."

"That's quite a bit of butter you serve up."

"Can't eat cornbread without butter," she informed him. "Not in these parts, anyway."

He smiled. "Fine with me. I'm only surprised someone in your fine shape can eat the stuff."

"Hiking."

"Works well," he said, a brazen glance to her lower body. "Where's Felicity?"

"She's staying at a friend's house tonight."

"Good. She doesn't need to be exposed to this."

Her sentiments exactly.

Nick inhaled half the loaf and groaned aloud.

Satisfaction swelled in her breast. It was her own recipe. Using the cornmeal Ashley ground for her from her garden corn, she made the bread once or twice a week.

"This is *really* good," he said and plopped the remainder into his mouth.

As he chewed, Delaney took pride in watching him enjoy her food. It gave her a sense of purpose, reward. Felicity raved about her cooking, but it was nice to hear it from a stranger. Her heart skipped a beat. And Nick Harris was a stranger—in her house—eating her food.

"It's incredibly moist. Sweet, too."

"It's my secret. I add pudding to the mix."

"Pudding?"

She nodded, though if her mother ever saw her put pudding into the cornbread mix, she would not have approved. Susannah Ladd Wilkins did not believe in tinkering with tradition.

"Can I have another?" he asked.

"Sure." Delaney reached for a separate napkin and fumbled a bit as she placed the golden loaf in the center. "They're better fresh from the oven," she said. Smearing another heap of butter over top, she thrust it toward him.

Accepting it, he winked. "Maybe I'll take you up on that one day."

Was he flirting with her? Delaney felt a warm flush, probably from the wine in her system. She glanced over the counter. Where was her glass?

"That wine looks good, too." He hitched his chin toward the counter behind her. "But that will have to wait for another day. No drinking on duty."

Delaney swallowed back her embarrassment. What did he think of her drinking alone? She collected her glass from the counter, a slight tremble to her grip. "I'm not a drinker."

"No?"

The could-have-fooled-me look rubbed her the wrong way. "I mean, I *rarely* drink. Only when Felicity's not home."

Nick raised a brow in question.

"Her father was an alcoholic," Delaney stated bluntly.

The revelation knocked the humor from his face. "Was?"

"Is," she corrected, growing flustered with the personal nature of the conversation. "I like to keep it away from her. The alcohol."

Nick nodded that he understood, but Delaney wondered if he could. Did he have experience with an alcoholic? Did he know what it was like to suffer the alcohol-induced outbursts? The scathing tongue? She shoved the memories from her mind and took a swallow of wine. Jack was a thing of the past and Delaney would allow him no power in her life.

When Nick finished the second loaf, awkwardness settled between them. She could feel him looking at her, curiosity swimming in the depths of his dark eyes. Was he thinking about the men, or was his mind delving into a more intimate realm? The realm of man and woman, attraction, desire...

Delaney hadn't played that game in a very long time, but she could recognize the signs. Men around town made advances, sniffed around like hound dogs for cues she was willing to engage with them. A few had been interesting, but none memorable, none worthy of her time. She was committed to Felicity. Whatever her daughter needed, she would have. They were a team, a unit. They were a family. Delaney regretted that her marriage hadn't work out, because it meant Felicity had to grow up without a father, without a man in the house to demonstrate what real male love looked like, how it treated a woman. How it *respected* a woman.

Morton Parker had filled in like the ace father he was, his boys stellar examples of how young men should behave. In fact, Delaney trusted Felicity with Travis and Troy without question. She only wished Felicity had her own father, all to herself. A man to guide her, to love her. But Jack wasn't that man.

Nick crumpled the napkin in hand. "Guess I'd better be heading out."

"You're leaving?" she asked, and blushed at the self-assured pleasure moving into his expression. She plunked the wine down. "I mean, it's okay if you want to, I'm fine on my own." Delaney fortified her diaphragm and added solidly, "I can handle things on my own, is what I meant to say."

"I'm sure you can," he replied, the sardonic gleam returning to his eyes. He scratched the back of his head and made a half-grimace. "But how about I hang around as back-up?"

"Whatever," she replied casually, replacing the foil over the bread plate. She didn't' want him to think she *wanted* him here. On second thought, she paused. "Would you like the last piece to go?"

A sweeping smile overtook his features, landing square in his dimples. "I'd rather come back for it later."

Delaney hastily sealed the foil back in place, tamping back a quick flight of nerves. A quiet noise hit the rear of her cabin. Her heart stopped. Nick whipped his head toward her bedroom, pressed a finger to his lips. His gaze became a heat-seeking missile, scanning the back wall. Her heart thudded like a locomotive. Was someone trying to get in?

Chapter Thirteen

As he pulled his gun from his waistband, Nick was surprised to see Delaney pull one out from beneath a plaid kitchen towel. Maybe she was more frightened than she let on. Smart woman.

Nick motioned for her to stay put. She shook her head vigorously, but he held up a stiff finger and pointed it at her. *One minute, you wait here.*

When she took a step toward him, he thrust her a hardened glare. *Back off.* The last thing he wanted to do was explain a bullet wound to her daughter, Felicity.

Delaney became still. She lowered the gun to her side. Satisfied she got the message, Nick moved softly in the direction of the noise that had come from the back room. He paused at the open doorway. Must be her bedroom. Jeans were piled in a basket in the corner, a dresser backed against the wall beside him. Next to it, a door sat ajar, presumably her bathroom. Fleeting images of Delaney naked in the shower zipped through his mind, but he squelched them. He edged along the wall, restraining his reaction to the perfumed scent lingering in the air. On the far side, there was a curtained window. Whoever was out there had the advantage. They could see in, but he couldn't see out.

Nick could feel Delaney standing by the door. Turning to her, he whispered, "Turn out the lights."

She disappeared and the living room went dark. Within seconds, he noted the drift of floral fragrance as she tiptoed up beside him. Her hand came to rest on his upper arm. "Did you see anything?" she whispered.

Although he couldn't see her, he could hear her breathing by his side. The hand on his arm assaulted his focus. Images of her T-shirted torso, her lean legs in the thin cotton pants flooded his mind. It was the steel pistol against his thigh that disconcerted him. "No," he managed. He scanned the blackness, but could see almost nothing. The cabin seemed to be embedded within the mountain itself, the window a wedge between a wall of wood and a wall of earth. Access to her room would be difficult from this angle. Not impossible, but difficult.

The soft pads of her fingers pressed into him. "What is it?"

"I don't know yet." He turned from the window. "Do you have a back door?"

"No." She slid her hand to his elbow.

"I didn't see anything outside," he said. The hard line of the gun in her hand was less than reassuring. He noted she left the gun hot. Last thing he needed was for her to misfire in the dark and hit *him*. "You wait here. I'll go check it out."

"Wait—" Delaney clutched at him. "I'll come with you."

"Scared?"

"No."

Nick chuckled softly.

"I can't *see* you," she said, then snapped, "And I'd hate to *shoot* you by accident after all your help."

You and me both. Placing his hand over hers, Nick gingerly removed her hand from his arm. "Thanks, but I won't be long."

Working from memory, he crossed the room in the inky blackness—which was easy—a route which fortunately was short and straight. As he rounded her bedroom door, the front porch light came into view. Once again, Nick instructed Delaney to stay put while he checked outside. Snaking along the wall, he kept an eye on the front door, toggling between it and the small window to the left. If someone was lying in wait outside, Nick needed to maintain an element of surprise. As he neared the door, he watched for signs of movement. Through the etched glass, the light shone white. Unlikely anyone would stand out there exposed, but he wasn't taking any chances. The man he met on the trail had already proven his boldness. Nick slid his hand to the door knob. Slowly, silently, he turned it. He raised his gun to eye level and poised his finger on the trigger. Easing the door open, he peered out through the slice of opening. Something moved. His grip tightened. His breathing stopped.

Down the trail, Nick spotted a dark figure running. He was almost positive it was a man. Slipping outside, he stole quickly across the porch. Through the screen, he sharpened his focus, but the swath of light wasn't enough for him to see with any clarity.

But he didn't have to. Someone had been here. Nick detected the scent of tobacco in the air. He turned and stopped suddenly at the sight of Delaney standing in the open doorway. "What are you *doing*?"

"Did you see someone?" she whispered.

Standing only feet behind him, she was an easy shot, should someone decide to take one. So was he. Nick tucked his weapon back into the waistband of his jeans and strode over to her. "Didn't I tell you to wait?"

"I'm not waiting in there like a sitting duck," she said, reaching for his arm again. She peered down the trail that led to Ernie's cabin. "Did you see someone?"

Nick's instinct was to lie, set her mind at ease. The protector in him wanted her to remain calm. But the man in him liked the way she grabbed hold of him for protection. "Someone was here."

Her expression registered the hit. "You *saw* him?"

Nick caught another whiff of floral and fruit and thought it might be her shampoo. "Yes," he said, glancing over her hair. Pulled up into a loosely tied bun, strands of creamy blonde fell into a frame about her face. It accentuated her dark brows, eyes black as coal within the dim light. Nick could see her unease catch fire as she imagined the man lurking outside in the darkness. "He's gone," he reassured.

She clutched at him. "Are you sure?"

He nodded. "Went down the trail."

Her eyes flicked down the trail, then back to him. "How can you be sure he won't come back?"

"I can't. Which is why I'm staying."

Delaney returned a look that nearly undid him. The tough girl had shades of vulnerability. "It'll be okay." He cast a glance around the porch and cupped his hand over hers. "The good news is, you only have one way in or out. I'll park myself here so you can rest easy. No one will get by me tonight."

"All night?" she uttered.

"All night." He took her by the hand and led her back into the cabin.

Delaney paused at the door, her slender hand softly pulling from his. "But where will you sleep?"

He smiled down at her. "Now what kind of body guard would that make me if I slept on the job?"

Delaney realized her error and faltered, "I—I…" She glanced about her porch, the furnishing limited to a couple of rickety rocking chairs and a wobbly wood table. "There's not even a place to sit, really."

He raked a hand through his hair. "I've spent time in worse."

A wounded look entered her eyes, her very beautiful, very vulnerable, very alluring eyes. He noted that the dim lighting softened everything about her. "I only meant that I'll be fine."

"Okay," she said hesitantly, as though debating her next move.

"I could use a glass of water, if you can spare it."

Delaney shook her head , as if to clear it. "Of course," she said.

Nick followed her to the kitchen, his attention divided between the gun in her hand and the lengths of hair falling about her neck and shoulders. She flipped on the light, but froze, her hand on the switch. "Is that okay?"

He gave a confident nod. "He's gone. You keep the curtains closed and you'll be fine." Nick watched the rise and fall of her breasts beneath the faded T-shirt as she inhaled deeply to calm herself. "Your daughter already handing out the university gear?" he asked, indicating the white emblem on the front of her orange shirt.

Delaney dropped her head and gently tugged the hem. "Oh, this?" She looked up at him and smiled tentatively. "Yes. Once she was accepted, her friends Travis and Troy bought her half dozen of these."

"Travis and Troy?"

For the first time since he'd been here, Delaney's expression relaxed into a smile. Easy, bright, it made her look healthy and happy and all the more attractive.

"They're boys she grew up with."

"Platonic, I assume?"

Delaney laughed and set her gun down by the dish cloth. "Not by their choosing."

Of course not, he thought. Felicity was as attractive as her mother, but with an entirely different appeal. Delaney had an air of strength about her, a determined set to her jaw, dark brows and spirited brown eyes that posed a sexy contrast to her long blonde hair, the color of pale wheat silk. Her body was petite, mostly covered from sight at the moment, yet she moved with a swagger that shouted confidence. Until tonight. He smiled inwardly as she handed him a mason jar with water. With a nod of thanks, he sipped, taking her in from over the rim. It was a swagger her jeans embodied well. And if there was one thing Nick liked in a woman, it was confidence.

Felicity was a different caliber entirely. Strawberry blonde, she was fair-skinned and he'd bet fair-hearted as well. From the two brief conversations he'd had with her, he could tell she was smart but had a gentle way about her. Unlike her mother who was accustomed to the hard work of horses and stables, Felicity was the product of indoor practice and study. She was refined, content to be part of the orchestra rather than take center stage.

Unlike her mother. Something told him Delaney could strut across a stage like nobody's business, the audience demanding encore after encore. An audience of mostly men, that is. Nick cooled his thoughts with a long, deep swallow of water and emptied the glass. "Thanks." He handed it back, purposely retaining hold as her fingers closed around his. "I needed that," he said, enjoying the slight bump to her gaze.

But he was best parked outside, where his mind had no distractions. Nick couldn't trust himself not to "touch" if he stayed inside with Delaney any longer. "If you need anything," he said, slowly arching a single brow, "I'll be right outside that door."

Delaney slanted a glance toward the door and said, "I feel silly having you sit outside all night."

"Would you rather I sit indoors? That sofa looks mighty comfy."

"Nice try." With her hands wrapped around his glass on the counter, a subtle smile drifted over her face.

And if Nick wasn't mistaken, he'd venture to bet she was harboring a hint of desire herself. *Perfect.* "I'll always try," he returned, indulging in the moment. As she walked him to the door, he added, "Try and get some sleep, will you?"

"Are you my father, now?"

"Oh no, far from it—of that, you can be sure."

Nick went outside and Delaney locked the door behind him. Lingering, she turned, hands encircling the cold metal knob. It was an odd feeling, knowing he was just outside her door. On the one hand, it felt nice, knowing he was there, should the stranger come back. She'd been surprised the man with the gun had the nerve to track her down. But he couldn't have followed her. Nick had run him off back on the trail. She turned, and gazed through the carved lines of the glass door. The only way the man could have known where to find her, was through Clem. He must have told Clem about her, and Clem had ordered him to come after the pictures.

But she couldn't believe Clem would really send an armed man after her. If she didn't cooperate—which she wouldn't—he might actually shoot her. Nervous energy pushed her from the door, propelling her to the kitchen. Did Clem really have it in him? He'd always been a low-life in her book, engaging in petty crime through the years, disorderly conduct and the like, but nothing ever serious. To her knowledge, he had never landed himself in jail.

Perhaps circumstances dictated desperate measures. If Clem knew she was on to his gold theft, he might indeed be capable of doing anything to cover his crime. Delaney rinsed and dried Nick's glass, her thoughts wandering to the front porch. Suddenly, she was glad he was here. She didn't trust anyone or anything at the moment. Anything except *his* ability to protect her.

Setting the glass on the dish rack to dry, Delaney went into her bedroom. Retrieving the camera from under her pillow, she sat on the edge of her bed and scrolled through the images again. There were three she decided were worthy for Ernie's viewing. Three she could use to prove there were men on the property who shouldn't be. She dropped camera to her lap. But she still had to prove their connection to Clem. Somehow, she had to get photos of him with his men. She had to prove her case beyond reasonable doubt. Ernie would defend Clem unless she could show him for the guilty scalawag he was. But how?

It was only a fluke she'd caught sight of them together in the first place. If only she could share her discovery with Nick. Maybe he'd be able to think of a way to draw the connection. He'd proven himself pretty handy so far. She glanced toward her front porch. The thought of him sitting outside her door evoked images of him staring down that man on the trail today, chasing him away from her cabin tonight. Nick was a brave one. A strong one. When the noise hit and the lights went out, she had felt totally safe in his presence. There wasn't the slightest doubt that Prince Harris would take care of whoever was outside.

Prince Harris. She smiled at her new nickname for the man. Had a nice ring to it. Delaney's thoughts detoured back to the porch. What was he doing right now? She glanced at the small clock on her dresser. It was eleven o'clock. Did he really intend to stay all night? Would he sleep out there?

Now what kind of body guard would that make me if I slept on the job.

The recollection threaded warm sensations of pleasure through her thoughts. Maybe he could use some coffee. It would get colder as the night went on. Abruptly, she rose. Grabbing a light jacket from her closet, she slipped it on and headed outside.

Turning the handle, she eased her head around the door jamb. Nick was sitting in the far chair, still as night. His eyes sought hers through the dim light. Only the rhythmic sawing of crickets and katydids came between them.

"You shouldn't be out here," he said.

"Why—do you think he's come back? Did you hear something?" Nerves drummed in her midsection as she glanced out into the black of night.

"No."

She breathed easy.

"That's not what I'm referring to."

"Oh." Her heart tripped. There was no mistaking the intent of his words. Spoken low, but spoken clearly, she understood what he was insinuating. She ventured out anyway. Well, he was a man, wasn't he? Men forever made innuendos were always on the prowl for a willing partner. It didn't mean anything if a woman didn't let it.

Besides, she wasn't out here to flirt with him. She was out here to help him. "Actually, I wondered if maybe you could use a cup of coffee."

"No thanks."

"But how will you stay awake?"

"It's not a problem."

Idling, she said, "That chair can't be comfortable." At six four, Nick dwarfed the rocker, the seat barely wide enough to accommodate him.

"It'll do."

"You know," she said, padding her socked feet closer to him. "I appreciate you doing this..." Delaney slid her gaze around the porch. "Standing watch and all." She felt a tiny rise of embarrassment, magnified by the slow grin pulling at his mouth. "You must be tired, and with the front door locked, I should be fine."

"It's no trouble, Delaney, though your repeated attempts to get rid of me are duly noted."

"What?" She evaded his quiet, knowing smile and objected, "I'm not trying to get rid of you. All I'm saying—"

Nick raised a swift finger to his lips.

Did he hear something? Delaney took two steps closer to him, stopping behind the rocker next to his. "What?" she whispered. "Is someone out there?"

He shook his head. "Just didn't want you to ruin the moment."

Indignation flared hot in her breast, fueled by his mocking grin. "If you insist on standing out here," Nick said, "why not have a seat? Less visible that way."

Delaney didn't know whether to kick his chair or sit, as he suggested.

Nick chuckled softly. "C'mon, I won't bite."

Wasn't he the one who said it wasn't a good idea for her to be out here? But sit she did, pulling the jacket more tightly around her shoulders. Not like she could sleep, knowing he was out on her porch, that someone might be lurking out in the dark. Delaney glanced to her side. "Aren't you cold?"

"Perfect temperature. Reminds me of the mountains of my youth."

"You grew up around mountains? Where?" she asked, suddenly intrigued.

He turned to her, his gaze roaming her seated figure. "Montana."

"Montana?" Why did that surprise her? Because she pegged him for a city boy? Delaney looked down at the planked floor. Of course, he did *look* as if he belonged in the mountains. She recalled that first day with him on the trail, when he interrupted her as she spied the men in the woods. It had struck her then how at home he seemed in the wooded terrain. Nick Harris had rugged good looks. Skin lined from years in the sun, his build strong and capable, he could easily pass for a rancher or a lumberjack. His attire contributed to the aura. Jeans and boots seemed to be the staple of his attire.

But mountain men didn't drive sports sedans. They drove trucks.

"Ever been?" he asked.

Delaney turned back to him. "Been where?"

"Montana," he chided gently.

"Oh." She shook her head. "No." Delaney hadn't been anywhere but Tennessee. In fact—she lifted her head and gazed out into the dark—she'd never been more than a hundred miles from here.

"It's a beautiful state. My parents still live there. In a small town outside Whitefish."

"Whitefish?"

"Ever heard of it?"

She shook her head, ignorance swelling in her heart, the late night hour crowding in.

Nick smiled. "Not surprised. It's pretty remote. Unless you're familiar with Glacier National Park, you've probably never heard of it."

Delaney wasn't. Couldn't pinpoint it on a map, couldn't find it without searching for it by name, because home was all she needed.

When she didn't reply, Nick remained quiet. Pulsating sounds from the crickets and frogs filled the porch, cold crept under the sleeves of her jacket. Neither said a word. Delaney wondered what Nick's life was like in Montana. Were those mountains similar to Tennessee? She'd heard they were bigger, grander, but mountain living was mountain living. Being surrounded by trees and hills couldn't be all that much different, could it?

Delaney tucked her feet beneath her, the position hoarding warmth as she sat motionless. Odd that she didn't feel uncomfortable in his presence. Odd she didn't feel the need to talk, to make conversation. There was something about Nick that felt easy, uncomplicated. It appealed to her.

"This is a beautiful property, Delaney." She tensed. The last thing she wanted to do was rehash his designs on her land. "You and Felicity, this small town... It reminds me of where I grew up."

Her ears sharpened. She wanted to hear more about Montana, how similar it was, how different, but she didn't want him to think she was interested. He might sense it as weakness on her part and try again to convince her to sell.

"The terrain is different, but the feel of the land, the people, it's all the same. Guess clean living and good people don't look all that different, no matter where you are."

Delaney tuned in.

"You're lucky to stay connected. Family and tradition is something you don't miss until you're thousands of miles away."

"Maybe you can understand why I'm fighting so hard to keep Ladd Springs, then."

He nodded. "I do. It's why my offer specifically included a section of land to remain in your name. Yours and Felicity's," he corrected.

"A section." Delaney looked away. "As though I'd be happy with part and not all."

"Sometimes life changes what we want into what we need."

She didn't need reminding she was in a bind—a bind that might cease—should she prove Clem's involvement with those men.

"I'm not here to take you away from your home, Delaney. On the contrary. I want to ensure this stays your home."

Latching her attention onto the outdoor light, the single floodlight hanging from the opposite end of the porch, she replied quietly, "It already is."

This cabin was her home. It was her mother's home. She wasn't sharing it with anyone. No one but Felicity.

"I'm sorry," Nick said. "I didn't mean to bring up a sore subject. After all," he added, and she could hear the smile in his voice. "You only came out to offer me coffee."

Chapter Fourteen

Delaney awoke early the next morning and dragged herself into a hot shower. She hadn't slept worth a hoot all night. How could she? Between visions of a stranger swirling around her cabin and thoughts of the formidable Nick Harris outside her door, she was lucky to get a wink in edgewise!

She was curious about his early life in the mountains, an existence that mirrored her own. Until he made it sound like she was after more, and she'd promptly dismissed herself from his presence. Truth was—she *didn't* trust herself. She was intrigued by his life but didn't want him to take advantage of her interest. Didn't want him to trip her up. There was no way this land would fall into his hands. She merely liked the idea that there was a positive side to the man.

The man. Knowing Nick was outside her door was far more pleasurable than she had believed possible. Finishing her shower in record time, she dressed, combed her wet hair, firmed her resolve and went to the front door. Unlocking the knob, she hoped he liked grits. It was about all she had at the moment.

"Rise and shine," she said and stuck her head outside. She glanced in both directions and her heart fell. Did he not stay for the duration like he said he would?

Disappointment seeped in as she slowly closed the door. Maybe the light of sunrise woke him. If he *did* stay, she couldn't imagine he stayed awake the entire time. He must have fallen asleep at some point. Bypassing her kitchen, Delaney decided against breakfast. She had too many things to do and not enough time to do them. Packing the camera, her wallet and cell in the backpack, she slung it over her shoulder and headed for the stables, wondering if she'd see Nick again today.

But by four o'clock there had been no sight of him. Not on her way to the stables, not at the house, no sign of his car on the road as she drove into town. Delaney parked her truck down the street from Fran's Diner. It was the only space available, which was unusual for a Sunday. Most folks around here were at home this time of day.

But not Fran. Her diner was seven days a week, breakfast, lunch and dinner. On more than one occasion she'd been known to quip how the Lord understood a woman who needed to work. His flock needed to eat and she was their servant. It was a sentiment that appealed to Delaney. A woman needed to do what a woman needed to do. From taking care of her family to taking care of business.

Delaney swept inside the front door, the clang of bells loudly announcing her arrival. She had yet to find out what had transpired between Nick and Felicity the other day but Fran would know. Delaney scanned the bar counter, the red stools, the slew of vacant tables. The place was empty. But this wasn't her busy time. It was the lull between the after church crowd and the dinner crowd, the latter not set to arrive for another hour or so. A few booths were occupied, but no one she knew. Which was surprising. Nine times out of ten, Delaney knew someone dining at Fran's.

"Hey sugar!"

At the familiar drawl, Delaney spotted Fran's red hair through the window to the kitchen, could even make out the blue eye shadow. The elder woman waved, then pushed out through double doors. Dressed in starched white uniform, red apron tied at her waist, Fran ran a zillion miles an hour, but she never passed up an invitation to visit. Give her a wink and a wave and she was all yours—so long as her patrons weren't waiting for food.

Delaney waited counter side. "Hi, Fran."

The older woman came over directly and met her with a warm embrace, a veil of Shalimar perfume enveloping them.

Pulling away, she noticed the scratches on Delaney's arms. "Good Lord! What happened to you?"

"Lost a fight with a tree."

Fran's brown eyes became saucers. "Did you fall *out*?"

Delaney smiled. "Something like that."

"Bless your heart, child, but you need to leave this minute and see a doctor about this!"

"It's not that bad."

"Not that bad? It looks like a bear tried snackin' on you for lunch!"

Delaney hadn't come here to talk about her injuries. She'd come here to talk about Nick. "It's nothing, really. Listen, I wanted to ask you—did you see Felicity here the other day?"

Fran's brow gathered in question. "Now, you know I was just about to ask about that pretty daughter of yours. Does she need a peach pie?" She cast a hand toward the front display case, golden pastry tops lining three levels of trays. "I have three on the shelves right now."

Grateful they had moved into easier territory, Delaney gave an exasperated shake of her head. "Between you and Ashley, the girl could eat her weight in pie!"

Fran frowned. "Now you know Ashley doesn't know her way around a peach orchard, let alone a peach pie."

Delaney laughed. "How about you tell her that, not me?

Fran brightened. "You know I do—every chance I get!"

It was the running feud. Peach or blueberry. Ashley and Fran swapped title at the county fair for who dished up the best pie, but both were delicious and packed enough calories to see a girl through winter. It was a feud smart money steered clear of. "Anyway," Delaney resumed the business at hand, "I wanted to know if you happened to see a man talking to Felicity when she was here the other day."

Fran fussed with the hair at her neck, several strands escaping the edges of her hair net. "What kind a man we talking about?"

"A tall man." A very tall man, Delaney mused, transported back to his side in her cabin last night. Standing arm-to-arm was when Delaney realized exactly how tall. She swallowed. "With dark brown hair?"

Fran's recollection snapped and she wiped her brow, followed by a light tap to her forehead. She pointed at Delaney and said, "Yes, I do, as a matter of fact. He was in here on Wednesday, talking to her. Why?" Instantly circumspect, she lowered her voice. "Is he trouble?"

"No, no," Delaney said. "I was just wondering if you happened to overhear what they were saying."

A wicked grin seized hold of Fran's mouth. "He was a handsome thing. You trying to keep him away from Felicity, are you?"

The statement struck Delaney. "Don't you think he's a bit old for her?"

Fran returned a full-bellied laugh. "Oh, sugar, don't be upset with me. When you get to be my age, they all start lookin' young!" She continued to laugh, but when Delaney didn't join her, she settled down and said, "Lord a'mercy, I didn't mean nothin' by it. You know I only had eyes for Deacon, but he's dead and gone." She fanned a hand over her mouth. "And you know me, I'm just a mouthful of tomfoolery."

"I know," Delaney replied, disturbed by the fact she had been upset by the silly remark.

"Anyway, I don't recall anything other than him talking to her about her flute and some hotel. Serenity Springs, I think he said. Seemed harmless enough to me, so I just kept an eye on him and kept to my business, you know what I mean? He didn't stay long. Line was a mile long out the door," she said proudly, pointing out the front. "And he knew it was best to get in it before he lost his chance altogether."

Delaney remained mired in two words. Serenity Springs. Was that a hotel he owned? Or the one he planned for Ladd Springs, should he ever get his hands on the title? Renewed urgency swept through her. If the man was already making plans...

Did he know something she didn't know? Was he closer to getting the property than she realized?

After a brief discussion of food, kinfolk and current events, Delaney passed on the pies and thanked Fran. Turning to go, she came face-to-face with Casey Owens. Long black hair hung limp around the teenager's face, her pale skin dotted red by the stress of hormones and a far from easy life. Her black shirt only accentuated the marks. A year shy of Felicity's age, Casey was Annie's daughter, a girl who hadn't fallen far from the tree. The hard line currently underscoring her piercing blue eyes raised the hairs on the back of Delaney's neck. Casey looked like she had a score to settle, and if Delaney didn't know better, she was looking to settle it with *her*.

Delaney side-stepped the teenager, but Casey stepped right with her. "Why do you hate me so much?"

About to push past the girl, Delaney hesitated. "What?"

"You heard me," she challenged. "Why do you hate me so much? I ain't never done anything to you."

Delaney suppressed the urge to respond. Best to keep this confrontation to a minimum. Casey had a reputation for getting into trouble, and Delaney wanted no trouble with her. But cut by the pain in the girl's voice, she replied, "I don't hate you."

"You want to cut me out of my inheritance all so you can have it for yourself. For *Felicity*."

"You don't understand, Casey. It's complicated."

The girl threw back her shoulders and angled forward, thumping her chest with her forefinger. "Yes, I do. You hate me, else you wouldn't be trying to cut me out of what's rightfully *mine*."

Delaney absorbed the sullen words, spoken by a child who was as much a victim as anyone. But filling her mind with venom was dangerous. When it came to Casey, arming her with animosity was like loading a shotgun and handing it to a child. Not smart. But wisdom never had been Annie's strong suit. "The property belongs to Ladds," Delaney said, as gently and calmly as possible.

Casey thumped her chest with fist, but her tough façade began to crack. "I'm a Ladd!"

Pity poured into Delaney's heart. They couldn't be sure of that. No one could, perhaps not even Annie. But voicing that would cause nothing but trouble—something Casey seemed already chockfull. "You need to be discussing this with your mother, Casey."

"I did! How do you think I know what you're up to?"

Fran walked over and with a cautious glance between the two, asked, "Everything okay over here?"

Casey sideswiped her with a hot glance, but Delaney knew the girl wouldn't go up against Fran. Fran was Annie's aunt and neither one of the women would put up with back talk from the girl. Casey knew she was on a tight rope and Delaney could see she was losing her balance.

"I hate you!" Casey cried, then spun around and ran out of the restaurant.

"Oh, Lord a'mercy on that child," Fran said fretfully. "I'm sorry about that, Dell."

Trailing the girl through the front windows until she disappeared from sight, Delaney nodded. "She's running on a short fuse."

Fran shared a look of parental concern with Delaney. "That she is, but I don't think Annie sees it. All she sees is a discipline problem, but that girl needs some attention." She wiped her brow. "The motherly kind, if you know what I mean."

"I hear you." Unfortunately, Casey was following the same path as her mother. And there was nothing Delaney could do about it. Handing over Ladd Springs to appease a girl raised by a mother who wasn't certain about the paternity of her child couldn't happen. If Casey were proved to be Jeremiah's, it would be different.

"You go on," Fran said. "Don't let her get to you."

Delaney looked into Fran's face, her heart bleeding for a child she had slim influence over. She understood the struggle, the heartache. Like Casey, Felicity had basically grown up without a father, but that's where the similarities ended. Delaney had made it her number one priority to fill the boots of two parents, where Annie hardly managed the one. Which was a shame. Casey was a bright girl. Given the right tools, Delaney believed she could do a lot with her life. She heaved a sigh. But Annie was more worried about Annie than Casey.

"I'll see you later." Delaney waved off.

"And take care of those wounds!" Fran hollered as Delaney pushed out the front door and into the warm sunshine. The heat was welcome against her skin, as though it could remove the chilly bite of Casey's accusation. The girl might not be her problem, but it didn't stop her from feeling sorry for the girl. It wasn't *her* fault she was born into a life of questionable paternity. She was an innocent victim in the mess, much like Felicity was a victim of her father's poor behavior.

"Dell."

Delaney halted, and whirled.

"Watcha doing?"

"None of your business," came the automatic reply as she pivoted to face Clem.

He smiled thinly, flicked a cigarette butt to the sidewalk and sauntered closer. The afternoon sun wasn't flattering to the yellow hue of his skin or the ratty denim of his shirt and jeans. "You don't look like you're workin' much."

"It doesn't matter what I look like I'm doing, it's no business of yours."

"Well maybe I wanna make it my business. You know, on account of you always meddlin' in mine."

Prickles raced across her skin.

"So where's your friend?" Clem pretended to look around. The sidewalk was empty, store fronts quiet.

"What friend?" she asked.

"Your big, strong man friend," he sneered. Clem stole a sideways glance to the street. Not a car in sight.

"He's not my friend."

"Ain't he?" Clem snickered, as though he knew better. "I think you're sleepin' with him."

"What the hell are you talking about?" she snapped, but knew full well what he was talking about—and the fact that he was talking about it was a bad sign.

"Wonder how Ernie would feel about that?"

Delaney forced herself to remain in place. "What I do is none of Ernie's business or yours, Clem Sweeney, and I'd advise you against stirring up trouble."

"Like you?"

"Like me, *what*," she demanded before thinking.

"You're a troublemaker," he hissed. "I know a secret about you and it ain't a good one."

Nerves snapped and popped. "You're wasting my time, Clem."

"Am I now?"

"Yes," she said and turned on her heel to go.

Clem grabbed her hard by the arm, his wiry grip steeled around her bicep. "Let me give you a friendly warning." His eyes glittered as he spit out in putrid breath, "Watch your back, Dell."

She yanked away, but his nails were dug in deep. She swung at him with her free arm, but he was ready and clutched her wrist. Anger percolated deep inside as her.

"You keep it up and those scratches on your arm will be the least of your worries."

"You don't tell me what to do," she said and threw her entire body into him, shoving him off balance. Clem lost his grip and tried to grab her again. "Leave me alone!" she shouted, hoping someone would hear the commotion.

But with no one on the sidewalk around them, Clem lunged at her. He grabbed both arms and this time Delaney lost her balance, careening into a parked truck. The side mirror edge jammed sharply into her shoulder. Rage streamed through her veins. "Nobody hits me," she growled and pushed off from the vehicle with her boot, ramming into Clem with everything she had. Nailing him in the chest, she pushed him hard into the cement wall of Fran's. He hit with a thud and shrieked in pain. Delaney jabbed her elbow into his upper body, his stomach, shoulders—anywhere she could make contact. Clem yanked a clump of her hair, jerking her head back.

She caught a glimpse of a black car, tires screeching as it swerved on the pavement and landed against the curb. A man jumped out of the car and ran toward them. Before his identity registered, Nick slugged Clem in the jaw. He reeled under the force, hitting the wall again and slumping to the ground.

"Get up!" Nick yelled. He yanked Clem up by the shirt and held his back to the faded blue wall. "I should beat the hell out of you right now."

"Don't." Heart pounding, Delaney squeezed the knot on her shoulder, her bicep beginning to throb.

"Give me one good reason," he bit back.

"He's not worth a night in jail."

Nick shoved Clem hard and warned, "I don't want to see you within twenty feet of her, you hear me? Twenty feet."

Clem's head bobbed up and down.

"If you do, the jail time will be worth the pleasure I'll take bashing your skull in." Nick gave him a push down the sidewalk. Clem pulled at his shirt, put a hand to his jaw, and scurried away.

Entrenched in place, they watched Clem clear the premises. Once he was gone from sight, Delaney retreated to her truck, Nick close by her side. She opened the door and stood facing him, her shoulders sagging. "You seem to show up when I need you most."

"We travel in the same circles." Concern drew his gaze to the shoulder she was favoring. "Are you okay?"

Delaney hung a hand from the top of her door frame, painfully aware of her shoulder. "I will be."

Tenderness mingled with danger in Nick's dark eyes. "You should have let me finish the job."

She shook her head. She had other plans for Clem.

"You need to let me help you, Delaney."

"And why is that?" she asked, her shock from the encounter not fully subsided.

"Because we want the same thing."

Delaney's hip fell back against her truck. "No, we don't."

"Yes we do. We both want what's best for this property and for Felicity."

Her heart thumped in defiance. "You have no right to bring my daughter into this conversation."

"Felicity is a nice girl. She deserves the best." Nick set a hand to the door frame alongside hers and the two faced off, the door hanging between them like a makeshift barrier. "My buying this property can give her that."

Delaney withdrew her hand and looked into her truck. Her backpack sat on the passenger seat, she the only one privy to its contents.

"Why won't you let me help you?"

Because she didn't trust him. She looked down the sidewalk to where she and Clem had been at each other's throats. She didn't trust anyone.

"What happened back there?"

"Old feud."

"Happen often?"

She turned to Nick. "Of course, not." His dark eyes grew impatient, but he held steady. *Did he not believe her*?

Delaney blew a fallen strand of hair from her face, cut another glance up the sidewalk and mumbled, "Doesn't matter. I know how to handle Clem."

Nick raised a brow in reproach but didn't say what had to be obvious to the both of them. Delaney hadn't handled anything with Clem. Who knew where it would have gone, had he not showed up. And they both knew it. Tempering her tone, she looked up at him. "Listen, can we talk about this some other time? I've got to get home before Felicity shows up."

"Why?"

"Just because." Delaney cast a wary eye down the street in either direction as she eased into the driver's seat. She grasped the door handle but didn't close the door. How could she? The man just saved her butt from who knows what—an occurrence that was becoming all too frequent—and she hadn't even thanked him. "Please. Stop by later? We'll talk then."

A smiled curved his lips into a near smirk. "Already planned on it."

Delaney slumped back into her seat. "You can't move into my front porch, you know."

He smiled smugly. "No desire to."

"Then what?" And with every fiber of her being, she wanted to know the answer. The *real* answer.

"I want to be satisfied you're not in any danger."

"That's why you've appointed yourself as my bodyguard?"

"Can't think of a better way to spend my time while I'm waiting for your uncle to come to his senses."

Memories from their conversation the night before loosened the knot in her chest. Nick wasn't a bad guy. Whether or not he wanted more from her remained to be seen. "Come by around eight. We'll talk then."

Nick smiled, producing those large dimples she had noticed from day one. It was as if they carved pleasure into the rugged lines of his handsome face. She closed her car door and gunned the engine to life. Memorable. That's what they were. Simply memorable.

Parked at her kitchen counter, Nick sat comfortably on a wooden saddle stool, one leg outstretched before him. Felicity was safely squired away at her uncle's home, playing her flute for him in what Nick found to be an act of pure grace.

From what he could discern, the man deserved very little af-fection. He certainly didn't dole it out to those around him.

Clad in tank top and jeans, both faded blue tonight, Delaney chomped on carrot sticks like they were the last food on the planet. Although he'd downed two loaves of her amaz-ing cornbread, she hadn't touched the first morsel. Claimed homegrown carrots were all she wanted tonight.

Nick scoffed. They'd work for about two minutes, but after that he needed something more substantial to fill his bel-ly. He'd already downed a plate of Fran's meatloaf. Could Delaney cook meatloaf?

"Want some more?" she asked.

"No thanks." He decided to hold his question about her cooking abilities for another day. Taking in the ugly patch of black and blue skin on her shoulder, he felt a fresh rise of an-ger. "Do you have any reason to believe Clem is involved with the man from yesterday?"

She angled her head, her gaze darting down to the floor before bouncing back to him. "No. Why do you ask?"

Because he didn't believe in coincidences. "This Clem fellow seems hell bent on making your life miserable, as does the man from the woods."

"So?" She held the carrot suspended before her mouth.

"So-o," he rolled out, "either those two have something in common or you have a damn good way of pissing people off." The muscles in her jaw visibly tightened. "Any idea which it might be?"

"No idea." She snapped off the end of a carrot with her front teeth and chewed more rapidly than necessary.

"Huh." He paused. White dots of light reflected in the black pools of her pupils as she stared at him. "And you have no idea why Clem accosted you this afternoon in broad day-light."

"Not the foggiest."

Nick knew a liar when he saw one. And he knew for a fact that Clem's appearance on the sidewalk was no accident. He'd been following the man since he left his trailer early this morning. After a few brief stops, one at a rundown house on the edge of town, the other at a pawn shop, Clem had turned his attention to Delaney. He'd spotted her at the post office and trailed her from there, as Nick trailed him, all the way to the diner. "Guess we have a mystery to solve," he said.

Pulling another carrot from the plastic bag, Delaney's hand stopped midair. "A mystery to solve?"

He nodded. "We need to find out why the man in the woods wants to hurt you, why your friend Clem wants to do the same. From my experience, there's usually a reason."

Dropping her hand to the counter, she swallowed hard.

Well, it was good to know the woman had the sense to be scared. She needed to understand this was serious.

Resuming her nibblefest, Nick wondered why she was keeping the truth from him—other than the fact that she considered *him* her mortal enemy—why cover the truth behind the attack? She couldn't be protecting Clem, could she? Memories of Clem's lunge at her in the woods came to mind. Was there was a reason he felt entitled to throw himself at her?

Nick had no use for a woman who lied, cheated or stole, no matter how good-looking she might be. And Delaney Wilkins was definitely a looker. He particularly liked it when her hair was pulled back, as it was now, into a bun of sorts, hanging low and loose in the back. It revealed the long, graceful curve of her neck, the creamy line of her collarbone, the one he could imagine running his lips over.

Nick enjoyed the view, there was no question. But if Delaney wasn't willing to cooperate, there was nothing more he could do here. "So." He slapped hands to thighs and lifted up from the stool. "Guess there's nothing more to discuss." He glanced over the contents of her counter, the half-eaten pan of cornbread, the clear plastic bag of carrots, her glass of iced tea that remained untouched. It was her turn to come to him. "What time do you go to retrieve Felicity?"

"Nine," she blurted.

"I'll shadow you down," he told her. "In the meantime, I'd be sure to ice that shoulder of yours." Her face dropped to the bruised skin on her shoulder. "It's gonna hurt tonight."

She nodded numbly and he turned to go.

"Nick—"

Pleased by the urgency in her voice, he turned back, slow and precise. "Yes?"

"Thank you." A small smile touched her lips, loosening the tension from her expression.

Nick felt an unexpected surge of desire deep and low. Delaney was opening to him. Her chest rose and fell with the acceleration of breath, soft brown eyes yielded entrance to her soul. She might not be revealing the details he sought, but it was a start. "You're welcome." He tipped an imaginary hat and said, "See you at nine."

Chapter Fifteen

Delaney breezed out onto the porch, closing the door in a whoosh of movement. Seated off to the side, she acknowledged Nick's presence. "I'm heading over to Ernie's," she announced and bent over to pull on her boots, her knot of hair falling to the side.

Nick approved of the thigh-length knitted sweater cardigan she wore. Best she didn't alert anyone to the mark on her shoulder. It would only invite question. And the off-white colored fabric would aid in keeping track of her in the dark.

"Are you really going to follow me all the way down?" she asked.

Nick stood, the muscles in his lower back tight against his gun. "I am."

She gave a flippant shake to her head and stood. "If you insist."

"Now you're getting the hang of it," he said, inflecting a carnal tone he couldn't resist.

Delaney rolled her eyes to the ceiling and said flatly, "Listen. I didn't tell Felicity you'd be here, so keep out of sight, will you? I don't want her getting the wrong idea."

Nick cocked a brow. "So long as circumstance doesn't prevent it."

She held him in her gaze for a long moment, but seemed to drop whatever follow-up swirled behind her eyes, and headed for the screen door. Crossing the porch in long-legged strides, she pushed outside and clamored down the steps, hitting the gravelly ground with a thud.

Nick kept his distance, but matched her pace. No moon to speak of tonight, he had to stay close. Delaney disappeared into the darkness, the thick chirp of crickets enshrouding her passage. In the dense foliage, the flicker of her flashlight as she bounded down the narrow path to Ernie's, her light moving in fits and starts, allowed him to follow her down with relative ease. She hit the clearing and crossed the small bridge, but he paused at the tree line. Scanning the black woods around them her for signs of light, movement, noise. Edging his way along, he was careful to stay out of the clearing as he tracked Delaney's progress to the front door. She entered, and he hung back, concealing himself within the tree line. Less than five minutes later, Delaney and Felicity emerged.

Nick wondered at the black box in Felicity's arms, but instantly realized it was her instrument. The women hurried down the porch steps until Delaney froze, Felicity nearly careening into the back of her. His antennae shot up, his body tensed. The man named Clem rounded the corner of Ernie's cabin. *What the hell was he doing here?*

Felicity hung back as Delaney's posture turned ramrod straight. In the yellow wash of light emanating from Ernie's porch lamp, a spray of insects swarmed above them as the confrontation unfolded before him. Nick couldn't decipher a word of the angry whispers, but when Felicity's body jumped, he moved toward them. Delaney flagged a protective arm over her child and shoved a finger in Clem's face.

Anger fanned out in Nick's chest. *What are you doing, Delaney?*

The only reason Nick wasn't standing between Clem and Delaney at the moment was Felicity. More specifically, her mother's request he remain anonymous.

Suddenly it was Clem's turn to play statue. Foreboding mingled in Nick's gut. Nick reached for his gun. Didn't the woman understand she was playing with fire?

Clem stomped off. Nick relaxed his grip on the cold metal handle. As Delaney stormed off in the direction of her cabin with Felicity trailing behind, Nick backed up, inserting himself into the landscape. To her credit, Delaney didn't look right or left as she passed him by. Instead, she made a bee line straight up the trail.

Good girl. Nick glanced back at Ernie's cabin before whispering his goodbye. *See you soon.* First, I have a spot of unfinished business to take care of.

You're gonna be sorry.

Clem's words reverberated in Delaney's skull. Seated alone on the porch, folded into her rocker, she pulled the cable sweater more tightly around her body. Where was Nick? He said he was going to be here tonight. Had he changed his mind, leaving her mind to run through the scene again and again? Telling Clem that he was a loser getting cheated by his own men had not been smart, but she couldn't help herself. He, of course, reacted with threats. But he couldn't seriously think he could have her killed, could he?

Her thoughts swerved back to the man with the gun in the forest. His intent seemed clear. The shots that whizzed by her head were real. Did Clem really believe removing her would solve his problem? Apprehension sank into her bones.

It would, wouldn't it?

With every noise, Delaney jumped. The light wind sounded eerie as it fluttered through the trees. The katydids drummed in a steady racket, their rhythmic song mind-numbing and ominously sound-neutralizing. They were so loud, the creek below was nearly drowned out of existence. At this rate, she wouldn't be able to hear Clem coming!

Her gaze drifted toward the porch door. Not a sign of Nick. And if the unseasonably cool temperature continued to fall, she'd be forced indoors, the soft knit insufficient to keep her comfortably seated outside. But she had to remain out here. She wanted to talk to Nick.

Rubbing the soft threads of material on her arms, she squeezed them close to her body. She *needed* to talk to him. Tonight she had made an error with Clem and she could only hope it wasn't a fatal one.

A sound cracked in the dark. Delaney whipped her head toward the doorway and into shaft of light outside. Her pulse hammered. It sounded like someone threw a rock. What if they threw a rock at her floodlight? She'd be left in complete darkness. She craned her head to peer down the trail but could see nothing, nothing but the white-gray rocks of the trail disappearing into the black canopy of forest. She saw no one, nothing out of the ordinary. An owl's screech punctuated the night.

Normally she loved sitting outside alone, relaxing into the calm of night. But tonight was no ordinary night. Tonight held uncertainty. She fingered the pistol concealed in her sweat pants pocket, the hard lines against her thigh reassuring. Where was Nick? He should be here by now. Was he waiting for Felicity's light to go out? Delaney drove her hands under her arms and pressed hard against her rib cage. *Was he watching her?*

It was eleven o'clock. Once again, Delaney involuntarily searched the trail, willing Nick's figure to appear, headed up toward her cabin as her protector. But he was nowhere to be seen.

Pulling her gaze back inside the screened confines, she relaxed into a soft focus on the porch floor, grown uneven from weather and age, the splinters numerous and perilous to the naked foot. She and Felicity kept the floor swept clean, but even so, they both wore thick socks to protect their skin. Tonight the socks also served to keep Delaney's toes warm.

She inhaled deep and full, then blew the air free in an anxious stream. Yet as her temper cooled, the air chilled and her heart filled with regret. She had allowed her tongue too much freedom and now it might cost her.

But what was she supposed to do? Clem's threat against Felicity could not go unanswered. Just hearing her daughter's name on his lips made Delaney cringe. But the mere thought that he might follow through was unthinkable. *Little old Felicity might just have an unfortunate accident.* Delaney shivered. If Clem laid the first hand on Felicity, Delaney would kill him.

"Hey."

Delaney jumped. At the sight of Nick, she balled the sweater into fists and burrowed into her seat cushion. "I didn't hear you come up."

"I'm a quiet guy," he said and let himself in. "The lights went off upstairs. Coast clear?"

"Yes," she replied, a shred of nerves still flapping within. "How long have you been out there?"

"Long enough to know you're the only one here."

She exhaled a sigh of relief. Nick was here.

He took his seat in the opposite chair, the transition silent as the night. "Quiet man" was an understatement. Three feet away from her, yet the rocker didn't make a peep as he lowered into it. No wonder she hadn't seen him. He was wearing a black button down and dark blue jeans. Add his dark hair and stealthy movements and the man blended seamlessly into the night.

"Aren't you cold?" she asked.

"Not a bit. Feels good." He smiled, his eyes penetrating the darkness. "Nothing like crisp mountain air to get the juices flowing."

Montana air. Home of the Rocky Mountains and one Nick Harris. She hadn't noticed earlier, but the black of his shirt enhanced his masculine features, deepened the tan of his skin, the depth of lines around his eyes, mere shadows beneath his heavy brow. She could feel him reading her.

"How's the shoulder?" he asked.

"Good," she said. "Tender to touch, but tolerable."

"What happened down there with Clem?"

Delaney spewed out her breath. So he had witnessed the incident. "I lost my temper."

"I saw that. Any particular reason?"

Delaney glanced away. How could she reveal what transpired without divulging her discovery? How could she let him know the extent of her concern without laying it all on the line, revealing everything?

"He's connected to those men, you know."

She turned and snaked her gaze around him. Oh, she knew. All too well.

"Wanna talk about it?"

The tenderness in his voice startled her. "Talk about it?"

Nick's eyes dashed to her shoulder. "You've had a rough couple of days. It could get worse." He paused, then added ever so gently, "I can help you."

She held onto the tender note in his voice, the fluid sway of his gaze. "You can't."

"I can."

You can't, she cried silently. Not without taking advantage of the situation. Not without taking the property from me, from Felicity. Once Nick learned there was gold on the property, he'd want the land all the more. Anyone would. Delaney shook her head and reverted her gaze back to the floor, taking refuge in the wood plank curving at the porch's edge.

"I followed Clem tonight." Like a fish on the line, Delaney jerked her face to him. "He met with those men."

"He did?"

"Shared some heated words with them, too."

Angst splintered her chest. "Did you hear what they said?"

"Some of it. I heard enough to know he's coming back."

"*Tonight?*"

Nick shrugged.

Delaney's heart fired with fear. He leaned forward and set a hand to her chair. She eyed the move with disquiet. The faint rise of his cologne caused her mind to sputter. Drawn into his black eyes, eyes that entrapped her, her insides trembled.

"You need to trust me."

She wanted to. It would make things easier. With his help, she could fight Clem and his cohorts and keep Felicity out of danger. Suddenly, Delaney wanted to trust him very much. But trusting him could jeopardize everything. And where did she start?

When she said nothing, Nick withdrew his hand.

"It's complicated," she said.

"What's complicated?"

"Clem, those men..." She dodged his questioning gaze. "Tonight."

"What happened down there, Delaney?"

She glanced askance and said, "Clem made threatening remarks about Felicity and I reacted." Nick remained mute, but Delaney could sense him harden. She turned to him. "Clem is trying to steal this property from Felicity and me, and I won't let him."

"That much, I gather."

"It rightfully belongs to us and I won't let him and his hoodlum friends con Ernie into giving it to them. I *won't*."

Nick eased back into his chair. He cast an appreciative glance around the porch, down the trail, and calmly proposed, "Why don't we start from the beginning?"

Delaney stared at him. Did she have a choice? She rubbed the chill from her arms and blew out her tension in one long, ragged breath.

Being alone on the porch with Nick held mixed emotion for her. Peaceful, serene—this was where she came to think, to "be." This was where she took her private time, her release from the stress of life. Last night had begun awkwardly, but grew easy. Nick was easy to talk to, easy to have around. She stole a glance at him, his expectant expression patient, knowing. He was easy on the eyes, too. Having him by her side felt cozy, like they were old friends. In fact, he was beginning to feel like someone she wanted to see more of, to lean on, to *need*.

But Nick was not a man to mess with lightly, that much she had seen. He worked hard to get what he wanted, and when trouble arose, he wasted no time in managing it. The man responded first, asked questions second. And he was asking them now.

Night pushed in around them, the katydids rampant in their song, their tempo urgent, pressing. Delaney felt compelled to talk, to share. Truth was, she *wanted* to talk. And she wanted to talk with him. Stealing a peek at Nick, a squiggle of nerves raced through her breast. "It happened just before my mother died," she said quietly. "Ernie and Ashley were with her, here." She tipped her head back toward the cabin. "They knew it was time and both wanted to be with her." There was no love lost between Ernie and Ashley, no emotional connection stemming from their commitment to Susannah. Only the fact that they alone shared her confidence. "My mother asked Ernie to will her share of the property to me and Felicity. He agreed, even wrote it down on a piece of paper." Delaney appealed to the business man in Nick as she added, "Ashley was witness to the event. She'll testify in a court of law."

"What happened to the document?"

"Ernie burned it."

Hope drained from his expression. "I see."

Delaney twisted the hem of her sweater in her hands. She refused to accept defeat. Not from Nick and not from Ernie. "My lawyer says an eyewitness to a deathbed promise will help in court."

"It can." Nick held her in his gaze, steady, confident. He didn't waver. He simply listened.

"It has to." Talking sense into the old man certainly wasn't working. "But Clem has been hanging around over the last months, like a shark that senses blood in the water. He's been working around Ernie's house, mowing the fields, trying to get into my uncle's good graces. He thinks Ernie will leave him something when he dies."

Nick angled away from her as he asked, "And apparently he thinks that time is coming?"

"Ernie's health isn't good. Hasn't been for years."

"Yet he's still kicking and screaming."

A smile pulled at her mouth. "You know the man well."

"Seems to me he operates on one channel and one channel only."

"He wasn't always this way. I mean, don't get me wrong, he's never been sugar and honey, but when my mom was alive, he was tolerable."

"She was his rock," Nick offered.

"My mother loved him. She took care of both Ernie and Albert when she was alive, but it was Ernie who held her affection. He was the oldest of the three and I think she looked up to him."

"Doesn't appear there's a whole lot to Albert."

Pity stirred in Delaney's heart. "There isn't. And what there is, isn't pretty. He has a couple of sons, but both are worthless. Albert never paid them any attention and they got into trouble."

"What about Ernie's son?" he asked, as though logging the information away.

"Jeremiah?" Delaney was surprised that Nick knew about him. "He and Ernie don't get along. He left town almost twenty years ago and hasn't been heard from since."

"Any chance the son might return to contest a will?"

"Not hardly. No one around here would bother to tell him. They know he couldn't care less if his father died."

"Until it comes to money," Nick said.

Struck by the comment, Delaney turned it over in her mind. "Would it matter if Ernie signed it over as a trust for Felicity before he died?"

"Anything can matter when it comes to the legal system." Nick picked at the denim on his knee and outstretched his leg. "One lawyer says it's settled, another disagrees, and the next thing you know, you have a court battle on your hands."

"You sound as though you're talking from experience."

He nodded. "Too much experience."

"Anyway," Delaney continued, finding the disclosure of information surprisingly freeing. "I've been trying to convince Ernie to stand by his promise so that it doesn't get to the courts, but he's resisting. Now Clem has reason to want this property for himself and will stop at nothing, pitting my uncle against Felicity and me."

"I doubt very much anyone could pit the old man against Felicity."

"True." Her angst slackened. "But she's tied to me and he detests me."

"Why?" Nick asked. "What have you ever done to him?"

She bit off a short laugh. "Where do I start?" At his confusion, Delaney said, "Well, let's see... I married his arch enemy's son, which lumps me into the enemy camp. I called him on his role in allowing my mother to die, which he can't face. I moved back into her cabin against his wishes—because Ashley forced his hand after my mother died. Guess she felt entitled, as she became a mother of sorts to me after my mom passed. Then of course there's Felicity. She resembles my mother, which aggravates him to no end."

Nick held up a hand. "I think I get the picture."

Really? Because she was on a roll and it felt good. It felt really good to get a decade of pain and suffering off her chest, even if it was with a stranger. A handsome stranger.

A stranger who stood to gain from her misery, she reminded herself shortly.

"But that doesn't explain the men with the guns or how Clem knows them," he said. "What do they have to do with the property and Ernie?"

She drew the sweater snug. "I told you." She glanced away. "They want the property for themselves.

"They seem pretty intent on a place they don't appear to be able to afford. Why take on the burden?"

"Greed."

"Greed?"

She nodded.

Leaning back into his rocker, Nick extended his second leg and crossed them at the ankles. Interlacing his fingers, he rested them low on his abdomen. "I guess I'll have to take you at your word."

Relieved that Nick had ceased his inquisition, Delaney eased back in her rocker. She took pleasure in the intimate conversation between man and woman. With Nick by her side, the black night had lost its power to scare. She no longer jumped at every little sound. With his imposing presence by her side, she felt safe, taken care of. It had been a long time since she felt this way. She sighed. Too long.

"Can I ask you something?"

She nodded, relishing the quiet strength in his voice. Nick was solid, formidable. An aspect to him she found particularly pleasing.

"Do you mind me asking why you left your husband?"

The memory sliced her heart in two. Ten years and more than a few nasty words later, Jack Foster still had the power to hurt. For better or worse, he remained a part of her life and would always be so. They shared a daughter. "My husband was abusive, Nick." Shadows of anger entered his eyes. "Mentally, emotionally and one day physically." She tightened her hands around the sweater ends. "He hit me and I moved out."

"You made the right decision."

The validation pulled at her. Delaney believed Nick could kill a man with his bare hands, but she doubted he would ever strike a woman. Although she had witnessed sparks of anger in him, Delany sensed his had more to do with self-defense than the intention to harm. "Most people said I should have stayed and tried to work it out, for Felicity's sake."

Nick shook his head. "A man willing to hit a woman once will usually hit her again."

She smiled. It was heartening to meet a man as intolerant as she on the subject. "That's what I said."

But the pleasurable feelings faded. While it sounded simple, leaving Jack was one of the hardest things she had ever done. It hurt. More emotionally than physically. To think the man she loved cared so little about her, about their child, had been heart-wrenching for her to accept. Jack was her first love, her only love. She had believed him a man of honor. He came from a good family. He performed well in school, in athletics. And he courted her with more romance than anyone she knew at the time. No one enjoyed the level of attention Jack showered on her. The first years of their marriage had been good. Until the drinking began. That's when life grew sour.

"He's an alcoholic," Delaney stated. "It was the drinking that made him lose control." She leveled her gaze with Nick's, relishing the tenderness she found in his dark eyes. "But he refused to give it up."

"He made his choice."

"He did."

"Why haven't you remarried?" Nick smiled, a smile that turned boyish. "I mean, it's been a long time since your split with your ex."

Delaney rolled her head side-to-side as she pondered the question. Because she had never met a man she deemed worthy? Never met a man she fully trusted? "Oh, I don't know." She settled her gaze on Nick and posed, "Will the proverbial 'haven't found the right one, yet' work?"

"If it's the truth, sure."

"Pretty slim pickings around these parts, or haven't you noticed?"

"I noticed you."

New emotions wound around her belly, her heart. "How about you? Ever been married, Mr. Harris?"

"Never been interested in settling down."

"Never?"

"Never."

"Doesn't that make for a lonely existence?"

He laughed softly. "I didn't say I spent my time alone."

"Oh—" Embarrassment flushed her cheeks with warmth.

"But like you, I've never met the right one." He grinned. "But Tennessee may change that."

"Tennessee?"

"Tennessee. You, in particular." Nick reached his hand over and sought hers. Delaney tried to appear unaffected by his touch, but the gesture felt like a zip-line tearing through her nervous system. "I like you, Delaney."

"You do?" she asked, and immediately felt foolish for asking, foolish for delighting in the feel of his hand around hers. It was big, strong and covered hers completely.

"I do. I like your combination of female and fortitude."

She suppressed a swell of satisfaction. She'd always prided herself on being independent. It was nice when a man noticed.

"I've never met a woman who's both tough and tender, silver and steel. I've run across a host of women who are hard as steel, pretty as silver, tough as nails, tender as a baby's breath, but never all rolled up into one. You're quite a find, Ms. Wilkins."

"Delaney," she said reflexively.

"Delaney," he repeated softly, his thumb caressing her hand. "You're coming to mean something to me."

Shivers of desire heated her, woke the woman inside her, as she hung on the edge of his sultry gaze. "I am?"

He nodded. "Is that okay?"

Delaney nodded before the first thought could enter her mind. At the moment, she could only feel.

Nick pulled his legs in, leaned over and brushed the hair from her brow, gazing at her cheek, her neck. "And I'll be honest. I'm worried about these men after you."

She wasn't. She wasn't worried about anything at the moment—except that *he* might make a move. A move she would have to answer.

"Clem is coming back tomorrow to check for himself about something."

Delaney gulped, her building desire stalled. "He is?"

"His exact words were, 'you'd better be right.'" Nick tipped her chin to face him more fully, the presumptive touch shocking to her skin. "Any possible idea what he could be referring to?"

She shook her head.

Nick nodded and pursed his lips. He allowed his hand to fall away, pulling it back to his armrest. Reclining in his seat, he tapped the chair. "Guess I'll have to figure this one out on my own."

Chapter Sixteen

Delaney lay in her bed, eyes wide open. She blinked, her vision unchanged between eyes closed and eyes open. It was dark. Too dark. She thought of Nick outside on her porch. Angst feathered across her arms. But what could she say? *Clem knows there's gold on the property and he and his men want it for themselves*? There was no reason for her to believe that Nick wouldn't want it for himself, too, once he found out it was available for the taking. The men had no qualms about looting her land. Why would Nick?

The presence of gold on Ladd Springs land changed everything. She and Felicity were no different. Once they held title, they stood to profit from the gold find. They might even avoid the necessity of selling their timber altogether. What she did know, was that Clem would continue to plunder the precious metal while she and Ernie hashed it out in court. It was a no-win situation. And if Nick learned of the gold, she'd be battling on all fronts!

Delaney pressed her eyes closed. The quiet sank in around her, flattening her to the mattress. What if Nick followed Clem to the site, followed him right to the gold, because *she* opened her big mouth? Her eyes popped open. She couldn't let that happen. She had to convince Nick there was another reason Clem said he was coming back to check on something. But what?

She clutched the quilted blanket to her chin. Lying and spying were not her department. She took care of horses, of finances—not lowlifes up to no good, attempting to tie them in knots with their own webs of deceit. Fine job she was doing of it. Shoot, she was lucky to keep *one* step ahead of them, let alone two or three!

Delaney glanced to her open door. The house was noise-less. Felicity was upstairs resting soundly. Nick was out front, standing watch. Or was he? She bolted upright in bed. He hadn't been there this morning when she went out to greet him. Would he be there now?

Yanking the blanket from her body, Delaney swung her legs over the side of the bed and planted socked feet on the floor. Deciding against retrieving the pistol from the drawer of her nightstand, she padded into the living room. She couldn't see the rockers from here. Since they were located on the other side of the solid wall, she would have to open the door to do so. What would Nick think if she poked her head outside?

Her breathing became shallow. Her thoughts raced to and fro. What could she say? *I wasn't sure you'd still be here. I thought I heard something...*

She took a few steps towards the door, but stopped. Delaney nibbled her lip, willing an excuse to take form. She flung her gaze up to the loft overhead, resisting the urge to check on her daughter. She'd only find the girl sleeping, safe and secure beneath her cotton comforter. Delaney and Nick had been here since she went upstairs. There was no need to double check.

Her gaze clung to the wall in a long stare, as though she could see through it. Should she go outside? Would it do more harm than good? A swell of exhaustion surged. The weight of her run-in with Clem anchored her to the smooth wood floor. Regret penetrated her gut. Running her mouth had made matters worse. Thankfully, Felicity was unaware of the dark turn their situation had taken, though that didn't pre-vent Clem from threatening to harm her. Seems he'd use whatever mechanism he could to threaten Delaney.

She slid a glance back to the front porch. Nick had come to her rescue, *twice*. She envisioned his daunting figure em-bedded in the small rocker, the chair two sizes too small for his body. But at the first sign of trouble, she imagined him springing from his seat and taking out the bad guy. She

smiled. Prince Harris was quite capable when it came to damsels in distress. His decision to follow Clem after their confrontation came to mind. No reservation, no doubt, Nick was
a man of action. He took charge when it came to defending
her. He took charge when it came to getting answers.

Delaney frowned. She hugged her arms to her body, the
muscles around her mouth tensed. Off the outside porch corner, the single bulb glowed, a faint swarm of insect activity
busy within the haze of light. Tomorrow Nick might learn her
secret. Worry pricked. If he did, what would he do with the
knowledge?

In the instant of decision, Delaney turned and trudged
back to her room. There was no reason for her to be out on
that porch with him. No reasonable excuse she could give that
would sound convincing, that wouldn't reveal her for the
comfort-seeking fool that she was. Longing pulled at her,
stronger, insistent. She wished they could be on the same
team. When Nick was around, trouble seemed to cower in the
shadows, surrendering in seconds beneath his intimidating
stature. Delaney slumped to a seat on the edge her mattress.
Elbows to knees, she buried her face in her hands. She, on the
other hand, seemed to have an uncanny ability to provoke
trouble into outright aggression.

As expected, Nick was not on the porch when Delaney
awoke the next morning. Removing the pot of eggs from the
stove burner, she submerged them in cold tap water. The grits
were ready, the bread browning in the toaster, the scent filling
the space around her. Delaney could only assume Nick was
chasing Clem into the forest. What else could Clem be coming back to check on? Clem and those men were connected.
Those men had been pillaging the gold. Of course Clem
wanted to check on the gold. Question remained, would he
unwittingly lead Nick right to it? It might only be a matter of
hours before she'd learn the answers to her questions.

Delaney shut off the faucet, tilted the pot and drained the
water through her fingers. As she transferred the eggs to the

island, rapidly moving legs caught her attention as they hurried down the narrow stairway. Felicity was ready for breakfast.

"Good morning!" she chirped. After depositing her backpack by the front door, she came over and plucked a napkin from the ceramic holder, a glazed and painted piece depicting a black bear and an evergreen—an art project she'd made in fourth grade. Felicity had been so proud of the accomplishment, but even more so that her mother prominently displayed it in the kitchen.

Delaney cracked open the eggs and deposited them into the grits. She tossed the shells into the empty pot, grabbed a fork from the drawer and slid both to Felicity, admiring the green plaid she wore over a cream tank top. "I always liked that shirt."

Felicity looked down as though checking to see which one she had chosen. "Thanks."

Delaney wondered if the skinny jeans—more leggings than pants—were comfortable. She had an affinity for Levi's herself, but the younger generation seemed to paint their pants on, but hip was hip and Felicity was among the "in" crowd when it came to teen fashion.

Felicity reached for the salt and sprinkled her breakfast before mixing and mashing the eggs and grits together.

"Are you ready for your test today?" Delaney asked. Taking pot in hand, she began washing it.

Felicity nodded. "I plan to ace it."

Of course she did. Felicity aced every test she took. "Well, don't count your chickens before they're hatched."

Felicity rolled her eyes. "Travis and Troy are coming over to ride this afternoon. Is that okay?" she asked, almost as an afterthought.

"It's fine." Delaney folded the kitchen towel in half, then set it aside. "Just remember what I told you."

"Stay together. Got it," she said, and downed a mouthful of eggs, a drop of thick yoke falling back into her bowl.

Delaney hoped Felicity understood loud and clear. She didn't need the added stress of worrying about her daughter alone in the woods, in addition to everything else on her mind. Leaning a hip against the counter, Delaney watched Felicity eat. Scooping the egg mixture onto her toast, the teen bit an entire corner piece off with her teeth. She chewed and swallowed.

Felicity caught her mother staring and asked, "Are you in a hurry?"

"Me? No." Delaney rapped her fingers on the butcher block surface, then flattened her palm on the counter and leaned forward. "Why do you ask?"

"You seem a little uptight."

"Uptight?" She shook her head. "No, I'm fine."

"Was that Nick Harris I saw heading down the trail this morning?"

Delaney's heart tripped. "*What*? What are you talking about?"

Felicity suppressed a grin. "I saw him when I woke up."

Delaney stiffened. Number one, what was she doing looking out her porthole of a window at that hour, and number two, so Nick *had* stayed the entire night.

The news tangled in her thoughts.

"You two an item?"

"What? She blew out a breath. "No—of course not! Why would you say such a thing?"

Felicity looked pointedly at Delaney's hands. Delaney followed her gaze to find her hands scrunching the dish towel within her fists. She tossed the towel aside.

"Wouldn't blame you if you were," Felicity added quietly, amusement dancing in the heather green of her eyes. "He is kinda good-looking."

Delaney's throat closed. This conversation was not happening.

Felicity shifted on the stool. "Besides, it's about time you found someone."

She glared at her daughter. "I haven't found someone."

"Mom. It's okay. We all need *someone*."

"I don't." Especially not *that* someone—the someone who wanted to take Ladd Springs from her. The someone who was about to learn there was gold on her land and who knew what he would do with that information. A thousand thoughts whirred into action, careening with raw emotion. An item? She and Nick?

He was good-looking enough of, she had to admit. Seemed smart enough. Visions of him from last night filtered in, his hand on her chair, his request for her trust.

"Whatever," Felicity replied dully, but underscored her point with a brief shake to her head. Silently, she concentrated her breakfast.

Delaney wanted to trust Nick. She did. It would make life easier is she could believe what he said about having their best interests at heart. But an item?

That was a bit of a stretch.

Felicity munched the last bite of egg and grits, scraped her bowl clean and downed the last of her toast. She cleared her dish, washed her hands and headed for the door.

Turning out the kitchen light, Delaney called out, "I'm right behind you."

Joining her at the door, Felicity asked, "Going into town?" When Delaney didn't respond right away, her daughter shrugged. "Do you want to ride with us later?"

"With who?"

Felicity opened the door. "Travis and Troy, remember?"

No, she didn't remember. Delaney couldn't think straight let alone remember what her daughter said ten minutes ago! But that was neither here nor there. "No," she answered hastily. "Thank you, but I have to work today." She tugged on her boots as Felicity did likewise.

What her "work" entailed remained to be seen. At the moment, she was only certain that her time today would be spent saving her daughter's inheritance. Somehow, some way, Delaney had to make sure her daughter didn't lose out due to Clem or Ernie or for that matter, Nick. *An item*. She scoffed. Did it get any more ludicrous?

Though she had to admit, it was heartening to know he had indeed camped out for the duration last night. Delaney stood and kissed her daughter on the cheek. "I'll see you at three." She closed and locked the door behind them. Would Nick be back this evening?

That depended upon his trip into the woods today.

Nick parked down the street from Clem's trailer. He sat just past the curve in the road, a nearby cluster of branches hanging far enough over the street to ensure he would remain unseen should it occur to Clem to look for him. Reaching for his coffee from the center console, Nick took a slow sip. He had no idea what time to expect Clem's departure, but with no place else to go, he had the time to wait. And think.

Delaney had been remarkably cagey about Clem and their dispute, much like she'd been when it came to the stranger on the trail. But sure as he was sitting here, Nick believed Clem and the men were tied together and she knew the reason why. Today, he would learn the facts for himself.

The cell phone vibrated on his dash. Nick picked it up and checked the screen. Malcolm again. Which was odd. It wasn't like him to be so insecure about a deal. But then it wasn't like Nick to take so long in securing a property, either. He answered the call with a brisk, "What's up?"

"Jillian is up."

"What now?" he asked, a twinge of memory firing in his groin as he brought coffee to mouth.

"She signed one of your investors for her project last night."

He yanked the coffee from his lips, the liquid searing his tongue. "*What?*" He glanced down at his lap, checking for spill spots. Thank God for lids.

"You heard me. I told you she was hounding us on this one."

"Hounding us, *hell*. Who defected?"

"Winters."

"Winters?" Nick couldn't have been more shocked if Malcolm had revealed himself as the turncoat. "Why would he do such a thing? He's one of our biggest supporters."

"Was."

"Did you talk to him? What the hell happened?"

"One guess." Malcolm's smirk leaped at him through the receiver.

Visions of Jillian's slender body undulated through his mind. "You're kidding me..."

"Wish I was, but I'm not. We can survive with the others, so long as you're close. Tell me you're close to a deal, Nick."

Crap. He wasn't close to anything, let alone a deal. Staring out the windshield, Nick's eyes glazed over, time stood still. The mailbox sat crooked by the road, the black metal box nearly in the path of oncoming traffic. Scruffy shrubs poked in and around the junk box Clem called home. "I'm working on it."

"Well, you better work fast or forget about this one. Jillian's closing the distance, no way are we playing second best."

"Damn straight we're not." Nick jammed his thumb on the end button. Because they weren't second best.

But if Jillian was up to her old tricks, competing would prove tough. She could wrap a man up in knots and steal his money before the poor guy had the first clue what hit him. But Winters?

That surprised him. Nick would have pegged him for an upstanding guy, a guy immune to such tactics. He and his wife seemed to have a great marriage—if such a thing existed—but sex sells. Sex cajoles, swindles and manipulates. It felt damn good while it was happening, too. Something he remembered all too well. Nick pounded a fist against the steering wheel. Damn it—where was Clem?

Through the windshield, Nick stared at the trailer. Dilap-idated was too kind for the place. It looked abandoned. Deserted. Was Clem even inside?

Nick had a mind to drive over and peek through the damn windows to be sure. But Clem had to be there. Last night, after driving into town to meet with the two men—something he'd have to take up with Delaney at a later date—Clem stopped here. Nick went to listen at the door. There were no other voices, other than those emanating from a television set. This was the man's home, Nick was sure of it. So where the hell was he?

Time was running out.

Delaney shouldered the Appaloosa's meaty chest to move him back as she dumped feed into the bin. The horse gave way with a low nicker, but once the sound of sliding nuggets had silenced, he pushed the rounded muscles of his chest into her back, his head bobbing anxiously for her to move.

"I hear ya, I hear ya," she said and stepped clear of the heavy animal. "No need to trample me over it." Delaney slapped him gently on the rump, followed by a quick rub, then tossed the bucket into its corner storage. "Don't make a pig of yourself, Sunshine."

Sadie neighed softly from across the stables and shook her buttercream mane from her eyes. Black lashes blinked over chocolate brown eyes as Delaney drew near. Sadie met her with a throaty nicker. "I'm going solo on this trip, Sadie. But maybe we can ride later with Felicity and the boys." She patted the mare's neck, stroked the solid length of muscle. Right now, she had to head Nick off at the pass—if that was even possible. For all she knew, Clem had already gone out to his "mining" site with Nick hot on his heel.

Stop. Delaney shook the pessimism from her mind. She stroked her mare's neck, down her backside, taking comfort in the smooth expanse of fur. Sadie grunted. Either way, Delaney had to be sure it was gold. Today, she'd take pictures of the rock itself and scrape off a sample. From what she'd read online, the bigger and more plentiful the fissures of a particular kind, the more potential there was for gold. And she wanted to know exactly what she was dealing with. Getting the gold out would be her next task, followed by selling it on the open market. Or did one go through a broker? She had no idea how gold was traded, but she would.

Delaney gave Sadie a pat on the rear, then kissed the velvety skin of the mare's nose, reveling in the sweet scent of her baby. "Time to go."

She snatched her backpack from its iron hook on the wall and took off for the trail behind the stables. It led up the backside of the mountain. By approaching from the upper ridge, she would ensure that no one saw her come in. She would see them, but they wouldn't see her. Once the site was clear, she'd climb down and get her pictures *and* her sample.

At the sight of the familiar red vehicle rounding the curve, Nick ducked his head. Alarm fired through his veins. Damn it, why didn't he take this into account? As Felicity's car approached, Nick snuck a peek over the dashboard. Was Delaney with her?

If so, he was a goner. There was no way she'd miss his car, parked off the shoulder of the country road. Felicity, maybe. But Delaney? Not a chance in hell. The car sped past and Nick let loose a sigh of relief. No Delaney. He sat upright and glanced down the road toward the property. Would she be right behind?

Nick stabbed the key into the ignition and gunned the engine, mindful of the half cup of coffee left in his console. He slid the gear into reverse and moved his vehicle farther from the road. If he backed up too far, he'd run the risk of missing Clem—provided the man hadn't already left. But the man didn't strike Nick as an early riser. More likely an "I'll-get-up-when-I-get-up type."

A fact which grated on him. Waiting on the lazy wasn't Nick's idea of a good time. Add Jillian's recent coup and he was feeling downright impatient. Waiting on others to get on with his business wasn't his idea of a good time. Unfortunately, alternative options weren't racing down the mountainside. He could always walk away from the project, but that wasn't gonna happen. He had invested too much time already and he felt close. Someone or something was going to break his way, he could feel it.

The hiccup with Jillian was something he could do without, but he knew how to handle that sly schemer. Thoughts of her bronze limbs intertwined with his, her lithe legs draped over his initial surge of desire. But she was old news. He'd moved on, even though she couldn't let go. Scorned and competitive to the bone, Jillian was out to prove she could do it without him and do it better. While he enjoyed a challenge, her hot-headed jealousy and controlling nature he could do without. Nick sipped lukewarm coffee, an eye on the rusty trailer. *Good luck, sweetheart, but mark my words...*

Serenity Springs will become a reality and will outshine whatever four walls you erect in its wake. It will be a masterpiece, a showplace like none other.

Ladd Springs was secluded, bordered by the USFS, and made all the more intriguing by trails and streams. With its plethora of springs, Nick would transform the property into his crown jewel, and he'd do it with Delaney Wilkins by his side. The image of her galloping bareback streaked through his mind. Delaney was a natural beauty, an earthy beauty—a nature girl through and through. She reminded him of Montana, of everything he loved about his home, the people, the land, the rugged landscape. Her appeal was entirely different than Jillian's yet even more intoxicating. She was a woman he wanted to see more of, spend time with, and during the course of building Serenity Springs, he would.

The thin aluminum trailer door swung open, folding back completely as it crashed against the vehicle's side. Nick downed the remainder of his coffee and set it back in the drink holder. He started his engine and closed a palm around the gearshift. Clem wasted no time hopping into his truck and peeling out over the shallow drive, headed toward Delaney's. Satisfaction coursed through Nick. *Bet whatever he's looking for is in those woods.*

Following at a safe distance, Nick traveled the two minutes to Ladd Springs and watched Clem's truck veer off the road onto Ladd property. He drove over to the trailhead where Delaney and he were confronted by the man with the gun. Clem's friend with the gun. Nick slowed his car and searched the vicinity for an inconspicuous place to park. The remainder of his trip would have to be accomplished on foot, but somehow he had to conceal his car. Up ahead, he spotted a dirt road, its drive overgrown with trees and brush. He flashed a look toward Clem's truck and grunted inwardly. The man had already parked and jumped out. Considering his rental vehicle, Nick bristled. The scratches the paint job would suffer would be brutal, but at the moment couldn't be avoided.

Nick turned and drove far enough off the road that his car couldn't be seen from passersby. While trespassing was a crime punishable by gunshot around these parts, he was grateful for one bright spot. Several yards in, there was a thinning of forest. He parked and hoped the neighboring property owner didn't have any plans this morning. If he did, Nick didn't expect his vehicle to be here in one piece when he returned.

Locking the doors, Nick took off for the road but jumped back. Old man Ernie's truck came barreling toward him, the antique Ford as loud as it was fast. *Someone's in a hurry.* Nick checked the Breitling on his wrist, surprised Ernie had plans this early. The car flew by and Nick wondered what could be so important to a man with nothing to do?

Wasting no more thoughts on Ernie, Nick jogged in the direction of the forest. Not yet familiar with the lay of the land, he couldn't afford to lose sight of Clem, though at the moment he'd done exactly that—lost him. But if Nick's suspicions were right, Clem was on his way to the spot Nick had found Delaney spying on two strange men a week ago.

Entering the forest, Nick kept his foot treads soft as he hurried, maintaining a good clip and a keeping a keen eye out for signs of Clem. This section of trail was wide, but according to his recollection, would soon narrow. Careful to avoid the jut of roots and rock in the dirt path, Nick tuned his senses to high alert. Mountain smells rose from the ground. The musty scent from the wall of clay beside him penetrated his nostrils. The passing cool front had infused the moist air with the scent of trees, a mix of pine and laurel. The temperature was cold but welcome as exertion warmed his body.

After he passed the falls, the trail opened up to a shallow ravine of ferns and rhododendron, littered with decaying logs. Nick slowed his pace, mindful of his current exposure. If Clem turned to look for him, he'd be wide open. Boring his gaze through the trees, over bushes, he searched for signs of Clem on the far side of the ravine. If he remembered correctly, this trail wound around to his left, ending up on the opposite side of the trees and creek below. Nick dropped his gaze briefly to the rocky stream and considered hiking straight across. The forest clutter below appeared passable. But not knowing how thick the lower ground might prove, it was wiser to stay on terra firma. Removing the gun from his waistband, Nick charged forth along the trail, running on the balls of his feet to keep his sound to a minimum.

Chapter Seventeen

Delaney reached for a limb dangling down from above and hauled herself up to the next level. The bruise on her shoulder throbbed, a painful reminder that reaching the ridge would not be easy. Winded, she sank to a seat on a fallen tree, its trunk split open near the base—lightning most probably the cause. The same fate that befell most downed trees in the forest. Mother Nature had a temper. Delaney peered down the path she'd just climbed and felt a sense of accomplishment. That had been tough!

With a heavy sigh, she dropped her head forward and breathed as deep as her lungs would allow. She knew she was wasting precious time. This hike shouldn't have taken her but a half-hour, max, but her muscles were screaming from the battering she'd endured in recent days.

She heard the muffled sound of her cell phone inside the backpack. It mounted in volume as she quickly unzipped the compartment and pulled it free. At the number on the screen, her heart leaped. She punched the answer key. "Hello?"

"Mom, I forgot my permission slip for the field trip next week. Did you ever sign it?"

Delaney raced through her memory. "I think so. You don't have it?"

"I don't. And I really want to go, but they're due today."

"Oh, *sweetheart*." Could Felicity have picked a worse time?

"Can you look for it and bring it to school? *Please*?"

"Yes," came her automatic reply, "though I don't know where it could be. If I signed it, I would have given it back to you."

"Will you check my room?" Felicity requested sweetly

"All right." Inwardly, Delaney groaned. Just when she'd almost made it to the top and happier trails. "I'll do what I can."

"Thank you!"

Delaney ended the call and stared down the steep terrain, the jagged pitch of rocks, dirt and brush. Trips down tended to be faster and messier than trips up.

But did she have a choice? Felicity couldn't miss her field trip to the symphony, not when she'd been looking forward to it all year. It was their last performance of the season. Delaney racked her brain. Did she sign that form?

At the moment, nothing was registering. Replacing the phone, she donned her backpack and stood. Glaring down the nearest branch, she grunted. Time to face the music.

Nick held back at the sharp turn, the odd-shaped boulder a dead giveaway that he was nearing the location in question. Lowering his weapon, he edged his gaze around the mass of rhododendron sticking out from the mountain above and saw what he was looking for. Clem had ventured off trail and stood in the middle of the forest inspecting a rock. He honed in on him. *Inspecting a rock*?

Straightening, Nick stuffed the gun back in his pants. Odd behavior for a man, even this one. Was it possible there was something hidden in the rock? Were Clem and his friends dealing in stolen goods?

From what Delaney said, the man was trash. Wouldn't surprise him if he'd squirreled away his loot in the woods. Is that what Delaney had discovered? Was she onto him and now he was trying to silence her? Nick clenched his jaw. Son of a bitch. But why would she protect him?

That was the part that didn't make sense. Nick watched Clem for several minutes but knew he couldn't stay. Clem, who was making a call on his cell phone, looked like he was only here to check on things. He could leave at any moment, and if he did, Nick was toast. If Clem left now, he'd be snagged. Glancing back down the trail, Nick tried to recall if he'd seen any hiding spots where he could conceal himself while Clem passed, but nothing leaped to mind.

With one last look at Clem, he logged the rock into his memory and re-traced his steps, lengthening his strides as he hunted down for a suitable hiding place.

After scouring the kitchen, Delaney climbed up into the loft and sifted through the papers on Felicity's desk. Thumbing through stacks of old homework, she tossed them aside and leafed through a second pile. There—she pulled the half-sheet of paper free. Caught between Felicity's science folder and a math test from the week prior was the permission slip. The signed permission slip. Delaney sighed. Just like she thought.

After straightening the papers back into some semblance of order, Delaney raced down the stairway and out the front door. Flicking a gaze to the rocker recently occupied by Nick, she wondered if he was in the forest.

If he was, there was nothing she could do about it at the moment. Felicity came first. Folding the paper in half, she tucked it in the outside pocket of her backpack, and with a determined step clambered down the porch steps, vowing not to let this little detour take more than an hour.

Nick's boot heel caught the edge of a rock, nearly tripping him. He cursed under his breath, whipped his gaze behind him, his pulse pumping in high gear. Clem wasn't anywhere near. But Nick had no way of knowing if and when Clem left his rock. *His rock*. Nick was willing to bet it wasn't the rock he was interested in. But he needed Clem gone before he could return to investigate.

Nick stopped suddenly. Above him, a narrow crevice reached deep into the mountain. Peering up into it, he noticed it led to a ledge—a ledge that would take him out of sight. No, the space was too small. He looked up the trail. If there was one, there'd be another.

A shout echoed through the trees. Nick froze. Was that Clem? Slashing his gaze sideways and back, he ceased his breathing and listened. When no more sounds came, he took a hesitant step forward, then paused. He scanned the surrounding area. Sunlight brightened the green overhead, the brown and gold leaves mounded at trail's edge.

Could be hikers. Ladd land bordered the USFS, but Nick wasn't familiar with where one began and the other ended. Moving forward, he remained wary.

Around the next corner, Nick found his sweet spot. The steep mountainous wall to his side opened up into a V-shaped gorge. Wide enough to accommodate his body, it offered enough rocks and branches to assist his climb. With one last glance up the trail, Nick hoisted himself up and into the mountain.

Wedging his backside into the hillside, Nick held gun in hand, aimed at the trail. Within minutes, he heard the pounding footsteps of someone running. Clem dashed by and Nick tracked his figure until he disappeared from sight. Was it Clem who had shouted? Was someone else at the rock?

Nick didn't know, but he'd find out soon enough. He waited another few minutes, then eased himself down, reaching from branch to branch to prevent tumbling into a full-fledged slide. Once he hit the clay trail, he headed straight back to the site. Detouring off trail, he trekked through brush, over the forest floor matted with dead leaves, the occasional rock. The gurgle of a creek wound through the earth on the opposite side.

Arriving in the vicinity where Clem had stood only moments before, Nick detected no signs of digging, only ferns, twigs and other foliage flattened from repeated foot traffic. At first glance, nothing appeared out of the ordinary. He moved over to the large rocks, the ones Clem had been inspecting. Gray boulders of irregular shape protruded between trees and rhododendron, their surface a sheen of moss, dotted with patches of white fungus. Nick touched one of the stones, finding it cold to the touch. He flattened his palm and leaned forward, exploring fissures and cavities, up and around. He took a step to the side, ducked his head and sucked in his breath. *Well I'll be damned...*

Instinct propelled him to check for onlookers. Through the black trunks of trees, leaves of green, over rocks and plants, he was alone. Nick exhaled and quickly rubbed the dirty streak in the rock, then examined his fingertips, holding them up to the scant rays of sunlight filtering down through the canopy above. The dust glittered ever so slightly as he turned his hand to and fro.

Son of gun—they'd found gold! Further scrutinizing the color variances, he noticed gouges in the jagged lines. He fingered them, studied them with a close eye. Definitely manmade. Someone had been chipping away at this rock, and by the looks of the damage, had walked off with quite a few chunks. Did Delaney know?

She must, he thought instantly. It explained her reticence to share. Explained her confrontation with the man with the gun. Explained Clem's high-tailing it in here, concerned his secret had been discovered, the gold gone. Nick smiled, admiring the natural wonder, the flecks of shimmery dust, the geological secret hidden away in layers of stone for millions of years... It was incredible. He didn't recall this part of Tennessee being known for gold. He dropped his gaze back to the vein. Yet here it was.

Nick looked around the immediate vicinity and searched for a rock, anything he could use to break off a chunk for himself. Spying one about the size of his fist, he grabbed it and struck the tip of the vein. Using the rock's edge like an axe, he hacked away as large a piece as he could. Turning the bullet-sized piece of mineral between his fingers, he shoved it into his front pocket. Ditching his makeshift tool, he brushed his hands together and headed out. If this was really gold, the stakes for Ladd Springs had just quadrupled.

After leaving Felicity's permission slip with the secretary in the front office, Delaney returned home, more eager than ever to get back to the site. She replaced her jacket with a long-sleeved jersey and headed up the mountain. The cool front had petered out, making way for warmer temps. Translated: she'd most likely be sweating before all was said and done. But the long-sleeves were necessary. She had no intention of adding to the collection of marks on her arms.

Trekking up the back side of the mountain, she made it to the ridge in forty-five minutes. Huddled between a twin pair of massive trunks, she downed the remainder of her water and slid the empty bottle into her backpack. Squatting, she peered down at the forest basin. There wasn't a soul in sight. Would someone venture by soon?

Anger welled. Probably. Those looters probably made daily trips in here to steal the gold. Well she was going to put an end to it, once and for all. Double-checking her phone was on vibrate, she took the path to her left and hiked down to the "golden" boulder.

Slinking through the trees and brush, Delaney kept a watchful eye and sharp ear out for any trespassers. If she saw or heard anyone, her plan was to run to the opposite side of the basin and hide behind the clump of rhododendron. It was her best chance for eluding detection.

But she was still alone when her discovery loomed front and center before her. She retrieved her camera and snapped off a few more pictures. Leaning close, she zoomed in on the vein of gold and snapped three pictures in rapid succession, then examined them on her small screen. The flash had washed out the impact of gold. Pulling back, she took a few more. On inspection, she judged them washed out but passable.

Tucking the camera back in her pack, she looked around for something to collect a sample. In a burst of foresight, she had packed a plastic baggy to carry her specimen, so she could have it tested to be sure it was gold. Then, she could show it to Ernie and tell him everything. He'd probably still fight her right to title, but she was fairly confident he wouldn't give it to Clem. Not with the knowledge the man was trying to swindle him, he wouldn't.

Deciding on a thick stick as a tool, Delaney scraped at the stone, a smattering a dusty brown falling free. She grunted. Not good enough. Picking up a nearby rock, she hacked away at the line in the stone and managed to chip out a small fleck. She stared at it in disappointment. Hopefully it would be enough to suffice as evidence.

She sealed the bag and stowed it away in her backpack. Turning, she headed back for the trail. At this point, she would take her chances and hike the main trail. If she heard anything or anyone, she could dodge them by heading straight up—the way she had done last time. She hoped it wouldn't be necessary, but it was best to be prepared.

Trudging through ground foliage, she kicked a branch with her boot and climbed up the narrow pass leading up to the main trail. Pushing up through a Y-shaped branch, she crawled up and onto the path. If Nick had meant what he said, he'd probably already come and gone. He didn't strike her as the type to "wait and see." And if what he said about Clem was true, she knew that greedy slime ball would have been here first thing. Her breathing labored, Delaney picked up her pace to a slow jog.

"Dell!"

At the familiar voice, she jerked her head up. Her heart thwacked at the sight of Clem. Standing dead center of the trail, he stared at her. "What's a matter? Ain't you glad to see me?"

Her heart pummeled against her chest.

"I see you been visiting my stone again."

"It's not your stone," she leveled, wrestling a building angst as the stakes were laid bare. Gun tucked in her boot, she couldn't get to it. The *camera* was in her backpack. If Clem learned of her pictures, it was game over.

He smirked. "I found it first."

"Trespassing on private property," she spat. Mentally, Delaney raced through her options. She could turn and run, possibly outstripping Clem. She could stay and fight, though it would mean more injury to an already sore shoulder. But if she could cause *him* injury, it would be worth it. She'd about had about enough of his attacks.

"That's where you're wrong," Clem jeered. "This place is gonna be mine, too, you watch and see. I already got Ernie convinced you're in cahoots with that hotel man trying to steal his property."

Delaney's jaw dropped open. "What?"

He smiled thinly. "Oh yeah, I told him you two was sleepin' together." He cocked his head. "Well, you know what? He wasn't too happy about hearin' them words."

Like a match to flame, the comment set fire to her resolve. "I will make you sorry you ever set foot on Ladd property."

He chuckled, mocking her. "Oh, will you now? And how you gonna do that when—" Clem lunged at her. Delaney jumped back. Managing to grab the end of her sleeve, he pulled. She yanked against him, slugging him across the side of his face.

"Get her!" Clem yelled.

The large stranger from the day before emerged from behind a boulder. He was on her in seconds, locking burly arms around her from behind. Delaney twisted, kicked and pulled, thrusting her heels into his shins. He lifted her from the ground, wrenched her head backward. Delaney shrieked in pain.

"What's a matter, tough girl?" Clem taunted. Rubbing a hand across his jaw, he spit on the ground. "You don't seem so high and mighty now."

"Clem," she bit out between gritted teeth.

"Yes?" he asked, leering at her undulating body.

Muscles screeched in her neck. The smell of sweaty, dirty man flared her nostrils. His panting disgusted her. Crushed between them, her backpack cut through the thin jersey of her tee, reminding her exactly what she stood to lose. "Let me down!"

"No can do. You and me are taking a ride." Clem gestured for the big man to follow. The third man materialized to join them, apparently lurking around the curve as the first two made their assault. He leered at her and licked his lips.

Panic rose sharply in her chest. She was the only one who knew about the gold. Other than Clem and these men, she was the only one who could prove that he was stealing from Ernie, from her. Unless Nick found it. But if these men were lying in wait for her, they may have already had their showdown with Nick. Damn them!

Delaney twisted against the man's torso, kicking her legs for a shot at Clem. He leaped out of reach, and once again the big man wrenched her neck in warning.

Delaney ceased. The fool could crack her neck without even realizing it!

"Lets' go," Clem ordered his thugs, and the two men followed, dragging her with them.

As they plodded down the trail, Delaney hung uncomfortably in the big man's hold. "Let me walk," she growled.

"Nope," Clem replied flatly. "You've proved you ain't trustworthy. Jeb, here, will escort you instead."

She stashed the name away. It could prove useful—once she freed herself. And free herself, she would. People would start looking for her when she didn't show up at home. *Home.* A horrible sinking feeling filled Delaney. As it stood, her daughter would be the one to have to report her mother missing.

Chapter Eighteen

Annie pulled into the Sweeney compound with her daughter, Casey, in tow. Candi Sweeney was Clem's sister and Annie's best friend—the only one of the bunch worth making the trip down the junk-lined road—and she needed to talk. Candi was like her other half, her soul sister. The two had met in high school. Annie thought she was pretty and sweet and perfect—until she met the Sweeneys.

The black sheep in the Sweeney clan, Candi was one member of the family not at war with the Ladds. She was the daughter who wanted to earn her degree and encouraged Annie to do the same. She helped her study, encouraged her to try out for the cheerleading squad, even to audition for the starring role in a school play. And it was Candi who had urged her to go after Jeremiah. She claimed Annie was the prettiest girl in school and could have whatever boy she wanted. Annie hadn't been as certain, but at Candi's insistence she went after Jeremiah, and to her surprise, he showed an interest. Annie had been beside herself at the time.

Jeremiah Ladd liked her.

It wasn't until he ran off to Atlanta with her sister Lacy that Annie uncovered the extent of his deception. Lacy was only the last in a long string of affairs. In the six months she and Jeremiah had been dating—or what she had believed to be dating—Jeremiah had slept with ten other girls. Ten. But Lacy was the most humiliating. Candi had been there for her, as sweet and caring as she could be, but it was Clem who took advantage of her devastation. One night, while out at the County Line Bar, he bought her drinks, danced with her, then took her back to his place. The rest was a blur, a nightmare Annie had been trying to black out of her memory ever since.

As they rolled past the rusted John Deere tractor, its front wheels flat, the weight of it sinking beneath years of neglect, Casey piped up, "I don't know why I had to come with you."

Annie glanced at her daughter. Sullen, moody, her jet black hair covering half her face, Casey wasn't happy to be anywhere at the moment. "Because you're grounded."

Disgust wrangled Casey's full lips into a frown, twisted her blue eyes into a knot of anger. "Which is *stupid*. I didn't *do* anything."

"It's not stupid. It's called consequences." Something Annie had been living with ever since that night at Clem's. Sleeping with two men and winding up pregnant was not a good mental place to be. While Annie was sure Casey belonged to Jeremiah, there always remained a seed of doubt. Nine months after Jeremiah left, nine months and a one-night stand later, Casey Melody was born. It was possible she belonged to Clem. But unlikely.

A mild tremor ran through Annie. She had slept exclusively with Jeremiah for six months. In all likelihood, Casey was his. She shook her mind free of old anxieties. Only *technically* was Clem a possible contender.

"Maybe you'll think twice next time before you decide to lie to your mother," Annie snapped. Lying only led to trouble, she added to herself.

Casey looked as if she could spit. "Whatever." She gave an indignant shake to her long, straight, glossy black hair and locked arms over her chest in defiance. Kicking a sneaker to the dashboard, she stared out the passenger window. "It's not like I did anything."

Not yet, maybe. But at the rate Casey was going, trouble would find her. It would stop her in her tracks, smack her hard. "Sneaking out with your boyfriend is what I call *something*," Annie replied.

"So. I told you—we didn't do anything. What's the big deal?"

"You're grounded because you lied," Annie informed her, hoping that what she claimed was true. For her daughter's sake. Annie gathered Casey in her gaze and exhaled heavily. She had such pretty blue eyes, a natural fire to her spirit and she was smart. So smart. If only she applied herself. *All I can do is pass on the lessons. What you do with them is up to you.*

Annie had learned hers the hard way. If she could alleviate a little pain and regret for her daughter, she would do so.

Pulling up to the cement block house, walls painted gray with white trim, Annie parked and eased out of the car. "C'mon."

Begrudgingly, her daughter followed. Heat rose from the arid mix of grass and dirt and clay, surprising Annie at how fast the temperature had soared. Gone was the misty nip she had awakened to, replaced by a scorching heat. While she preferred sunshine to rain, a few passing clouds would be nice. Especially since the air-conditioning had gone out in her car. If she was lucky, it was only a matter of Freon.

But Annie's life wasn't littered with luck.

Navigating the crooked line of stepping stones covered by weeds, passing a lone clump of purple hydrangea, she walked up to the front door and knocked. The bleached-out metal door exuded the stale scent of cigarette smoke. Boasting an oval glass etching in its center, it had been pretty in its heyday. Annie remembered when they installed it. Candi had been so proud, showing her friend how the gold lines glittered in the sun, the beveled glass sparkling as she opened and closed it. But like everything the Sweeneys touched, they only touched it once. Weather and time and neglect took over from there.

Candi opened the door and greeted Annie with a warm hug. She invited her inside, where the remainder of Sweeneys were embroiled in a heated discussion.

"It don't matter to me *what* he does. I ain't interfering."

"Now Buford, who said anything about interfering?" Mrs. Sweeney's generous figure was wedged into a recliner, the mauve material faded and worn. Her silvery curls were un-brushed, her housedress a pink floral, and on her feet she wore blue terry cloth slippers. "I said go and talk to the boy. He can't be hosting people at all hours over there, not when I can hear the racket from my front porch."

"Clem," Candi said when Annie looked to her for explanation.

Enough said, Annie thought. Uninterested in hearing anymore, she looked to her friend. She was here for a visit but preferred it didn't include Candi's family.

The stocky Mr. Sweeney paraded across the square room, his lower stomach protruding from beneath his white T-shirt. Like his wife, his salt and pepper hair could use some attention. "Ethel, I'm going to put my foot down."

"Stomp it in the mud, for all I care," she replied with a wave of her hand, a lighted cigarette hanging from between her fingers, the smoke snaking its way through the air toward Annie. "Just make sure you get the boy to quit or *else*."

Mr. Sweeney thrust out his hefty barrel-shaped gut. "Or else what?"

Candi shook her head in frustration, highlighted blonde streaks forming distinct sections between her natural brown. "How about we take a walk?" she whispered to Annie.

"Good idea." Annie turned to Casey and found her staring down the youngest member of the family. Sulking in the corner, the elder Sweeney's grandson Jimmy seemed content with staring right back at Casey, his dark brooding looks partially covered by the long swath of artificially black bangs. Dressed in black T-shirt and black jeans, the boy worked hard to project his new Goth image.

"Wanna wait here?" Annie asked her daughter, knowing the answer before she replied.

"No way." Casey spun on her heel, making a bee line for the front door.

Annie followed as Candi waved off to the family, "I'm going out for a while."

No one acknowledged she had said a word as Mrs. Sweeney stared down her husband, announcing, "Or else I'm gonna leave this house and never come back."

"Hah!" He flung his arms high into the air. "I been trying to get you to do that for thirty years and look at you..." He swept a beefy hand in her direction. "You're still sittin' here."

Annie caught Mrs. Sweeney's icy glare on her way out and thanked God once again she hadn't been born into this family. She might have issues with her own kin, but nothing compared to poor Candi.

Outside, the air suddenly felt fresh and clean. Bright, sunny. Happy. Annie turned to Candi as she closed the door behind them. "When are you going to move out of that house?"

"When I save up enough cash to pay first month, last month, utility deposit—" Candi frowned. She glanced askance at the house beneath lowered lashes, thickly coated with mascara. "You have no idea what it's like on a daily basis."

Annie hated the sadness pouring into her friend's big brown eyes. She'd had it rough of late, and if Annie could have helped her, she would. But barely managing on her own with Casey, she had nothing to spare. She'd already offered her couch, but Candi refused. She wasn't going to bog down her friend with her troubles. She'd handle them herself.

"But I'm getting close," Candi said, and took off walking. "Which is what I wanted to talk to you about."

Annie walked with her, but Casey declined. "I'll wait here," she said and leaned against the car door.

"Fine." Annie was in no mood to argue.

"But first you. How's your lawsuit going?" Candi asked, her gaze glittering with curiosity.

"Nowhere, yet. The lawyer says I have a chance, but it would be better if I could prove paternity."

"Which means you'd have to call Jeremiah."

Annie nodded, unable to mouth the words.

"Are you sure he wouldn't agree? I mean, don't you think he'd want to know for sure?"

"No." And she didn't want to hurt Casey any more than his absence already did. It was one thing to know your father lived in another state, had his own life, had his own issues. It was another to know he rejected you outright. At least that's what Annie told herself. Early on, she had tried to persuade Jeremiah to acknowledge Casey was his, tried to talk sense into him about doing right by his own flesh and blood. But he'd refused. He was a selfish bastard and some things never changed. "I think it would only complicate matters."

Candi gawked at her. "Seems to me it would make your life easier."

In the sense of money, yes. But not emotionally. Which was the problem. Going after her rights to Ladd Springs was churning up some dirty water. Casey was firing insults and sucking mud, starting to hang around with the wrong kids at school. It was no good. But Annie believed in her heart that she was doing the right thing, that it was time to set things straight and give her daughter her due.

She only wished it wasn't so difficult in the getting. Seeing Jeremiah again would open old wounds. It would remind her of everything that happened, unravel everything she had worked to build for herself and Casey. No. Jeremiah would only be trouble.

"Do you want me to call him?" Candi ventured.

"No—absolutely not!" Her pulse fired in rejection, but the question of how Candi could pull it off quickly flooded in. She cupped a hand to her brow, shading her eyes. Did she know where Jeremiah was? Annie assumed he was still in Atlanta, but she didn't know for sure. She'd stopped checking years ago. Stopped wondering and hoping and gave up on her last fantasy that he would do the right thing. Jeremiah Ladd was a son of a bitch, same as his father. It was in their blood, Delaney proving herself no different. Dropping her hand, she allowed thoughts of Jeremiah to subside. "I've been talking to a lawyer. I think I'll let him come up with a plan."

"If you're sure..."

At the relief in Candi's expression, Annie nodded. "I'm sure." She kicked at a beer can lying in her path and asked, "What's going on with you?"

Candi's eyes brightened. "I want to open my own salon."

"Really? But how are you going to manage that when you have no money?"

"Well, I'll need investors."

At Candi's averted gaze, Annie asked, "What kind of investors?"

"People who believe in me."

"Well, that's easy. You're the best hairstylist this side of the Mississippi!" Candi blushed at the compliment. "That ought to be easy."

As they rounded the corner of a stand of trees, a flowering dogwood reflecting bright white in the sun, Clem's trailer came into sight. Annie's insides clenched. Now there was a great way to ruin an afternoon, she mused. Dents marred the entire back side of the trailer, the result of a drink-induced parking attempt by Clem's brother Hank. After a night of carousing the two had returned home, and Hank managed to nail the entire back end of trailer. Sober, he couldn't hit the broad side of a barn. She shook her head. Both brothers were losers, with a capital L.

Candi glanced at Clem's trailer. "If he knows what's good for him, he'll steer clear of Daddy."

"Steer clear?" Annie asked, surprised. "I didn't think the two spoke."

"They don't. But even so, he manages to cause trouble."

"How?"

"He's been carrying on with some guys the last couple of weeks, playing his music loud into the night, probably drinking... Momma is none too happy about it, I tell you."

"Is that what they were talking about when I walked in?"

Candi nodded. Turning to Annie, she rolled her lips together. "Momma wants Daddy to kick him out."

"I thought he already was kicked out."

"Off the property, kicked out. She wants Daddy to have his trailer towed."

Annie savored the vision of Clem's rust-pit being towed away, never having to bear the sight of it again. A nice image. She glanced over again and wished Mr. Sweeney would do just that. Tow the dang-blasted thing away.

"Daddy won't do it," Candi said.

"He won't?" Annie asked, her mind split between Buford Sweeney's possible reasons against the idea and the sight of a blonde-headed woman sitting inside Clem's trailer. Annie strained to see through the dirty, sliding glass doors of the trailer.

"I think it's because he's too cheap to pay for the service, but Momma doesn't care. She wants Clem out."

Candi continued walking. Annie haphazardly kept up, her attention wrapped around the woman in the trailer. She could see Clem's figure, standing over her. Annie's thoughts stilled. If she didn't know better, she'd swear that was Delaney in there! Not too many women in this town had long, white blonde hair running down their back. Not near Delaney's size and not talking to Clem. *Coincidence*?

Realizing Annie had fallen behind, Candi stopped. "You okay?"

Annie kicked into motion. "Yeah, sure," she mumbled, her gaze stuck on the scene inside Clem's trailer. When he noticed her, he rushed over and whipped the curtains closed.

Could it really have been Delaney?

Delaney hated Clem, maybe even more than Annie. Why would she be in Clem's trailer? Was she talking about the property? Trying to scare him away from Ernie? He did seem to be hanging around there quite often these days...

In fact, every time she'd stopped by, Clem was there.

Annie wrestled with her curiosity as Candi waited for her. Hope twirled around her heart like the floating ribbons of sky-bound balloons. Could this work to her benefit some-how? Could she convince Ernie that Delaney and Clem were teaming up on him? Which didn't make sense. Delaney was queen in her own mind. She thought she could conquer the world. She didn't need Clem Sweeney.

Annie's brows rose and her pulse sprinted. *Was something else going on?*

Felicity breezed in through the front door of the cabin. "Mom, I'm home!" she called out and climbed the stairs to her room. Travis and Troy were riding over in ten minutes and she had yet to change, but her band coach had stopped her after class to inform her that she was up for another scholarship. Another scholarship!

Goosebumps raced across her skin. She couldn't believe it. Another one—and this time it was money she could use for *any* musical cost she wanted. Maybe even a new flute. Felicity peeled off her good jeans and pulled on a pair of torn, faded Levis. Riding bareback would ruin a pair of designer jeans faster than Travis could jump the creek. Pleasure ripped through her. She couldn't wait. He said he had a present for her. A present.

For what? Her birthday wasn't for three months! What could he possibly have and why? Buttoning her fly, Felicity rushed into the bathroom. She checked her hair in the tiny mirror, checked her makeup, her reflection revealing a goofy smile. But so what? Travis was the only boy she ever cared about. She liked Troy, but Travis was the one she preferred. Smart, sweet, he always kept her guessing. Troy was predictable. Outrageous and daring, but predictable in his quest for attention. Felicity ran a quick brush through her hair than hurried downstairs, the silken waves in need of a wash.

Travis had a gift for her? What could it be? Leaping past the bottom stair, Felicity yelled, "Mom, I'm leaving now!" She swept into her mother's bedroom, catching herself at the doorway. Poking her head inside, she glanced about, surprised to find it empty. The bathroom door was open, the light off. She looked around, perplexed.

Huh. Her mom was always here when she arrived home from school. Walking back into the kitchen, Felicity glanced around the living room, the kitchen, noting nothing out of place. Everything was as it was when she left this morning.

Maybe she was already at the stables. Felicity grabbed a green apple from the basket by the refrigerator and headed out the door. Wait until she heard about Travis' surprise!

But when she arrived to empty stables, Felicity became worried. Something was wrong. Her mom was always here when she got home from school. Always. Sadie came up to Felicity and nudged her soft muzzle against her. "Where's Mom, Sadie?" Felicity asked, absently scanning the woods around them. *No riding in the woods alone.*

Felicity grew uncomfortable. "What happened? Was her mom okay?

With no choice but to meet the boys, Felicity gathered her black mare. Using the barn stool parked off to the side, she hopped onto her horse's back. She gave a brief shake to the reins and clicked her mouth. "Let's go, girl."

Travis would know what to do.

As Felicity emerged from the trail into open field, she saw Travis and Troy Parker waiting for her just past Uncle Ernie's cabin. They sat idle on two chocolate-colored Quarter horses, bareback as always, the only movement the occasional swish of a black tail. The day that begun with a nip in the air had warmed considerably, though Felicity was gripped by a building chill. When she called her Mom's cell phone, it went straight to voicemail. It would only do so if her mother had turned her phone off. Why would she do that?

Felicity trotted past the main house, looking past the empty rockers for signs of life inside. Ernie's truck wasn't here, but what about Uncle Albert? He never went anywhere. Had he decided to go somewhere with Ernie?

"Hey Felicity, hurry on up!" Troy shouted.

She turned toward the brothers, but her eyes focusing on Travis. As though he could sense something was wrong, he kicked heels to horse and rode toward her.

Relief trickled in as she stopped her mare and waited for him.

Travis was by her side in seconds. Long brunette bangs partially covered his brown eyes but couldn't conceal his concern. "What's up, Felicity?"

"My mom. She isn't home."

Confusion rippled across his face. "She isn't?"

"No," she replied quietly.

He shook the hair from his brow, his brown eyes closing in. "Where do you think she is?"

Felicity shrugged, but her heart caught at the sight of Nick's sedan pulling into the driveway near Troy. Travis followed her gaze. "You expecting someone?"

"No." But she was grateful for Nick's unexpected arrival. "He's a friend of my mother's."

Travis probed no further, turning his horse so the pair of them faced Nick as he drove in and parked. Rising from the vehicle, he pushed the door closed and strode over, his white polo shirt crisp against navy blue jeans. He checked out Travis with an almost dutiful paternal once-over and said, "Hey, Felicity."

"Hi."

"Is your mom around?" he asked with a hopeful smile.

She shook her head. "No."

Nick paused, scrutinizing her face. "Everything okay?"

"My mom isn't here," she said, as though he would understand the significance.

He nodded. "That's what you said. Any idea where she is?" Nick set hands to hips. "I'd like to talk to her."

"No—and that's the problem," she said, her words suddenly tumbling out. "She's always here when I get home from school. Always."

His brow rose, cutting deep lines across his forehead. "Well I'm sure she'll be here soon." Nick offered an appeasing smile, but Felicity was having none of it.

"You don't understand, Mr. Harris. She's always here when I get home. Always. It's not like her to be gone. She didn't even leave a note."

Finally, the magnitude of her plight seemed to register in his expression. "She's never missed a day?"

"No. Never. I tried to call her cell phone, but it went to voicemail." Scary shadows crossed his eyes. "Do you have any idea what could have happened, Mr. Harris?"

Nick stepped toward them and Travis' horse took a restless step, his ears pricking back and forth.

"Where are you guys going?" Nick asked.

"We're going for a ride," Travis responded, protective steel lining his voice.

Troy trotted over, casting an appraising eye to the situation. "What's going on over here?" Sporting the same brown hair and dark eyes, the brothers were nearly identical, save for the scar on Troy's cheek and his more muscular build. Troy lifted weights. Travis did not.

Felicity waved him off. "Nothing, Troy. We're fine."

But the Parker boys were defensive that way, always on the lookout for someone moving in, trespassing. Tempers fired quickly around these parts, and these two were known for their hard-hitting response time, Troy willing to flaunt his strength more readily than Travis.

"Felicity," Nick prodded, ignoring the interruption. "When was the last time you talked to her?"

"This morning when I left for school. Actually—wait—no. I talked to her when I realized I didn't have my permission slip for a school field trip. I called her and she brought it to school for me."

"What time was that?"

"About nine-thirty, ten."

"And she brought it to you? You're sure?"

"Yes. She left it with the office and I gave it to my teacher." As Nick digested the information, Felicity asked, "Why? Did you see her today? Do you know where she might be?"

"No." But he had a funny idea he knew where she was headed. The golden rock. He had checked his sample with a local jeweler in town, and it was legit. Ladd Springs had gold on its hands, and he'd bet his life Delaney knew about it, probably suspected he'd find out, too.

"Should we get my Uncle Ernie?"

Nick glanced back to the cabin behind him. "No. Not yet. Let me do a little checking first." He looked up at the young man next to Felicity, the boy next to him. These must be the twins Delaney had mentioned. They were friends of Felicity's and, by the looks of them, both strapping and courageous in their own right. Nick could entrust them with the girl's safety. No telling what Clem might do if he found her alone. After all, she was an extension of her mother. "Listen, you boys live around here?"

Travis nodded and pointed up the road. "We do. Just up yonder, around the bend."

Troy scowled at his brother and asked Nick, "What's it to you, mister?"

"I want you to take Felicity with you." Nick turned to her. "Can you stick with them while I look for your mom?"

She nodded. "Do you think you can her?"

"I do."

Relief softened the tension around her mouth. "Okay. Tell her I'll be at the Parker's. She can call my cell."

"Will do."

Chapter Nineteen

Standing in front of the "golden rock," Nick scanned the abundance of trees, the trunks black sticks against a backdrop of sea green. Swells of earth formed walls of red clay on either side of him, boulders and roots rose free from a blanket of brown leaves and decaying branches. But there was no sign of Delaney, no clue to her whereabouts. "Damn it," he muttered. "Where are you, Delaney?"

Nick's gut told him Delaney was in trouble, and the more time he wasted, the more danger she faced. If she wasn't here, he had a sneaking suspicion that Clem might know where to look. He was the only person who had demonstrated a will to hurt her, he and his pal with the gun. The three men together had it out for Delaney.

She was a fighter, he'd witnessed that much firsthand. If it came down to fists, she'd get away from him. Bumped and bruised for her time, but Nick would put money on her to walk away the winner. If it didn't, things didn't bode well for Delaney.

Nick half-ran, half-jogged the trail out of the woods. Once he reached the clearing, a plan formed in his mind. First stop, Clem's trailer. If he knew something, Nick would get it out of him. Beat it out of him, if need be, something that would give him great pleasure. Then he'd get Delaney, and the two would return to Felicity. Sadness pricked at his heart. He hadn't liked seeing the naked fear in her young eyes. If Delaney was harmed, the bastard responsible would pay. Nick could only hope that bastard was Clem.

As Nick jogged through the tall meadow grass, Ernie's cabin came into sight. His truck was back, along with another car. A white sedan, unfamiliar to him.

When Nick reached the gravel driveway, he spotted a woman speaking to Ernie. Huddled in his rocker as usual, he appeared unhappy to see her. Nick strode over and heard the black-haired woman demand, "You mean to tell me you're not the least bit concerned?"

"I ain't."

Rounding the edge of the cabin, Nick noted Albert Ladd, peacefully rocking to and fro as the disagreement heated beside him. Nick shook his head in wonder. The man was innocuous to a fault.

"Well, you should be," the woman snapped. "Those two are up to no good."

"You're the one who's up to no good." Ernie looked to Nick. "Along with this one."

The woman whirled around. "Who are you?"

"Nick Harris," he said, wondering at her identity, as well. The woman was fairly attractive, with a slim build. Her black hair, all one length, framed a round face marked by two big blue eyes. Two incredibly beautiful blue eyes. "I'm here to speak with Mr. Ladd," he told her.

"Mr. Ladd?" Annie blinked, as though confused by the reference to Ernie.

Scaling the steps, he asked, "Ernie, I'm looking for Delaney. Have you seen her?"

"No."

"Any idea where I might be able to find her?"

He scowled and dodged Nick's gaze. "She ain't no concern of mine."

Nick swallowed the first words that came to mind and said calmly, "Felicity is concerned about her mother. Says she wasn't home when came home from school." This sparked the first sign of interest in the watery red-gray eyes. "Any idea why that might be?"

Ernie flicked a look of annoyance toward the woman standing beside him.

Nick turned to her. She took a step away from him and pursed her lips. "And you are?" he asked.

She brought a hand to her neck and covered her throat, her fingernails painted as blue as her eyes, coordinated with the blue flowers of her willowy blouse. "I'm Annie."

The name didn't mean anything to him. "Do you know Delaney?" Nick asked. Ernie had looked to her when asked about Delaney. There had to be a reason.

"Yes."

He stepped toward her. "Any idea where she might be at the moment?"

Annie brushed hair behind an ear and dropped her gaze to the planked floor.

"It's important," Nick urged. "I think she might be in danger."

She flipped her face up to meet him directly. "Danger? What do you mean, *danger*?"

"I can't really explain," he said, feeling certain the woman knew something. "Do you know where she is?"

Annie bit her lip back and glanced sideways to Ernie. Nick caught the briefest hint of acknowledgment in Ernie's gaze. Were the two discussing Delaney when he walked up? Were they hiding something? Anger welled. He moved closer to her and said, "Listen, you must believe me when I tell you her life could be at stake. If you know something, I need to know. *Now*."

"I, I..." Annie cowered away from him. "I'm not really sure."

Nick's patience snapped. "Tell me—"

"I think she's at Clem's but I'm not sure..." Annie darted a glance to Ernie and sputtered, "But I didn't see her face, so I can't be certain!"

Ernie grumbled and shook his head. He jabbed the pipe into his mouth.

"You saw her at Clem's trailer?

"Yes, yes, inside. I think it was her." Annie thrust her gaze around like a helpless female in search of miraculous assistance, the kind that would pop out of thin air. "She was sitting," she said quickly. "He was standing, talking to her."

Her blue eyes rounded. "But I'm not sure—I was far away, and he closed the curtains when he saw me."

"Why do you think it was her?" Nick pushed, beginning to doubt the veracity of the woman before him. She was sketchy, dodgy. When he walked up, it sounded like she was instigating trouble.

"Her hair," she exclaimed. "I saw her hair through the glass doors."

Nick had to agree. It was pretty distinctive, even from afar. He turned on his heel, leaped across all three stairs and hit the ground running. If Delaney was at Clem's, he'd have her out within five minutes.

"C'mon, Dell." With Delaney's arms tied behind her back, Clem manhandled her toward his truck, shoving her inside. "We're going for a ride." He slammed the door closed and walked around the front end, climbing into the driver's seat.

Struggling against the ropes cutting into her wrists, Delaney shifted in the seat until she was sitting upright. The stench of his vehicle was overwhelming, a combination of cigarette smoke and rotten food. "Where are you taking me?"

"Pipe down. You'll know soon enough." Clem stuffed a lighted cigarette between his teeth and turned the key in the ignition. The engine started with a loud pop. As he yanked the vehicle into reverse, Delaney's body lurched forward then back, as he jammed his dusty boot to the accelerator. Both of their bodies bounced around on the bench seat as he pulled out onto the pavement. With a screech of tires, Clem took off in the direction of town.

As they drove, air rushed in through the open windows, blowing hair across her face, her neck, several ends sticking in her mouth. Delaney spit the strands out as best she could, but at the speed they were traveling, it was no use. More took their place within seconds.

Clem rested his elbow on the open window frame and drove as though he didn't have a care in the world. His expression was blank as he looked to the road ahead. He puffed from his cigarette without hurry, the smoke assaulting her nostrils as he exhaled.

Delaney remained incredulous to his audacity. He'd actually commanded men to kidnap her—*kidnap her*—which was nothing short of a felony. She glared at him from the corner of her eye. It was a federal crime, one she would make sure he paid for dearly.

As Clem slowed for a stop sign, Delaney pulled her hands from beneath her rear end, adjusting her weight to relieve the stress on her shoulders. The bruised one ached, her hands were beginning to tingle. The seat was growing hot and sweaty against her back. She needed to make a plan. She needed to be prepared to escape when the opportunity presented itself.

Delaney eyed the door handle. There was no way she could grab hold of it, let alone open it. Analyzing the floor layout, she made note of the hump in the floor of the center console. Clem drove an older model, a barebones model truck, meaning the only thing between their feet was the gear shift—nothing substantial she could brace her boot against for a leap out the window. She glanced outside, currently a blur of trees and mailboxes. Of course at his speed, jumping out the window could mean broken bones.

She turned to him, repulsed by his nicotine-stained fingers, his bony jaw covered by a scraggly layer of light brown facial hair. "You're not going to get away with this, Clem."

He snickered. "That's what you think."

"They'll know it's you."

Clem looked over at her and smiled thinly. Glancing between her and the road, he pulled a drag from his cigarette, the ashes turning bright orange, then blew the smoke straight into her face. "Ain't gonna be me."

She struggled not to cough in the cloud of smoke. Wasn't going to be him? But he'd sent the men away. Who, then?

The first sliver of icy fear passed through her stomach. Up to this point, she believed it was going to be a matter of him and her. A battle between her and Clem was one she could win. Had she miscalculated? Should she have fought harder? Delaney dropped her gaze to her boots. He'd taken her gun. He'd taken her backpack. She could only hope he didn't have the sense to check her camera.

"Now what you got to say, Dell?" he chortled. When she didn't reply, he added, "That's what I thought." And spit a wad of saliva out his window.

Clem drove toward town but turned off on a country road before making it to the official town limits. Delaney recognized the mostly rundown area for what people referred to as the wrong side of town. She wouldn't be caught dead here at night. Her pulse fluttered. Actually, she would. That's exactly what could happen to her after dark in this neighborhood. She turned and centered on Clem. He wouldn't really go that far, would he?

Nick pounded the empty trailer's door. "Damn it, where are they!" he shouted. Whipping his head around, he fought the urge to go back and wring that woman dry for information. She was a local. She knew the Ladds, Clem—she must have some idea where he might have gone.

But he didn't have time. He only had time to act, to *move*. Nick ran to his car, jumped in and keyed the engine to life. Heedless to oncoming traffic, he peeled out of the drive, cutting off a station wagon as he headed toward town. He was going to the only other place he thought Clem might go.

Clem stopped his truck outside a wooden shack. A cloud of dust billowed around the truck and for once Delaney was thankful to be inside. One end of the home's eave was collapsed, the front porch hung precariously from the exterior wall. He honked the horn twice and the screen door opened. The man known to her as Jeb walked out. He nodded to

Clem, held a hand up, his fingers and thumb spread wide. *Five minutes.*

Clem nodded he understood. The man disappeared back into the house.

So...she had five minutes to figure a way out of this mess before the next leg of her journey began. And she had no doubt it included Jeb, perhaps even his cohort from the woods. She swallowed, the move doing nothing to lubricate her throat. It was dry, tight, painfully so. She glanced askance at Clem. Maybe she could talk some sense into him. Maybe belligerence wasn't her best option.

Retrieving a pack of cigarettes from a cubby in his dashboard, a dashboard covered with white, nasty ashes—Clem pulled a cigarette free and stuck it in his mouth. He drew a lighter to its tip and flicked on the flame. His cheeks hollowed as he sucked in hard.

"What do you want, Clem?"

He turned to her, his yellowed teeth clutching the cigarette butt as he spoke, "I got everythin' I need, Dell."

"We can make a deal," she said. "It's your find. I'll give you some rights to it."

"Some rights?" He guffawed, and took a long drag from his cigarette. Exhaling, he smiled. "How about I take all them rights, instead?"

"It's Ladd property. I think Ernie would have something to say about that."

"Ernie ain't got nothin' to say about things he don't know about."

"He'll find out, Clem. You have to know that."

He cocked his head to the side and peered at her quizzically. "And how's he gonna do that? By traipsin' out into the woods?" He laughed and shook his head. "You really get me, Dell."

Stupid. This was stupid and going nowhere. He wasn't going to listen to reason. She needed to escape, that was all there was to it. "I need to go to the bathroom."

His cigarette hung from his mouth, the smoke curling around his fingers, around his face, his stringy, greasy hair. He appeared to consider her request, but replied, "Hold it."

"I can't. And I don't' think you want me messing up your truck." The hair around her shoulders and neck was growing warm, uncomfortable as it stuck to her skin. With no clouds in the sky, the sun was baking the vehicle. "I need to go. I'm sure they have a bathroom in there."

He squinted at her, wary of her motives. "Don't you go try nothin', Dell. Jeb ain't the friendly sort and he don't much care for women." Clem's lips pulled the ends of his mouth into an insulting smile. "Kinda like old Jack."

Delaney tensed but kept her mouth shut.

Suddenly agitated, Clem withdrew the short cigarette from his mouth and flicked it out the window. "Let me go check." He pushed out his door and traipsed over to the flea-bag of a house and entered. Delaney, wrestling with the rope at her wrists, her skin burning from the repeated friction, could only imagine what it looked like inside the rundown shack. Bending her fingers around the rough braid of material, she fought to loosen the knot to the point where she could slip her hands free.

Clem came out of the house and she stilled. Trailing his figure to her side of the truck, she breathed a sigh of relief. He was letting her go to the bathroom. He opened her door and instructed, "Get out." Delaney stretched a leg down to the running board and sliding the other over, hopped down to the ground. "You got two minutes and then we're leavin'," he said. Wrapping skinny fingers around her bicep, he propelled her toward the house.

The place was a dump, the yard littered with beer lids and cigarette butts, a rearview mirror, a rusted pipe, miscellany of bricks. "What do you plan on doing with me?" she asked, careful not to trip over the random cement blocks in her path. Broken in two, it looked as if someone had hurled the thing there and left it.

"You ask too many questions," Clem said. He yanked the screen door open and thrust her inside. She cringed. The stench was overwhelming. Stale beer and old tobacco permeated the air. Fast food containers lay opened and abandoned on the table, the couch, accompanied by shreds of lettuce, bread crumbs and smears of ketchup-covered paper wrappers. A few empty soda cups sat nearby. Jeb stood by an olive green refrigerator, downing a can of beer. His skinny friend was in tow, eyeing her with a lascivious gleam.

Her insides recoiled.

"Bathroom's in there." Clem pointed to the narrow door in the back. "And hurry it up. We ain't got all day."

Thankfully, no one questioned how she was going to perform the task. Delaney strode through the tight quarters and entered the bathroom, reaching tied hands behind her to close the door. Inside the small confines, the toilet bowl was a burnt-orange color, the water line blackened by mold. The mirror was a mess of smudges and stains—whose origins of which she didn't even want to consider. The pedestal sink was white porcelain, its drain hole dark and rusted.

Delaney peered at her reflection and for the first time felt the full brunt of her situation. Jeb looked like a man with nothing to lose, his friends oblivious to any consequences of their actions. Clem had always been a loser, and not a very bright one. Her thoughts veered toward Felicity. For all intents and purpose, she had already lost her father. Felicity couldn't lose her mother, too. She dumped her gaze to the sink. Staring at the grimy tiled-floor, pressure built in Delaney's chest. She had to find a way out of this mess. She had to break free. She couldn't let this be the way her life ended. She looked into the mirror, desperation exploding in her chest. Sure as she was standing here, death waited just outside the door.

Grateful to find his car in one piece, Nick drove as fast as he could, his speedometer tapping numbers it had no business touching. Hugging country roads with his precision vehicle, he almost wished he had a squad car on his tail. Might prevent him from doing something stupid when he landed in town.

If Clem and those men had Delaney, as he believed they did, they were going to get what was coming to them. Whether it came from his hand or not, they were going to regret the day they ever touched her. Thoughts of her ex striking her crossed his mind and stirred fury, deep in his gut. Only a weak man hit a woman. A coward, in every sense of the word. Alcohol didn't excuse the actions, it only accentuated them. Delaney might be a fighter, but she didn't stand a chance against a man. Sheer mass worked against her. Visions of last night on her porch pulled at him. The first time she revealed her vulnerability—the feminine need to be protected and cared for that every woman harbored.

A need he wanted to fill.

Nick jammed his foot to the pedal and the car lurched forward. All eight cylinders rumbled as he gunned the engine to max capacity.

Delaney jumped at the fist pounding on the door. "Hurry up in there!"

"I'm almost done!" Heart pounding, she continued to work her hands back and forth across the radiator pipes, rubbing and tugging against the sharp edges. Her skin burned from the friction, but the process was working. She could feel the knot tighten, the fibrous threads tearing apart. She lifted her leg and hit the toilet handle with her boot. The bowl flush drowned out the sound as she yanked her hands hard against the rusted metal.

She could feel Clem's impatience on the other side of the door. Her time was up. Pulling her body erect, she backed up to the door handle and opened it, turning to face Clem as she walked out. She squeezed arms to her back, mindful of covering any sign of the loosened rope with her fingers.

Jeb and his cohort were waiting outside. The smaller man opened the passenger door to a blue truck and gestured for her to climb in. "Where are you taking me?"

"I done told you, Dell. It doesn't matter." Clem scowled. "Now go on and get in the truck."

Delaney stood firm. "We don't have to do this, Clem." She glanced at the men, then back to him. "I won't say anything about your involvement with the gold. I won't tell Ernie. Just let me go and you all can go free." Jeb glowered but she continued, "I promise. You can walk away and no one will be the wiser."

"Too late," Clem said, and Delaney thought she detected reservation in his voice.

Could it be? Was he debating the wisdom of this decision?

"You don't have to do this, Clem. You'll go to prison for life." Delaney avoided Jeb's dark frown stabbing at her from across the faded hood of the truck. "Listen to me. You won't get away with it. They'll find you. They'll prosecute you."

The wiry man holding the passenger door of the truck became fidgety, darting glances between Jeb and Clem. Silver medallions rimming the crown of his hat glinted in the sunlight.

"We've got to get on with it," Jeb barked.

Clem flinched. "Get in the truck, Dell!" He pushed her and she nearly tripped over a metal tire rim. She shook the hair from her face and stumbled toward the truck. An inkling of finality was creeping in. Should she run? Should she wait?

Would they shoot her in broad daylight? Despair seized her. She glanced at the cluster of surrounding houses, empty, abandoned. Was there anyone around to notice what was happening? Eyeing the truck's cigarette smoke and sweat-drenched interior, she had no doubt that was not the place to be. From everything she'd heard—getting into the perpetrator's vehicle was the *last* thing she should do.

Clem shoved her forward. "I'm sorry, Dell. But you left me no choice."

Climbing in, she scooted into the middle. Jeb and the other man eased in and flanked her on both sides. Sitting rigid between them, she felt trapped. Fear peppered her heart. A looming sense of dread filled her.

Clem stood beyond the hood. He lit a cigarette and stared at her.

Loathing filled her. The man was a coward. He couldn't even do the deed himself. Jeb gunned the engine to life and pulled out onto the road. As they passed a row of seemingly deserted houses in varying degrees of neglect and decline, Delaney saw no one to act as her witness. Like rats in the light of day, no one showed themselves in the streets. Were they huddled in the slums of their miserable lives, unwilling to help an innocent woman? *Misery loves company. It's not my problem. Mind your own business.*

As Jeb picked up speed, Delaney tried to keep from touching the men. Tried to ignore the smell, the fear rising inside her. Tried to keep her wits about her. She had to make a plan.

But getting into this truck may have sealed her fate.

Nick careened around the corner and drilled the accelerator to the floor. The house Clem had gone to the other night was down this street. It was the third one around the next corner. Downshifting, he took the curve with a screech of tires. The sight of Clem's truck unleashed a band of rage in him.

Clem's exhaust pipe discharged a puff of smoke as the truck's engine jerked to life. Nick nailed the accelerator. His car reacting with the power of a jet engine, he pulled in front of Clem and cut him off with a violent jam to his brakes. Clem jerked his truck into reverse, but Nick was already out of his car, the gun pulled from his waistband trained on Clem.

Clem's eyes widened in horror.

Nick pulled the driver side door open, hauled Clem out with one hand and slammed him against the truck. "Where is she?"

Clem glanced at a blue truck, four blocks down, then looked to Nick. "I don't know what you're talkin' about!"

"Where is Delaney?" Nick demanded once more.

Shaking, Clem glanced toward the truck again and back to Nick. "I don't know!" he shrieked. "I swear!"

Nick followed his gaze. Taillights lit red, then extinguished as the truck turned the corner. Delaney. It had to be. "Liar." He slugged Clem in the face with everything he had. The man staggered, fell flat on his back. Nick kicked him in the side, his boot connecting with a thud. Clem curled up into the fetal position, moaning loudly.

Disgust rolled through Nick. "You haven't heard the last of me," he promised. After a final kick, he ran to his car, jumped in, and headed in the direction of the blue truck.

Chapter Twenty

Jeb took the main road, turning at the first light, the route out of town and into rural wasteland. A mix of forest and fields, there wasn't much here. Farms had vanished, homes abandoned as people had given up wrestling with the land and moved out. Alarm shredded Delaney's thoughts. Did they intend to shoot her and dump her in a remote area? She shuddered. Who would find her out here?

No one.

Resolve fired through her. She had to come up with a plan!

Jeb glanced in the rearview mirror and Delaney felt him tense. He crushed the accelerator with his massive boot and tightened his grip on the steering wheel.

"What are you doing?" the smaller man cried. "You're gonna cause the cops to follow us!"

"We've got company."

Delaney twisted around and saw the familiar car racing toward them. Relief flooded her. *Nick had found her.*

The skinny little man looked back and shrieked, "Who's that?"

"Not sure." Jeb looked to her. "You know him?"

Excitement swelled, but Delaney didn't respond.

Jeb looked over her head to his friend. "Hold on."

Angst zipped through her. The little man grabbed hold of the hand grip above his door. Delaney pressed her feet to the floorboard. Not much else she could do as Jeb spun the steering wheel sharply to the left, sending her into the man beside her. He sped down the dirt road, the truck's frame jostling her bones as the large wheels hit deep grooves and ruts.

Knocked back and forth between the two men, Delaney, heart racing, craned her head for another glimpse of Nick. He was following, but it was clear his car could not handle the uneven terrain like the truck could. Delaney glanced at Jeb. Maybe he wasn't as dumb as she thought.

Hanging on for dear life, the skinny man locked a white-knuckled grip to the hand hold above as the road curved up ahead. Several tree trunks stood near the road as it narrowed into the forest. "Watch out, Jeb!" he hollered.

Jeb barreled forward in determined silence.

Delaney braced herself. Using her feet and shoulders, she pressed her body into the seat back. Adrenaline flushed through her. She tried to keep centered, praying no cars were traveling in the opposite direction. *Was Jeb crazy*? They could all be killed!

Gone were the grass and shrubs. Trees and curves dominated now, reducing visibility to nothing but leaves and tree trunks. It was darker in the shade, the scent of trees permeating the interior of the truck. She couldn't tell if Nick was still behind them or not. This wasn't Ladd land. She had no idea what lay up ahead.

Did Jeb know where he was going?

The truck slowed as they drove deeper into the woods, only because the landscape was getting in his way. Maybe it would give Nick a chance to catch up. The truck hit a massive rock, uprooting her from her seat. If his car would hold up, that is. Nick's low-lying sports sedan tore at her spirit. This was tough going, even for a truck. There was no way Nick's car would make it through.

She had to get out. Delaney glanced sideways from man to man. Sandwiched between them, she couldn't jump out. She surveyed the road ahead. There remained one option. She had to stop the truck. They were traveling slowly enough now, it might be possible. And if she could manage to stop the truck, she might be able to escape into the woods. They could shoot at her, but with all the trees, she had a fighting chance. Besides, she doubted they'd pursue her with Nick on

their tail. Jeb had already proved he wasn't completely ignorant. He must realize Nick would catch up with them, and he
knew Nick had a gun.

In a split decision, Delaney made her choice. Inching her
left boot toward Jeb's as they approached the curve ahead,
she calculated the distance and counted—one -two-*three*. She
jammed her boot onto Jeb's and braced against her seat back,
locking her legs into rods of steel.

"What the—"

But it was too late. As the truck hit a tree trunk with a
sickening crunch, Delaney drove down into the lap on her
right. Her head and shoulders hit the dashboard with a painful
whack, her body bouncing back like a rag doll.

Nick jammed the brakes to the floor. *Damn it*, there was
no way his car would make it any farther. Not without dropping a chassis—which would be worth it if he thought the car
stood a chance at catching up. But it wouldn't.

He jumped out, pulled his gun and took off running. He
had no idea how far ahead the men were, but he would close
the distance. He had to. Delaney was with them.

There was no way he was going to let them hurt her.
Spotting the curve up ahead, he cut through the forest. Time
was of the essence.

Momentarily stunned, Delaney popped her head up. She
gauged the situation. Jeb was slumped over the steering
wheel, his head a sticky mess of red. The scrawny man next
to her shrieked, "What were you thinkin'?"

Waves of pain rolled through her head, sharp and dull at
the same time. Twisting her aching body, she swung her legs
over his bony ones and kicked at the door. Sharp spasms
erupted in her head, her shoulders. "Get out!" she commanded.

Eyes slanting toward the inert Jeb, he froze.

"Get out!" she yelled. Wedging the toe of her boot into
the door handle, she tried to pull it open. "Open the door,

damn it!" Delaney pulled frantically at the rope around her wrists.

As though roused by some unseen force, the little man pushed his hands between her boots and thrust the door open. Visibly shaking, he slid out ahead of her, his gaze darting nervously about. Probably checking for Nick's whereabouts.

"He's coming," she warned him, shock and adrenaline firing her temper. A sweep of light-headedness made her pause. Shaking the dizziness, she scooted her bottom along the seat cushion behind him—until a hand grabbed her by the hair. The pain to her scalp, quick and severe.

"You're not going anywhere," Jeb growled.

Tasting escape, she fought against Jeb, but he wrenched her head back. Fearing he would rip her hair out, she scrambled in his direction. Delaney worked to keep the loosened rope at her wrists concealed as he hauled her free of the vehicle.

She might still have a chance to use it to her advantage.

Dragging Delaney to her feet, Jeb snarled, "That was a stupid move."

Blood ran down the side of his face. Danger poured from his eyes.

"What are we gonna do now?" came the bedraggled voice from the other side of the truck. "That man's comin' to get us! He's comin'!"

"Shut up, Willie!" Jeb yelled.

Jumping about, the smaller man cried, "He's gonna kill us! He's gonna kill us!"

"I'm gonna shoot you myself, you don't shut your pie hole."

Willie struggled to remain still, bobbing about as though he needed to pee. Delaney turned to Jeb. His hand on her arm was hurting, but she had to delay. "He's right. But if you let me go, you can walk away. Right now." Nick needed time to catch up with them.

Jeb jerked her roughly. "Don't take me for a fool. Your boyfriend's car can't handle these roads. He'll be lucky to make the first half a mile."

He wrenched her arm, she cried out in pain.

"Let's go, girl. And don't try anything stupid—I already have orders to shoot you." Her heart thwacked. "I'll do it here if I have to."

Delaney managed to keep on her feet as Jeb forced her through the heavy brush. Her head had dissolved into a dull ache, most of her pain now coming from the hand digging into her arm. She wanted to work her hands free, but with Willie bringing up the rear, she feared even a slug like him would take notice and alert Jeb. And Jeb meant business, of that much she was sure.

He stopped. She followed his gaze to a small house in the woods and her heart sank. *What a perfect place to dump a body.*

Jeb plowed forward, an added spring to his step.

With renewed panic, Delaney struggled for ideas. She couldn't let it end this way! She had to fight! Had to escape! Willie looked at her, but quickly averted his eyes. Seemed he, too, understood what was at hand.

Delaney's throat went dry, her lungs filled with pressure. With each step closer to the abandoned structure, fear shredded her insides. Four cement walls and collapsed roof, it was all Jeb needed to conceal her body. She tugged and pulled against the rope. If she could only wrangle a hand free—

Jeb kicked in the front door and pushed her inside. Dust flew into the air. Delaney coughed, turning mouth and nose into her shoulder.

"Stay out here and watch for him," Jeb instructed Willie.

"Ye-ye-yes sir," Willie stammered. He glanced around the woods and looked like he expected to see a ghost.

A shot rang out. Delaney dropped to her knees.

Jeb swore, released her. A second shot nicked the door frame with a piercing ricochet. She ducked instinctively—thrilled. Nick had found her!

Willie squealed as he ran into the house. Arms and legs flailing, he slipped and fell, crawling the rest of the way inside. Like a scared mouse, he scurried for safety behind Jeb.

"Why didn't you say anything?" Jeb yelled, firing off a shot, taking cover behind the front wall.

"I didn't see him!" he wailed. Cowering with hands over his head, Willie looked as if he were trying to blend into the wall.

Delaney quickly worked the rope from her wrists. *This was her chance.*

The next bullet shattered the window, sending shards of glass tumbling across the floor near Willie

"Let her go!" Nick called out.

Delaney jumped up to run, but Jeb grabbed her by the arm, pulling her to him. He jabbed the barrel of his gun beneath her chin. Cold metal drilled into her skin.

No one made a move. No one made a sound. She could feel Jeb's heart pound at her back. The slick sweat of his arms moistened her shirt, his odor sour.

Jeb moved Delaney toward the open doorway. Plastering his back to the safety of the cement wall, he eased his head between hers and the door jamb, breathing hard against her hair. He searched for sight of Nick.

Trees, leaves, a dapple of light, but no Nick.

"Last time," Nick yelled. "Let her go or I'm coming in after her."

She and Jeb looked toward the direction of his voice. Other than the shimmer of sunlight through the jungle of green, she saw nothing. But he was there. Beneath the weight of Jeb's meaty arm, her chest rose and fell with the hope of him. He was here. For *her*.

"Go round back," Jeb ordered Willie. "Run around and act as a distraction."

The man glanced up in horror. "What?"

"You heard me," Jeb hissed. "Go on."

Out back was nothing more than a hole in the wall—an avenue for escape if Willie decided to take it.

Delaney seized the opportunity. "Save yourself, Willie. I'll tell Nick not to shoot you, if you run now."

"Shut up!" Jeb barked into her ear. Delaney winced. Willie remained in place, though his expression registered the offer. "Go now, or I'll shoot you myself!" he yelled.

Willie scrambled to his feet. Wary of Jeb, his gaze flitted in and out of the house. He looked to Delaney, to Jeb. "I— I'm going out..." he stuttered, backing toward the far wall. "I didn't mean to hurt nobody, I *swear*."

"Shut your trap—she's lying about helping you!"

Willie double-checked with Delaney. "You didn't do anything," she reaffirmed, and with an intent look from her eyes, willed him to run. "It's not you they'll want."

Jeb jabbed the pistol into the base of her head. She cried out. A bullet clipped the wall outside. As Willie wailed and dashed out the back, Jeb raised his gun and shot blindly into the woods out front.

Willie could be heard hollering "Don't shoot! I surrender, I surrender!"

Jeb reeled off another shot and Delaney jabbed the heel of her boot into his knee. She was finished playing victim. With all her might she pushed away from him, but he yanked her back. Again, she kicked ferociously at Jeb's. The time her effort threw him off balance, and the two of them fell through the front door, landing in a heap on the ground.

Delaney kept up her struggle, hoping to give Nick the time he needed to move in. If Jeb was going to shoot her, now would be the time. She muttered a silent prayer, then bit into his forearm. Jeb yelped and rolled to his side. With a hand to her throat, he scanned the vicinity for Nick, and froze. Delaney peered up, coming face-to-face with the towering vision of Nick Harris, his gun trained at Jeb's head. "Move a muscle and I blow your head off."

Jeb remained still as stone. Heart pounding, Delaney did likewise.

"Toss the gun," Nick said. Jeb did so. "Now get up. *Slowly*."

Delaney watched in stunned disbelief as Nick handled his weapon like a pro. Would he really shoot Jeb? Did he have it in him?

Once Jeb was standing, Delaney rolled free and sprang to her feet. She burrowed into Nick's side. "Thank God you're here," she rasped, pulse skittering through her veins. The large, masculine bicep of a man never felt so good.

Maintaining focus on Jeb, Nick told her, "Call the police. And this time, no argument."

Giddy with relief, Delaney almost laughed. *Protest?* Then it dawned upon her. "I don't have my phone. Clem took it."

Jeb stared at the two of them, and Delaney felt a rush of angst.

Nick pulled the phone from his back pocket and handed it to her. "Use mine."

With trembling fingers she dialed 9-1-1. The call was answered immediately. "I'd like to report a crime," she said.

"I know of more gold on the property," Jeb interrupted. He focused on Delaney, his eyes devoid of emotion. "Let me go free and I'll show you where."

Delaney's attention split between the emergency operator and Jeb. More gold?

"It's bigger than the one Clem knows about."

So they really were trying to swindle Clem...

Jeb tossed a glance toward Nick. "Your man here knows about it, too."

Staunch by her side, gun pointed at Jeb's head, Nick replied, "Don't listen to him. He'll say anything to avoid jail time."

Delaney gaped at Nick, then Jeb.

"He's lying, Delaney."

"I'll show you where it is," Jeb said urgently. "Now— before lover boy cleans you out."

The operator was asking her something, but Delaney missed it. "What?" she asked into the phone and the woman repeated the question. Delaney glanced around. The three of them were faced off in the quiet of trees and brush, the ano-nymity of isolation. "We're near an abandoned house, off old Miller Road. Maybe a mile or two into the forest," she told the 911 operator.

"You stand to lose a lot, Ms. Wilkins," Jeb continued, a new tone of respect in his voice. "I can help you keep what's rightly yours."

Delaney clenched the phone to her ear. "I don't believe you," she told him. Prodded by the operator, Delaney said, "Yes, yes, I'm still here. Yes, I'll hold the line."

"You're making a big mistake," Jeb said.

Chapter Twenty-One

Nick pulled into the drive for Ladd Springs, slowing his car to a stop alongside Ernie's truck. He slid the gear into park and turned to Delaney. He made a striking picture, with his white shirt collar opened at the neck, black curls of hair poking up through the V of his shirt. She basked in the familiarity of his cologne, his raw maleness, the concern stirring deep in his eyes. "You okay?"

Riddled with tension, inundated by doubt, she nodded. "Yes. I'll be fine."

He reached over and took her hand, resting it on her thigh. His long fingers were strong and gentle, his skin warm and soft to the touch. It was a reassuring gesture. A silent motion that said he stood with her, they were in this together. Drawn to the old homestead, Delaney peered at Ernie's cabin with renewed courage. She had her proof. Willie had agreed to testify against Jeb and Clem in exchange for lesser charges. Ernie would finally understand she had been telling the truth about Clem all along.

Delaney repressed the urge to stare at Nick. They had barely spoken during the ride back home. She had been on the phone with Felicity, he content to drive in silence. But Jeb's words lingered. Did Nick know about more gold on the property?

Nick gave a light squeeze to her hand, then rose from the vehicle and rounded the hood to open her door. With a quick calming breath, she took his hand, placed boot to ground and allowed him to help her from the seat. She doubted it. This time, the two of them were on the same side. Her shoulder ached, her head maintained a mild throb, her knees were bruised, but she was okay. She was ready to face Uncle Ernie. Delaney cleared her throat and said, "Let's go."

"Mom!" Felicity called out, sprint flat-out across the tiny bridge in a bee line for her mother.

Tears welled in Delaney's eyes. *"Felicity..."* The afternoon's events melting away at the sight of her daughter, Delaney took off running. Careening into Felicity, she lifted her from the ground in a powerful bear hug.

"You're okay," Felicity whispered ferociously, hugging Delaney hard.

"I'm fine." Great, now that she had her child in hand. With Clem out of the picture, her baby girl would be okay. She would be okay.

Delaney continued the squeeze, the two swaying back and forth as they reconnected, the late afternoon showering the grounds in soothing streams of golden light.

Releasing Felicity at last, Delaney took her hands in her own. She gazed into her child's eyes, thankful for the ease she saw in them. She had not shared the details of the day, only that she was fine and the two of them were going to be okay. "Sweetheart," Delaney said. "I need to talk to Ernie."

Felicity nodded.

"Are Travis and Troy here?" she asked.

"No. Mr. Parker rode home with me."

Of course he did. Morton was that kind of man, that kind of father. "Okay. Sit tight, will you?" Delaney didn't want Felicity learning about the gold find this way. She wanted to sit down with her later and go through everything. All of it. Just the two of them.

Delaney joined Nick cabin side and briefly wondered how Ernie would take the news. No one wanted to hear their trust had been broken, even a cynical old man like him. But he had to know, and it had to make a difference. Her heart lurched. *It had to.*

When Delaney stepped up onto the porch, the door swung open. Beady eyes took her in with menacing suspicion behind the lens of his glasses. Ernie walked out and raked her with a once over. "What happened to you?"

"I had a run-in with Clem."

Ernie addressed Nick. "What kind of run in?"

"Clem tried to have me killed today," she replied, but as she said the words, the shock of reality finally set in. Clem tried to have her killed. *Killed.*

"What are you talkin' about?" he demanded, clearly annoyed by the accusation.

"He's been working with men to steal from you, Ernie."

"He ain't stole nothin' from me," he said, as though she were a silly child, then headed for his rocker.

Bolstered by Nick's presence, Delaney followed, keeping a few steps behind the old man. "He found gold on the property, Ernie. He's been mining it for himself, unbeknownst to us."

"Gold?" His small eyes widened within the black rims of his glasses. "We ain't got no gold around here."

"Yes, we do. We have a vein in a rock over by the west end of the property, just off the trails that run parallel to park land."

We may have two sources. Sharing a glance with Nick, Delaney maintained focus on Ernie. It was a sentiment she wasn't willing to voice. Delaney had no way of knowing whether or not Jeb was lying. She could only trust her instinct. She trusted Nick. "I saw it for myself," she continued. "It's legit." In the few words she and Nick had ex-changed in the car, he claimed to have discovered the gold only this morning. Which made sense, especially in light of their conversation last night.

"You're lyin'." Ernie waved her off.

"She's telling you the truth," Nick said. "Two men were arrested today on kidnapping charges with the intent to commit murder. They kidnapped Delaney per Clem's instructions. The police are looking for him now."

Ernie whipped an angry glance at Nick. "You set this all up, did you? Think you're so smart?" he rambled on, ignoring the reality at hand.

"I had nothing to do with it," Nick replied quietly.

"Fillin' her head with lies about Clem, about gold on the property."

"I saw it for myself, Ernie," Delaney interjected. "Ladd Springs has gold!"

"I don't believe you." He turned away from them. "And I'm tired of you startin' trouble where there ain't none." Ernie pushed off from the ground, rocking to and fro as if he hadn't a care in the world.

Albert emerged from the house. "What's all the fussin' about?"

Ernie glared at him, then returned his attention to the wood railing. "Nothin.'"

Nodding, Albert plodded over to his chair and took his seat alongside Ernie. "Okay."

Delaney couldn't believe what she was hearing. Was Ernie insane? In denial? "Ernie, I can prove it to you. I have pictures." Had them, but could get them again. Once she recovered her backpack—the one Clem took from her. "I have photographs of the rock and the gold in it."

"Don't matter to me."

Delaney and Nick exchanged a stunned glance. "You don't care that the value of this land has just skyrocketed?" she asked. "And that you were considering giving it to a man who was robbing you blind?"

Please, God—tell me I'm not having this conversation! At the sound of the car pulling into the drive, Delaney turned. Relief flooded her body at the sight of Ashley Fulmer's SUV. If anyone could talk some sense into Ernie, it would be Ashley.

The four waited in silence as Ashley made her way to the porch. Wearing turquoise cowboy boots and sequin-covered dress to match, she was toting an oversized basket of fresh garden produce, with carrots, collards, okra and more.

"Hey, darlin'." Ashley waved cheerfully.

"Hey," Delaney murmured in return.

Ashley pounded up the steps and announced, "Ernie, I brought you some vegetables."

"What am I gonna do with those?" he grumbled.

"Boil them. Eat them fresh." She came to a stop before him. "I don't care what you do with them, so long as you swallow them. Ask Albert, he can help you."

At the mention of his name, Albert smiled. "Course I can!" he replied good-naturedly. "I got me a ham hock, too." From his rocker, he surveyed her basket. "You got any beans in there?"

"You know I do!" Ashley sang out, then seemed to notice Delaney's appearance for the first time. Her blue eyes became saucers. "Good Heavens, darlin'! What happened to you?"

"It's a long story, but it ends with Clem Sweeney going to jail," Delaney returned flatly, a fact that brought no small measure of satisfaction.

"*Jail?*" Ashley balked. "What in tarnation has the boy done now?"

"We have gold on the property and he's been stealing it for himself."

Ashley could have been hit with a cast iron skillet. "*Gold?*"

"Gold." Delaney waved a hand toward her uncle, then crossed her arms over her chest. "But Ernie won't listen to a word of it. Maybe you can talk some sense into him."

"Not now, honey." She glanced at Ernie. "I need to get these to the kitchen." Without another word, she disappeared inside.

Delaney stared after her, dumbfounded. Her loyal ally abandoned her for a trip to the kitchen? Had the world tipped upside down?

Delaney checked on Felicity. Sitting near the wishing well, her daughter seemed frozen in place, like a stone statue. Delaney searched Nick's expression for direction.

"How about we come back?" Nick suggested. "Let the news sink in for a while."

"C'mon back with some cornbread, Delaney." Albert smiled broadly. "I'll make up some collards and we'll have some real fixins' for supper!"

Delaney felt as if she stood in a time warp. No one was connecting the dots from one conversation to the next. It was as if each and every one of them were living in their own world, existing in their own universe of reality. She was stumped.

Ashley breezed outside and chirped, "Okay, then. You boys enjoy your veggies. I'll be back tomorrow with some more."

"Do you have any pie, Ashley?" Albert asked shyly.

"You know I do! I'll bring you some tomorrow, honey." To Delaney, she said, "It's getting late. Let's leave them be, and you come tell me all about this gold you've been talking about." Ashley took Delaney by the elbow and steered her toward the stairs.

Dully, Delaney allowed herself to be removed from the porch and ushered to the cars. She glanced at Felicity, who instantly rose and came over to meet them.

Ashley continued her hold on Delaney's arm even as they came to a stop.

"I'm not sure what just happened up there," Delaney muttered.

"Listen, honey," Ashley said. "Your uncle hasn't got much time left." She glanced up at the cabin. "He's real bad off and you need to know about it."

Delaney gaped at her. "What are you talking about?"

Nick and Felicity were intent on Ashley continued.

"Yes, darlin'. It looks like he only has months to live, if that."

What was Ashley talking about? Delaney flung her gaze to Ernie's cabin. The cancer didn't look like it was making a dent—the man was as ornery as ever!

Ashley's blue eyes were serious, intent. "It's moved to his pancreas, darlin', and his doctor said he'd be surprised if the old man made it through the summer."

"Summer? How do you know this?"

"Well," Ashley began, a tinge of shame mellowing her gaze, "I'm not supposed to know anything, but Ida heard her niece Mary Beth talkin' about it to her momma, who said she was plumb crazy over the whole thing. How could it be that Albert didn't say anything to her 'bout it, giving her proper notice so she could come pay her respects."

Delaney nodded. Ida was Ashley's hairdresser and Mary Beth's mother was Albert's ex-wife's sister.

"It's a shame—even though he is an old coot," Ashley said. "No one deserves to die alone, with no one to look after them. I can't imagine what I'd do if it were Booker." She tossed a heartfelt look toward the house and added, "Bless his heart, but that rascal Ernie didn't say the first word about it to anyone."

Delaney understood the vegetable delivery. It was Ashley's way of helping. Whether Ernie wanted her to or not, he was Susannah's brother and Ashley would not let him die alone.

Tears filled Felicity's eyes and Delaney suddenly felt the same heaviness in her heart. Ernie was a lot of things, but he was family. He was blood, her mother's brother. And family came first. All thoughts of gold and Clem and the property fell away. "What can we do?" Delaney asked.

"There's not a thing we *can* do, honey. Just pray the good Lord takes him quick and painless, I reckon." She wrapped an arm around Felicity's shoulders and glanced between Nick and Delaney. "What more is there?"

As Delaney worked through her second glass of wine, she was grateful for Nick's company. The three of them had retreated to her cabin, absorbing the news in the privacy of their own space—like a family. Felicity had retired to her loft, claiming a need to be alone. Nick and she were parked out on the front porch.

Nightfall was submerging the forest around them, injecting the air with a crisp chill. Trees emitted their fragrance, the scent accentuated by the hint of humidity. Showered, Delaney felt one step removed from the day. Her body hurt, but the shock was finally wearing off, reality settling in. "Amazing how life can change so drastically in the span of twelve hours, isn't it?"

"It is," Nick agreed. After a trip to his hotel, he too was freshly showered and cleanly shaven. And he smelled good, Delaney mused. He smelled good and he looked good.

"It doesn't seem real that Ernie is going to die so soon."

"It's a shocker," Nick commented bluntly.

Delaney cradled the glass in her lap and turned to him. Was he being sarcastic? "We knew he was sick, but only months to live?"

Nick cast a look of reproach. "You knew?"

"Yes." But staring down the actuality of his death felt entirely different.

"I'm surprised you're so concerned," Nick said. "It's not like there's a whole lot of love between you two."

"True." Delaney considered the observation. Nick didn't appear to be insensitive on the subject, simply immune to the significance. Could it be they viewed things differently in Montana? "You have to understand," she said. "Ernie's family. He loves Felicity," she asserted. "That counts for something."

It counted for a lot. Though she could see how someone might not understand. Delaney sipped from her wine. Unless you were raised in these parts, it did seem kinda strange, this love-hate relationship they shared.

"Well, Felicity's an easy girl to love."

Delaney smiled. "She is. But she's his blood. She's Susannah's granddaughter, and he'd never abandon her. He could have turned us out onto the streets, but he didn't. For that, I'll always be grateful."

"Does Felicity know about her father?" Nick asked.

"About the drinking, yes. She doesn't know that he hit me." The first hint of disapproval entered Nick's eyes and she defended, "He's her father, Nick. I don't want to tarnish him in her eyes any more than I have to. It hurts enough to know he doesn't come to see her. Do I really need to add insult to injury?" No pun intended, she mused.

He hesitated, and she saw a myriad thoughts pass behind his eyes. "I've found that honesty is always the best course," Nick said.

"You don't have kids. A child changes things, changes you." She paused on the thought. "Did you ever want children?"

"Never seemed a good fit for my lifestyle. I don't stay in one place very long."

Delaney stared into the bowl of her wineglass. The statement cut through the fog of the day with surprising clarity. Nick moved around. He didn't settle. He didn't reside in one locale. He went where ever the next hotel was going up. That was his lifestyle. She set the glass on the wooden table between them. *Foolish to get tied up with a man like that.* Delaney stood abruptly.

"Where are you going?" he asked, mild alarm in his voice.

"I'm tired," she lied. "It's been a long day." She tried to inject humor into her tone, but fell short.

Nick stood and came to her.

"I appreciate everything you did today," she said, realizing at once how completely inadequate her words were. She came close to losing her life this afternoon and if it weren't for this man, she might not be alive this minute. Felicity would be without a mother. Tears swamped her lids. "I don't know how to thank you." She felt her voice break. "You didn't have to risk your life for me, but—"

"I did," he whispered, and cupped her face. "I would have killed them if they harmed you. With my bare hands."

Delaney turned her face into his palm and breathed in the scent of him, the feel of him. His skin was soft, warm. Nick leaned down and kissed her cheek. Slow, supple, his lips sought hers and kissed them. The surprise move buckled her knees.

"Nick," she protested, uncertain as to why she felt the need to stop him.

He gathered her into his arms. "I want you, Delaney. From the first day I saw you, I've wanted you."

She remembered that first day. Rugged, strong, he was a natural in the forest. At the time she had viewed him more as a threat than an object of desire. But his appeal hadn't gone unnoticed. Delaney had been drawn to his smoldering dark eyes from day one, the sheer strength of him, the power he exuded. Nick was a big man, all man and she yearned for a connection with him. A lasting one.

He stared into her eyes, his as black as night. Delaney shivered. It felt as if he could see right through her, could see that she wanted him and planned to take full advantage. "Do you want this as much as I do?"

Old animosities, old doubts bombarded her brain.

"Do you want me, Delaney?"

"Yes, but..."

"Is it that man's words today?" His eyes searched hers. "Did what he say bother you?"

"What?"

"The gold, Delaney," he said, as though she were playing dumb. "Do you think I know of more gold and I'm not telling you?"

"No." Incredibly, she had forgotten about it. But now that he mentioned it...did she?

"The truth," he said.

"I didn't know you knew about the first location," she hedged.

"I told you, I didn't until today. And if you recall, there wasn't exactly time to tell you about it."

She surrendered to a small smile.

"Jeb is a liar." Nick declared. "He'd say anything to save his skin, you need to believe that."

"Why?" she asked without thinking. "Why do I need to believe it?"

Nick's eyes became hooded. "Because if you and I are going to be together, we need to be honest with each other."

Be together? Her lips trembled under his hot gaze.

"I don't know about any other veins, Delaney. In fact, I doubt their existence. From what the jeweler told me, it's a fluke that you have the one."

Her research indicated the same, yet there it was. Gold on Ladd Springs.

"Either way," Nick said. "I don't know about any other gold and if the gold that is here, it belongs to the Ladd family. Ernie, you...and Felicity. I'm not interested in plundering you." He dipped his head down and kissed her. "I take that back," he murmured, hovering inches from her. "I do want to plunder you—your body."

Longing curled her toes.

"What'll it be, Ms. Wilkins? Are you up for a night you'll never forget?"

Nick was asking to make love to her. He wanted to cross the line from whatever it was they were to lovers. Delaney's eyes shot to the loft where Felicity was sleeping. He smiled. "I can be quiet." He pecked her nose. "Can you?"

Chapter Twenty-Two

Nick left at sunrise, per Delaney's strict orders. Where he and Felicity might see no harm in her having "someone" in her life, she wasn't about to move the man in after one night. She still wasn't sure how she felt about it. Lusty desire pulled at her. But a future together?

It was too much. It was too soon. There were too many things to see about before she started entertaining a new relationship, the first of which was Ernie. Delaney's chest constricted. The thought of Ernie dying unleashed a tide of memories. It took her back to the last days of her mother's life, when she knew the end was near. It had been agonizing for Delaney, yet her mother had been oddly calm, as if she knew. She hadn't told Delaney she felt it was time. She'd said her goodbyes earlier in the day, when Delaney had brought Felicity by for a visit, and those were the last words they shared.

Felicity had been six at the time and during the visit, drew pictures of heaven and God for her grandmother, as if she knew, and wanted to assure her all would be well.

Delaney had simply talked. She shared her heart, shared her dreams. It was the only thing she could do at that point. When Ashley told her the next day her mother was gone, Delaney had been crushed. Her mother didn't include her in her last moments?

Ashley told her Susannah wanted her daughter's last memories to be of life and love, not death and sadness. Did Ernie feel a sense of calmness as his last days neared? Had he told Albert, the one person most likely to be at his side?

Delaney shook her head and wrapped the last loaf of cornbread, sliding it into the paper bag with the others. It wasn't hers to decide. What mattered is that they were here for him, that they made sure his last days on earth would pass as easy as possible.

At the sound of Felicity's arrival home from school, Delaney set the bag of bread aside and reached for a plate of fried gizzards. "Don't take your boots off," she called out. The bread was still warm and she wanted to hurry and get the food over to Ernie, but she had been waiting for her daughter.

Felicity poked her head inside the door. "Did you call me?"

"I did," Delaney said. "Keep your boots on. We're going to Ernie's."

Lifting her nose, Felicity sniffed the air. A gleam entered her eyes. "Chicken gizzards?"

"They're his favorite." Delaney rarely made them, due to the odor. Since the cabin had few windows to open for ventilation, the scent had a way of soaking into every nook and cranny, lingering for days. But if fried gizzards couldn't bring a smile to Ernie's face, nothing would. "I want you to come with me," she told her daughter.

"Okay," she replied happily.

The two headed down the path. In the open clearing, Felicity stopped just shy of the creek. Placing a boot on the bridge she stared at her mother. Clouds passed overhead, the babble of water the only sound between them.

"What?" Delaney asked her.

"Should we say we know?"

"Why wouldn't we?"

"Well..." A light breeze blew the hair from Felicity's face as concern crowded her gaze. "Didn't Ashley say she wasn't supposed to know?"

"Foolishness. I know, and he's going to know I know."

"Are you sure? Don't you think he might get mad?"

Delaney wanted to laugh. "Let him. Ernie gets mad at everything." Ornery old *fool*. But it was probably his temperament that had kept him alive this long.

"If you say so." Bag of cornbread in hand, Felicity fell into step and followed her mom over the arched wooden bridge and to the house. Up the steps they trekked and Delaney rapped on the screen door. "Ernie!" Without waiting for a reply, she entered.

Albert looked up from his chair. He spied the plate in her hand and his eyes lit up. "You brought us some vittles?"

"Gizzards and cornbread," she told him. Glancing up the stairs, she asked, "Where's Ernie?"

Ernie hobbled out of the kitchen, cane in hand. Pounding the end of it onto the floor he said, "I'm right here." When he saw Felicity, his demeanor softened a degree. He glanced between the women and asked, "What do you want?"

"We brought you some food."

He eyed the plate and bag like they concealed a rattle-snake. "What for?"

Delaney walked over to him and lowered her voice. "We know about...your condition."

Ernie's eyes nearly burst from his skull. His skin flushed red as he demanded, "Who told you? That's privileged in-formation!"

"Doesn't matter. We know and we're here for you." She extended the plate toward him. "We made you some gizzards and cornbread."

Felicity took that as her cue to approach. "Here, Uncle Ernie." Her voice broke, tears lined her eyes. "Fresh-baked cornbread."

"I didn't want nobody knowin' about this!" he wailed.

Delaney tried to calm him. "It's okay, Ernie. We're fam-ily."

"No it ain't!" He jabbed a crooked finger toward Felici-ty. "Look at her! She's cryin'!"

Felicity had a heart of gold but not an ounce of stoicism to her name. "She's upset. As am I." Delaney inwardly shrank from the wrath twisting his features. The man look possessed.

"No you're not! You want me dead! Don't lie. You think you can take the property easier without me in the picture!"

"Ernie, *stop*." Delaney swept a glance around the room, set the plate down on the dining table to free her hands, in the remote possibility she needed to defend herself from physical attack. "We're here because we *care*."

"You don't care about me—never did!"

Felicity, bag clenched to her midsection, stood shaking, an utter look of horror pasted on her face. By contrast, Albert sat placidly in his ratty chair, hands folded over his enormous coverall-clad stomach.

"Please." Delaney tried to quiet Ernie. "Can't you see you're upsetting her?"

His eyes tore into Felicity. Visibly struggling with his emotion, he worked hard to reel himself in, his thin lips trembling. To Delaney, it looked as if Ernie had so many things he wanted to say to her, so many things he wanted Felicity to know. Then his gaze turned glassy red, and Delaney's heart ached at the sight of him. Even from ten feet away, she could hear him breathing, his breath raspy and labored. For the first time, she recognized the signs of physical stress. Ernie didn't have long.

For a long moment, the old man stood rigid in place, looking from child to mother, mother to child. Delaney wanted to intercede, to placate him, but how? It was obvious what he thought of *her*. For a long moment, the old man stood rigid in place.

"Ernie, we do care," Delaney insisted, keeping her plea soft, non-threatening. "We've had our differences, but it doesn't mean we don't care what happens to you. We're *family*." Doesn't that mean anything to you? she wanted to ask, but refrained. Her goal was not to provoke him. It was to provide compassion as he faced his last days.

Ernie stalked over to his recliner and took his seat in silence.

Did she dare try and take a seat herself?

Felicity suddenly walked straight over to her great uncle, leaned over and kissed the top of his bald head. "I love you, Uncle Ernie."

Tears swamped Delaney's lids.

Felicity set the cornbread down on the coffee table before him and asked, "Would you like me to go get my flute?"

Ernie didn't respond.

Albert asked hopefully. "Is that cornbread, you got there?"

"It is," Felicity answered him. She wiped her eyes and placed it on the sofa table. "There's enough for you two to share. If you'd like, I can bring down some more later, when I come to play my flute." She turned to Ernie. "If it's okay with you that I still come..."

He looked up at her and Delaney swore he was about to cry. "Of course I want you to come play for me, child."

Felicity smiled. "Thank you."

If her daughter had won the Nobel Peace Prize, Delaney wouldn't have been more proud of her. Her daughter was strong and selfless, gracious and generous—but mostly, Felicity was pure love. Delaney went over, wrapped an arm around her shoulders and admired how her slender frame stood erect and firm within her grasp.

Ernie hardened as he turned his attention to Delaney. "Ain't you gonna tell me about our court date?"

"I'm not," she returned quietly.

"Why ain't you?" he demanded, as though angry she wasn't rising to the bait.

"It's not important."

Ernie practically came out of his chair. "It sure seemed important last week!"

She nodded. "That was last week."

Ernie scowled at her. "I don't believe you."

She shrugged and bowed her head, defeat settling heavy upon her shoulders. Demanding that a dying man head to court, so she could fight him for title to the property didn't seem right. His last days should be spent with family, but in a good way, not haunted by feuds and greed. The police had called this morning and informed her that Clem was in custody and she could pick up her backpack at the station.

With Clem out of the picture and in no way able to get his hands on the property, Delaney had to resign herself to the facts. If Ernie wanted to will the property to Felicity, he would. If not, who else? Jeremiah? Albert?

It was out of her control. But either way, fighting her mother's brother to the edge of his grave was not going to happen. Delaney turned to go. Felicity turned with her.

"You can't pay the taxes," Ernie muttered behind her. "You want this place so dad-burned bad, but you can't even pay for it."

Pay the taxes? Delaney pivoted slowly, a slew of resentment rising hot in her breast.

"Do you even know how much they are?" he asked.

"Do you mean yearly, or the balance you haven't paid in the last three years?" she asked, unable to keep the anger from slipping into her tone.

"I got better things to do with my money," he grumbled.

"*Than pay the taxes?*" she asked, incredulous to his total disregard.

"I'm donatin' my money to breast cancer."

Delaney almost fell over. The breath emptied from her lungs. She grabbed hold of Felicity, as though she needed to steady herself. *Breast cancer?* Was he serious?

Ernie looked away, avoiding the onslaught he must surely expect to be slung at him this very minute and with good reason. Breast cancer killed his sister. The same breast cancer diagnosis he refused to believe, the treatment he refused to fund. Yet now he was going to support cancer research with the money that should be going to property taxes? Taxes to save the property he'd promised to bequeath to his sister's daughter and granddaughter?

Delaney felt nauseous.

"Mom," Felicity asked. "Are you okay?"

"I'm fine," she replied, sadness curbing her anger. "Fine."

Ernie reached over to the side table alongside his chair and pulled a white envelope from the lower compartment. He thrust it toward her. "Here."

"What's that?"

"What you've been wantin' so badly."

Delaney walked over and took the envelope from him, turning it over in her hands. There was no name, no address. It was completely blank.

"It's title to the land."

Delaney's jaw went slack. Was he kidding? Her eyes went quickly to Felicity as she slid a shaky finger to loosen the flap.

"It's in Felicity's name," he said pointedly. "It belongs to her, not you. And she don't get it until I die."

Delaney looked inside and couldn't believe it. Was the title to Ladd Springs really inside this envelope she held?

Felicity placed a hand to her forearm. Comfort. Solidarity.

"But I ain't payin' the taxes," he said, avoiding any eye contact with Felicity. "Them there is your problem."

"But why, Ernie?" Delaney asked. "Why give us the property now, after all this time, after everything we've been through?" It didn't make sense. None of it made any sense.

Delaney received no answer. And in that moment she realized she never would. Most likely, Ernie didn't have an answer to give. He'd made his choice back when his sister was alive—for inexplicable reasons—and he was doing so again. Poor choices, good choices, did anyone know what drove them to act as they did?

Delaney dropped her gaze to the envelope in hand. Excitement bloomed. Felicity could go to college and stay in college, get the training for the career she wanted to pursue! When Delaney looked up at Ernie, she felt the urge to hug him. Instead, she gave the nod to Felicity.

The girl hurried over and encircled him with her arms. "Thank you, Uncle Ernie!" She hugged him fiercely. *Thank you so much.*

Delaney leaned against a wood column on her cabin's porch and stared out into the thick mass of forest. Trees and brush and mountainous earth cradled her mother's cabin, protected it from the harsh elements, the world at large, making it indeed her safe haven. Felicity was down at Ernie's a bit earlier than usual, playing to both their hearts' content while she stood alone with her thoughts. It had finally happened. No more lawyers, no more fights. The property belonged to her and Felicity.

Delaney didn't care that only her daughter's name appeared on the title. The two were a team. They could stay on Ladd land and live their lives the way their ancestors had—among the mountains and streams, springs and serenity. *Serenity Springs*. The name took form in her mind. Had Nick seen in this property what others took for granted? Had he seen the potential and believed it worth fighting for?

The screen door creaked and Delaney's hand flew to her throat. "Good grief—" She whirled around to see Nick step inside the porch. "*You scared me*," she exclaimed breathlessly.

"You seemed a bit faraway there." He neared, affection mingling with concern. "Everything okay?"

Heartbeats thrashing through her chest and shoulders, she nodded, breathing in and out to calm the hammer of her pulse as he approached. It was not quite dark out, the embers of sunset glazing the porch in golden tranquility. Nick leaned down and kissed her softly on the lips, his fresh drift of cologne mixing with the rich scent of forest hovering in the air. He lingered, and kissed her again, sliding moist lips across hers.

Delaney's insides groaned with pleasure. That was nice.

"So how's Ernie?" he asked. "Is the illness hitting him hard?"

"I'd say so. He signed the property over to Felicity."

Nick arched a brow. "Come again?"

"Handed us the papers this afternoon," she said, suddenly overwhelmed with joy. A part of her felt guilty over celebrating at a time when her uncle was facing such misery. But another part of her was excited for the future.

"You must be thrilled."

Her pleasure quickly faded. "I am."

"That's about the saddest happy face I've ever seen."

Delaney tried to smile. "It doesn't feel quite right, you know?" She glanced down toward Ernie's home. "He's facing the end and we're facing the future." Delaney yearned for Nick to make her feel better, convince her that everything was okay and she wasn't a bad person. "It's not right."

Nick placed a finger beneath her chin and held her in his gaze. "It's life."

"But his is ending so awfully."

"It didn't have to be this way," Nick said. "Your uncle chose to be angry, chose to drag you through the muddy river before agreeing to what should have been a no-brainer. You have nothing to feel guilty or ashamed of. This property belongs in your family."

"But you wanted to buy it." The blunt force of her words caught him on the jaw.

"I did. Until I came to know you and Felicity."

"And now you don't want it anymore?" Delaney grunted and turned from him. She locked arms over her chest. "I find that hard to believe."

Nick placed his hands on her shoulders and turned her back to face him. Dark eyes smoldered as they normally did, usually when he was about to take charge. "I never said I didn't want it. I simply don't need to own it."

"I don't understand."

"I want to build my hotel here. I can do that with you and Felicity."

A tremor of excitement shimmied up her spine. "*What*?"

"You heard me." Nick lightened his hold, slid his hand up and down her arms as though warming her, then untied her arms and intertwined his fingers through hers. The connection was gentle, intimate. "I want us to build this hotel together."

"Together?" She balked. "But I don't even have the money to pay the taxes. How am I going to help build a hotel?" Though she found the proposition enticing. Build a hotel with Nick? That would take years, right? Side-by-side, day after day. It certainly would ensure that he wouldn't be going anywhere any time soon—a proposition she liked even better than the first.

"I may be able to help you with that." A wry smile tipped the corner of his mouth upward.

"By buying the property," she said glumly, swallowing her disappointment. Why did she let herself fall so easily?

"By signing a hundred year lease."

She pulled back. "A what?"

He squeezed her hands, his smile turning into a grin. "Technically, ninety-nine years, but who's counting? It gives us one to grow on, he added with a wink."

"Nick. Be serious."

"I am." Lifting her hands to his mouth, he pressed his lips to her fingers. "It'll give me enough time to get to know you better."

"Nick, *stop*." Delaney meant his teasing, though the feel of his warm lips against her skin reminded her of their night together—a night she wanted to repeat. But a hundred years? Was a lease that long even possible?

"The 99-year lease is a business arrangement used to ensure the lessee rights to the use of a property, without actually holding title to it." He cupped his large hands around hers and held firm. "You own the property, but give me a 99-year lease. I build my hotel, at my expense, while paying you for the use of your land. It's a win-win."

"What happens if I decide I don't want to be in the hotel business anymore?"

Nick cocked his head. "Giving up on us already?"

Delaney ignored the spray of nerves, his adorable pout and said, "I'm being realistic. What if things don't work out between us, what then?"

"We re-negotiate the terms of the deal."

"Would I be stuck with a hotel?"

He laughed and relinquished her hands. "Good grief, woman! You make it sound like a punishment!"

"Well... I can't afford the taxes. I doubt I'll be able to afford a hotel."

Nick slid his arms around her waist and pulled her to him. Warm within his embrace, she tried to evade the amusement dancing in his devilishly black eyes. "You wouldn't have to buy it. I would have to sell to someone more your type and let you two run off on your merry way while I found a hole to curl up and die in."

"*Nick.*" She squeezed his muscular torso, luxuriating in the solid feel of his body next to hers.

"If you're planning our future demise, I have to be realistic, don't I?"

"I'm not planning our future demise."

Nick leaned down and planted a kiss on her forehead. "You're not?"

"No." She tilted her head up and his mouth sought hers. "I'm not," she murmured as he kissed her—the way she wanted him to kiss her, yearned for him to kiss her.

Nick sighed. "Can we start planning our hotel, then?"

Delaney giggled like a school girl. "Are you using me for my land, Mr. Harris?"

"Not at all. It's all about your body, Ms. Wilkins." He enclosed his mouth over hers again, sliding his tongue in and around, as if he couldn't probe deep enough, hard enough.

Delaney matched his tempo, an urgency building inside her. Last night with Nick had meant something to her. A lot of something. To think that he felt the same way was everything she wanted. More than she could have hoped for. And if the surge of desire she felt was any indication, she wanted him right now.

The sensation of Nick's mouth and hips ran together in her mind, her body, fusing the pleasurable feelings inside and outside into one. She ached for him to hold her, to love her. Everything about him was masculine, strong. Delaney did not consider herself a weak woman, but she was powerless to resist him.

Boots pummeled up the stairs, the porch door swung open.

Delaney gasped, jerking away from Nick. "Felicity!"

Her daughter stood in the doorway, her body a narrow silhouette against the backdrop of the fading sun. Horrified that her daughter had witnessed the two of them, Delaney could only hope that her child was not appalled by the scene. But she couldn't see her face.

Delaney held her breath, straightening her shirt as Felicity strolled toward them. Her daughter's face came into the glow of cabin light. "You two need to get a room." Calmly, she deposited her flute case by the front door, then proceeded to tug her boots free

Relieved by the hint of humor in her daughter's voice, Delaney realized Felicity was encouraging her...*again.* Delaney cleared her throat. "I have a room, thank you."

Felicity chuckled. "You might try using it." Picking up her case, she opened the door and wiggled her fingers goodbye. "Night, Mr. Harris."

Nick grinned broadly and raised a hand. "Night, Felicity."

Delaney gaped after her daughter. "Did that really just happen?"

"It did, and she's right." Dropping his sultry gaze to her mouth, he murmured, "We need a room."

Chapter Twenty-Three

Delaney grabbed her gun from the dresser top. Fear skirted through her pulse. Nine o'clock in the morning, who the hell was pounding on her front door? Had Jeb gotten out of jail?

Nick and Felicity had gone, leaving Delaney alone. She edged her way along the wall and peeked around the corner. Holding the gun low by her side, she cocked the pistol and steeled her arm.

"Delaney Wilkins! I know you're in there!"

Delaney bolted erect. *Annie?* What the heck was she doing here?

Uncocking the gun, she slipped the pistol back into her boot, pulled her jean pant leg down and walked to the door. With a shake to her hair, she braced her nerves and opened the door. "Do you mind not destroying my property?"

Annie marched past her and whirled. "So you've done it. You've finally done it."

As Delaney stared into Annie's fiery blue eyes, her demeanor primed for attack, realization dawned. *News travels fast.* Delaney set hands to hips and stood astride. "Done what, Annie? Secured the rightful ownership of Ladd Springs?"

"Oh, save your high and mighty tone with me," she fumed. "I'm sick and tired of your holier-than-thou attitude. I've come to inform you that this is not over. My lawyer will contest the transfer of title."

"Since when is a man not within his rights to sign over his property?"

"Since he's working under duress."

"Duress?"

"Duress." Annie stepped forward and jabbed a finger toward Delaney's face. "It is illegal to unduly influence a person to gain power over their property."

Delaney bit out a laugh. "You might want to get your terms straight. Which is it? Duress, or undue influence?"

"Don't get smart with me."

"Get smart with you? How about I educate you on the facts?" Staring her down eye-to-eye, Delaney could almost feel Annie's heart pumping as hard and angry as her own. "Ernie signed the property over to Felicity. That's the only thing that matters."

"What about Jeremiah? Don't you think he'll have something to say about it? He'd have to release his rights for Felicity to get Ladd Springs."

Annie sucked the wind from Delaney's confidence. "What?"

Now it was Annie's turn to gloat. "Oh, yes. Or didn't you know?"

"But it was Grandpa Ladd's name on the title, not Jeremiah's."

"Tell a court of law. The fine print says otherwise."

Fine print? What the hell was Annie talking about?

"Oh," Annie added. "And don't do anything to the property I wouldn't do. It won't be yours for long."

Nick exited the jewelry store and pulled out his phone. The sidewalk was deserted, most folks somewhere else at two in the afternoon. After one call to his attorney this morning, his plans were moving forward. He dialed Malcolm's number. Once the paperwork was drawn up and Felicity signed on the dotted line, he was in business. The irony struck him. Felicity would have to sign. His new landlord was barely eighteen years old. He chuckled. Definitely new territory for him!

"Nick."

"Hey," he responded, glancing at the bags of manure and pine mulch piled in neat stacks outside a hardware store. "I have good news."

"I heard. Lanny called me right after he got off the phone with you."

Nick smiled into the phone. "Stealing my thunder, is he?"

"Saving your butt. I've been on the phone with investors all morning, steering them back on course. Jillian almost snagged another one, so you can thank me later."

Well-acquainted with Malcolm's paybacks, Nick smiled. "How much will that cost me?"

"Plenty. But listen, I don't have a lot of time at the moment. When are you coming back? We need to get started on drawing up the plans."

"Well, that's one of the things I'm calling you about, Mal." He swung his gaze into a thrift store, where ladies' dresses lined the display window. "I'm going to have a survey done on the property. I have some leeway as to site location, so I plan to stay another week or so and explore the land by foot."

"Is that really necessary? I thought most of it was forest land. Seen one tree, you've seen them all, right?"

Nick laughed. "Malcolm, haven't I taught you better? You must become one with the land, get to know her secrets before you can exploit them for highest and best value."

"You met someone?"

Nick laughed again, but this time it reached deep and low into his abdomen, stirring old feelings of want. "You know me too well."

"Yes, and sometimes your penchant for women translates into trouble for Harris Hotels."

"Jillian hasn't made a dent in our reputation."

"Not for lack of trying!"

Slowing as he neared his car, Nick chided, "Yes, well, who knew she was psychotic?"

"She hides it well, I'll give you that," Malcolm replied. "But I thought you would have learned your lesson about mixing business with pleasure."

Nick stopped just short of his car. "Except this time I think I'm in love."

"Yeah, I'm in love *every* time—the point remains the same."

Nick shook his head and replied, "Touché." Pressing the key fob to unlock his door, he said, "Listen, don't worry about my love life. This deal is sweeter than we could have imagined. But I need you here. How soon before you can catch a flight?"

"To Tennessee?"

He chuckled. "Well... I'm not in Bali."

"Are you kidding me? I'm up to my eyeballs in paperwork! I can't come down there. What could possibly be so important that you need me on site and not in the office?"

"Gold, Malcolm."

"Gold?"

Nick nodded. "In more ways than one."

Delaney resisted the urge to place another call to her attorney's office. She'd called twice, the man had her number, he'd return her call when he was free. She paced the kitchen, checked on the cornbread again and chastised herself aloud, "The bread won't bake any faster, you keep looking at it!" She tossed the oven door closed.

She spun on her socked heel and dropped back against the counter. But she was going crazy. Was Annie right? Did she have a point? Delaney didn't recall any fine print referring to Jeremiah. What could she be talking about? Was there more to the title than what was listed in the public records? Were there other papers, other documentation regarding the property? If so, how did Annie know about them and Delaney didn't?

She wanted to call Nick, but she didn't want to appear ignorant—especially after all the plans they started laying out last night in bed. Her lawyer could answer the legal questions about title and rights. He'd know what to do.

But she wanted Nick to help her. She wanted Nick to make this go away—they were planning a hotel together! Maybe even a life. She couldn't let Annie ruin her plans before they even got started.

Footsteps sounded heavily across the front porch and Felicity burst in through the front door. "Mom!"

The frantic call of her name gutted Delaney. She rocketed from the counter.

Fear popped in Felicity's delicate features. "It's Casey!"

"*Casey?*"

"She's in the hospital," she cried.

"The hospital?" Delaney clutched hold of the island, alarm crawling through her. "What on earth for?"

"She overdosed."

Standing in the emergency room waiting room, Annie Owens was a wall of anger. Beneath the stark lighting, worry carved deep lines around her mouth, across her forehead. Ice filled her gaze and she raised her chin indignantly. "What is she doing here?"

Waved off by Ashley, Delaney hung back, Felicity hovering by her side. With no time to change, Delaney still wore a tank top smudged with cornmeal and buttermilk, her hair pulled back into a hapless ponytail. But then again, there weren't many folks who would see her. The waiting room was practically empty.

"I invited her," Ashley stated crisply. She took a step forward, inserting herself between Annie and Delaney, her hot pink dress and boots ridiculously out of place in the somber environment. As usual, the woman looked as if she were headed for the dance floor and not a family crisis.

"What for?" Annie asked. "She's the one who caused this."

"Malarkey!" Ashley exclaimed. "That's nothing but tomfoolery, Annie, and I won't stand for you saying another evil word. Delly didn't cause this any more than you did."

But the accusation stung. Part of Delaney felt it may be true.

Ashley moved closer to Annie and lowered her voice. "The child is troubled, Annie. She needs help. This is just her way of cryin' out for it."

Annie turned her back on her godmother, but her wrath didn't dim. It scorched the room and everyone in it.

Delaney hugged arms to her body. The girl was troubled, but drugs? She never suspected it had gone that far. After turning Casey away at Fran's, an overdose was the last thing Delaney expected to happen. How had she fallen so far into depression? Felicity and Casey were friends at school. They ran in the same circles. It's how Felicity learned of her condition. *Did you hear? Casey Owens overdosed.*

From there, word spread like a Tennessee wildfire through the rural high school.

"Annie," Delaney murmured. "If there's anything we can do..."

Annie turned on her, fury setting the pain ablaze. "Do? Haven't you done enough already?"

"Annie—"

"Don't Annie me," she spat. "You all but called my daughter illegitimate to her face—*and you wonder why she's upset?*"

Delaney balked. "I did not."

"'The property belongs to *Ladds*,'" Annie mimicked. "Ring a bell?"

Delaney shrank in the wake of indictment. Casey must have run straight home to Annie and repeated the encounter verbatim.

"Whether you like it or not," Annie said, daggers shooting from her eyes. "Casey belongs to Jeremiah. She's a Ladd, same as you."

Delaney didn't come here to cause trouble, but she wasn't going to roll over and play dead, either. Noting Ashley and Felicity had faded into the background of the confrontation, Delaney took the reins, she stepped forward and said,

"Annie, whether she is or isn't hasn't been established. So under the circumstances I think it's fair to say the property rightly goes to Felicity."

Resentment pulsed through Annie's features, colored the blue of her eyes with an unsettling mix of worry and anger and hate. "Do you think I care any less for my daughter than you care for yours?"

"Of course not."

"You divorced, Jack. We're both single mothers." Annie screwed her face into a display of disgust. "Tell me how we're so different again?"

Delaney shifted her weight from heel to heel. "Annie, please. You're not even sure who Casey's father is," she quietly accused.

"I am. It's Jeremiah Ladd." Annie hesitated for the briefest of seconds, like a cat ready to pounce, but then her expression calmed and Delaney's skin tingled. She flashed a glance to Ashley, as though warning sirens would ring out any moment. "I wonder how he'd feel," Annie added, "knowing that you're stealing his inheritance." Delaney felt the hit swift and firm to her gut. "Perhaps someone should call him." Annie's nostrils flared. "Before it's too late."

Delaney was floored. Annie Owens was a lot of things, but calling Jeremiah? Was she out of her mind? She knew how Ernie felt about his son—how Jeremiah felt about his father. Was she that bitter? Hell bent on destroying the family to get what she wanted, no matter the cost?

The mere thought of Jeremiah entering the picture was toxic. Pure poison.

Staring at Annie through a haze of disbelief, the waiting room felt like it was suspended in time. Delaney ran a hand over top of her head, down her ponytail and asked, "What's the point, Annie? Is it money you're after?"

"I'm after what rightfully belongs to my daughter, same as you," Annie declared.

Placing a hand to her forehead, Delaney drew it halfway down her face and stared. Deep down, Delaney had the sneaking suspicion that, given the chance, Annie would sell the place and run with the money. She didn't care about the legacy of Ladd Springs. She didn't have memories that bound her to the land, family members buried in its soil. She wanted money. Legitimacy. Delaney spewed out a sigh. "This is stupid."

"I agree." Ashley stepped in and seized the opportunity to bust them apart. "Hissing at each other like two angry possums isn't gonna solve a thing." She pointed toward the emergency ward, bracelets clanging at her wrist. "We've got a child in their fighting for her life. She needs all the support she can get, and I demand you two put your differences aside and focus on what's important." She checked with Felicity, as if seeking her agreement.

Felicity nodded, her green eyes glistening.

"There's plenty enough time later to argue over who deserves what. Right now, we've got to come together, bow our heads and pray for Casey." Ashley reached out and grabbed hold of Annie and Delaney, drawing them to either side of her. Felicity filled in between her mother and Annie. "We're family," Ashley declared and bowed her platinum head of hair. "Let's start acting like it."

Nick was waiting for Delaney at the cabin when she arrived home. The sight of his car parked near Ernie's was a welcome sight—more so than she could have imagined. Like a mountaintop breath of fresh air, the knowledge that Nick was here to help her through this maze of legal wrangling and emotional bribery eased her spirit. Throughout the entire ordeal, Nick had managed a calm mind, a firm hand—a can-do attitude. Unfortunately, it was more than she could say for herself.

Delaney hurried up the last stretch of trail, looking forward to losing herself in his capable arms. She had dropped Felicity off at Travis and Troy's home, securing Betty Ann Parker's promise to drive Felicity home after dinner. In the wake of Casey's tragedy, Felicity wanted to be with the boys. And Delaney? She wanted to be with Nick.

He met her at the door with the warm hug she had been yearning for. "Delaney..." he murmured her name into the top of her head and squeezed her to him.

She slid her arms around him, the hard line of his body warm and reassuring as she buried her face in his chest.

Nick squeezed harder and asked, "Is she okay?"

She will be, Delaney thought. But as it stood, Casey was facing an uphill battle. According to Ashley, this wasn't the girl's first experience with drugs. She'd dabbled with pills before, but never to this extent. "I hope so."

Nick pulled away and peered into her face. He brushed the hair from her eyes, glided his thumb over her cheek. "You look tired. Come in and let me get you something to eat."

The offer pulled a smile from her. Nick was in her home, offering her something to eat? She shook her head. Now there's a twist! A twist she liked.

It was a twist she liked. Nick helped Delaney pull the boots from her feet, taking the pistol from her as he escorted her inside and onto the sofa. He set her gun on the end table and settled in beside her. He gathered her in his arms and asked, "What'll it be? Cornbread? Grits? What do you southern girls eat around here when in need of some comfort?

Nestled in his warmth, Delaney laughed. "Would you know how to make either one?"

"Not exactly." Nick returned a sheepish grin, rendering his tough masculine features to boyish innocence. "It was a side of him she enjoyed. But I'm always game for experimenting. Found a half-baked loaf in the oven."

"Didn't have a lot of notice when I left." Delaney leaned into his shoulder, burrowing into the crux of his chest and arm. "Thanks for the offer to cook, but I'm not hungry."

"Glass of wine?" he asked. Pulling the elastic band from her hair, he stroked the length of it.

She laid her head against him. Such a simple gesture, but she found it incredibly soothing. After their nights together, his tender way of lovemaking, she found him incredibly soothing. "I think I'd like to sit for a while." She looked up at him. "If you don't mind?"

He gently pushed her head back. "Not a bit. This works perfectly for me."

The two sat in silence for several moments, the wooden interior of her cabin painted in gold as sunlight simmered into evening. Delaney contemplated the best way to broach the subject of Annie's threat. The fact that she had the audacity to bring Jeremiah into the picture terrified Delaney. As Ernie's direct descendent, Jeremiah Ladd was the one person Delaney feared could interfere with her daughter's future with regard to Ladd Springs.

"Why so tense, Delaney?" Nick asked, rubbing his hands up and down her arms, the length of her thighs. "What's the matter?"

Everything. She hugged him closer, relishing the solid feel of him, the warmth of his body. Nothing. Not with you by my side.

Nick slid a hand along her cheek and pushed the hair away from her neck. He massaged the muscles along her neck and shoulders, his large hands pulling the tension from her, replacing it with desire. It felt good to have Nick touch her, but right now, she needed his brain. With a fierce squeeze, she pulled away from him—but not too far. She needed the feel of his body next to hers, the sense the two were connected, that they were a team. "Annie made some threats at the hospital this afternoon."

"Threats?" Black eyes and brows gathered like a building storm on the horizon. "What kind of threats?"

Gazing into the depths of his dark gaze, hot, fluid—unreadable—Delaney hesitated. After all, she and Nick weren't family. They might be becoming important to one another, but they weren't family. She searched Nick's eyes, as though she could detect the truth. She wanted to trust him, to build a future together. She knew Jeb had most likely been lying to save his own skin, but... After all, how much did she really know about the man?

Nick moved the hair from her eyes. "Talk to me, Delaney. Something's going on, I can see it."

"Annie threatened to call Jeremiah."

"Jeremiah?"

"Ernie's son."

"I thought you said no one would call him?"

Delaney didn't like the sudden pour of concern into Nick's eyes. Tentatively, she revealed, "Annie says Ernie doesn't have the power to transfer title to Felicity without his son's approval. Something about the fine print."

Nick stiffened. "And you believe her?"

"I don't know," she answered meekly.

"Listen," he said, and pulled her up from the sofa. "Enough of this negative talk. We'll deal with things when and if they arise. In the meantime, I have something for you."

She paused, swamped by confusion. "Have something for me?"

"Yes. I've been waiting for the right time, but there doesn't seem to be a right time around here."

Delaney followed Nick over to the kitchen island where his briefcase sat. He reached into the outer pocket of the soft leather bag and pulled out a small velvet box. A quick lump formed in her throat. Oh my—was he proposing? Her pulsed skyrocketed through her chest, her limbs. He opened the box, and her heartbeats fluttered wildly. Inside laid a gold pendant. "Nick?"

"I had this made from the gold piece I chipped off from the rock in the woods." Nick pulled it free, gathering the delicate chain in his fingers. "It's a wishing well."

"A wishing well?" she asked, trying to unravel the odd look in his eyes.

"Yes." He unclasped the chain and placed it around her neck. The brush of his fingers tingled across her skin as they secured the chain behind her neck. Drawing his hands forward, he tenderly held her face and gazed into her eyes. "I want you to think about all your hopes for the future, all the possibilities that await you in life."

Delaney touched the petite chunk of gold at her collarbone, the metal cool and heavy against her skin, heedless to the tremble of her hand. "You had this made?"

He nodded. "After I had it tested for authenticity, I had the jeweler in town form it into a wishing well." Admiring the piece, he said, "He does good work."

Delaney laughed nervously and fiddled with the pendant, she said, "He's been there for years."

"Well, it looks great." Nick dropped his gaze to her lips. "*You* look great," he murmured, then kissed her, soft and sweet. Delaney's insides melted and she privately scorned her ridiculous leap to conclusion. *Propose*. They'd only been together a few weeks!

But truth be known, Delaney would have said yes.

Nick's dark eyes moved between the pendant at her breast and her face. He rubbed his thumb over her fingers and murmured, "Diamonds would suit you, too."

# # #

The End

Delaney's Southern Cornbread

2 cups yellow cornmeal
2 cups buttermilk
3 TBSP melted bacon drippings, extra to grease pan
1 egg
1 tsp baking soda
1/2 tsp salt
1/4 cup vanilla pudding mix (optional ~ to add moisture)
2 TBSP sugar (optional ~ for the sweet tooth!)

Preheat oven to 400°F. Grease bottom and sides of 10" cast iron skillet with bacon fat. For crispier crust, pre-heat skillet for 10 minutes before adding batter. Mix all ingredients above together and pour into greased pan. Bake for 30 minutes. Serve warm. 8 servings.

***Mind you there are tons of variations for this recipe, like adding bacon bits, fresh corn kernels, jalapeño peppers ~ but whatever you do, don't tell my mother I added sugar and pudding mix, 'cause she'll have my hide!

However, there's one modification she will approve and that's Grandma Lulu's way. Combine the buttermilk, cornmeal (self-rising), salt and pepper and whisk until smooth. Heat a small cast iron skillet to medium on stove top. Melt a slice of butter in pan, then pour a 1/4 cup of batter into the pan, spreading it out pancake style.

Cook several minutes or until bottom is golden brown, then flip (I add another swatch of butter before the corn cake hits the pan for the second time!). Cook until underside is golden brown (won't take long), then remove from pan and eat immediately!

All I can say is "Yum." My family thought this method tasted like a regular pancake and I could only shake my head in wonder. Those kids are crazy as a dizzy goat, I tell you. Plumb crazy.

About the Author:

Dianne Venetta lives in Central Florida with her husband, two children and part-time Yellow Lab Cody-boy! An avid gardener, she spends her spare time growing organic vegetables, surprised by what she finds there every day. Who knew there were so many amazing similarities between men and plants? Women, life and love and her discoveries along the way provide for never-ending fun on her garden blog: BloominThyme.com.

You can also find her on twitter @DianneVenetta and facebook.com/DianneVenetta. Plus, learn how you can become a member of her street team, Bloomin' Warriors, where you'll be eligible for special discounts, advance excerpts, author swag and unique gift items throughout the year. For full details, be sure to check out her website, DianneVenetta.com.

Other novels by Dianne Venetta
Romantic Women's Fiction
The Gables Trilogy:
JENNIFER'S GARDEN
LUST ON THE ROCKS
WHISPER PRIVILEGES

Women's Fiction
CONDEMN ME NOT

Mystery/Romance Fiction
Ladd Springs Series:
LADD SPRINGS #1
LADD FORTUNE #2
HOTEL LADD #3
LADD HAVEN #4
LOSING LADD #5

Read an excerpt from Ladd Fortune...

Chapter One

Lacy Owens tamped down the flutter of pulse skirting through her chest. Parked across the street from the salon, she stared at the day spa, the mirrored glass display window splashed with fancy lettering. Trendz. Inserted between a sandwich shop and an insurance office, it was painted glossy black and stood out like a bald eagle in a blue sky. The hoagie shop to the right had been there for as long as Lacy could remember, its exterior faded to drab beige. The insurance agency was new and remarkably boring, its window marked by white block letters spelling out the company name and agent. Beyond the building, the green hills of Tennessee rose into the sky, a batch of patchy white clouds floating lazily in the distance.

Would Annie be happy to see her? Would she be angry? Lacy's breathing grew shallow. The temperature in the car was rising, heat pressing in on her. Their reunion could go either way. Knowing Annie, she'd try and toss her baby sister out on the sidewalk with a kick to the rump—which would hurt, in more ways than one.

While Annie might throw her out on sight, Lacy had to try. It was meant to be. She knew it the minute Jeremiah Ladd walked into the lounge, announcing to his girlfriend, Loretta Flynn, they were headed for Ladd Springs. Ladd Springs. Tennessee. *Home.*

It was her opportunity. The stars were in alignment. That very day her horoscope said it was time for a return to the fold. Lacy nibbled at her lip, fiddled with the steering wheel. Atlanta had never been home. Atlanta had been her escape.

A woman pushed out through the front door of Trendz, her brown hair straight and shiny in the midday sun, her clothes fitted and chic. Lacy wondered if the woman had had her nails done. Was Annie in there? Lacy glanced at the clock on her dashboard. Three o'clock. She slid her gaze back to the salon. Annie would have to be, wouldn't she? She still worked full-time, didn't she?

Nerves sputtered and popped. Grabbing a slim leather purse from the passenger seat, Lacy pushed opened her car door and headed in. It was now or never. Hopefully, Annie would understand. Hopefully, she'd forgive her. Hope was all she had. As Lacy crossed the street, her legs felt boneless, like she'd dissolve into a mess on the street, this instant. It was a wonder she could even walk! But walk she would. She'd walk straight into that salon and face her sister, once and for all. It was time. This mess between them had gone on too long and it had to stop.

Lacy opened the salon door and was immediately sucked in by the strong scent of hair products, nail polish and per-fume. Her heart thudded as she scanned the salon's interior. A line of mirrored stations manned by a bevy of women dressed in black created a corridor down the center. Each stood by their chairs wielding blow dryers, flat irons and scis-sors over their clients. From above, drips of blue hung down in the form of ceramic lighting. Lacy thought the subtle hues very modern, very sophisticated. Venturing in a few steps, she noticed the nail station was empty. Her spirits fell. No Annie. She heaved a sigh, eyeing the receptionist who sat smiling behind her check-in desk. She was a perky young blonde who didn't look a day over fifteen.

"May I help you?" the girl asked.

"Um..." Lacy hesitated. She looped short curls of hair behind an ear. Should she ask about Annie? Should she leave her name, thus warning her sister of her arrival?

Absolutely not. A surprise visit was best, sort of a spon-taneous reunion where she could gauge her sister's reaction on the spot and respond accordingly. "Well..." Lacy paused, suddenly second-guessing her entire scheme. "I was wonder-ing about having my nails done."

"Great! We have a nail tech who's the best in the business."

Lacy didn't doubt it. When she and Annie were kids, her older sister forever practiced on her nails, creating stripes, polka dots—the works. Lacy had always been amazed by her sister's uncanny ability to "stay within the lines" as she painted and wished she could have done as well, but she never could. Polish forever smudged and dripped. Annie was good with hair, too. Lacy could apply makeup, but hair and nails were Annie's area of expertise. "Hm," she hedged, "do you happen to know her name?"

The receptionist looked at her queerly.

Dingbat—of course she did! She worked here, didn't she? Flummoxed, Lacy clarified, "I mean, I want to make sure it's the same woman my friend recommended."

"Annie Owens. Is that who you were looking for?"

Lacy's heart raced at the confirmation. She nodded.

Flipping through pages in her appointment book, the receptionist said, "She has availability Friday afternoon, and then next week." She dragged her pencil lightly down the page and said, "Tuesday morning and Wednesday afternoon." Checking with Lacy, she asked, "Will any of those work for you?"

But Lacy didn't answer. In the back of the salon, Annie had emerged and currently stood immobile in the center aisle. Dryers whirred, conversation chattered, but Annie only had eyes for Lacy.

Lacy gulped. Without looking at the young woman, stammered, "Um, let me think about it, okay?"

"Sure thing," the receptionist replied.

Annie came to life and approached Lacy with a hard line in her gaze, a chop to her step. Familiar blue eyes bore into her. Annie's wrath arrived ten steps ahead of her, followed by a sharp whoosh of displeasure, which strummed in the air around them as the woman stood face-to-face. "What are you doing here?"

Despite her sister's animosity, Lacy thought Annie looked good. Her hair was shorter now, cut into a cute page-boy, her black-clad figure trim. Her makeup was flattering in shades of pink and other than the vile look in her eyes, Lacy discovered her sister had grown into an attractive woman. "Hi, Annie." Lacy gave a short wave, flushing with an uncomfortable awkwardness.

Apparently catching onto the underpinnings of anger between Lacy and Annie, the receptionist closed her book and busied herself with something on her desk.

"I asked you a question," Annie repeated flatly.

Lacy shuddered beneath the caustic tone. People could hear her! "I wanted to let you know that I'm back in town," she ventured softly.

"Why?"

"Um..." She bit her lip, averting the gaze of the receptionist, the inquisitive glances from hairstylists. "Because we're family, why else?"

"Is Jeremiah with you?"

Without thinking, Lacy nodded.

Loathing poured into Annie's expression. "So you two are still together."

"No!" Lacy exclaimed, pressing a hand to her chest. "Oh, no, we're not together at all!"

Annie's eyes narrowed to slits. "Then why would he be here same time as you? Coincidence?"

"No. He's with my friend Loretta. Loretta Flynn."

"Your friend?" Annie asked, disbelief crawling through her eyes.

"Yes, yes—we work together at a lounge in Atlanta." Or did. She'd quit on her way out the door as she headed home for Tennessee. "That's how I know he's here. He told Loretta he was coming home and I...I..." Lacy didn't know exactly how to say it. *I needed an escape*? *I wanted to come back home*? By the icy nature of Annie's reception, it didn't seem like her sister much cared why Lacy had returned. Only that she had—and it wasn't good news.

"What do you want?"

Lacy glanced about the immediate vicinity. Was the middle of the salon's entrance really the place to be having this discussion?

As though taking her cue, Annie stalked off toward a white leather nail chair. Beside it sat a square black ottoman, a pristine white towel draped over one side. A myriad polish bottles lined the work table, shades ranging from the sheerest of pinks to the darkest of plums. Files and clippers were lined neatly to one side, the workspace made all the brighter by a petite but powerful black lamp. Lacy thought her sister had come a long way from the rinky-dink salon in which she started her career as a teenager. From what Lacy could tell, Trendz was top of the line, as nice as any in Atlanta and a surprise find in this backwoods town. When Lacy lived here, the fanciest store they had going was the flower shop, and they only stayed afloat because of weddings and funerals.

Struggling to continue the conversation with something harmless, Lacy decided on a compliment. "This is a nice place you work in."

"This isn't a social call."

"Isn't it?"

Annie glowered, crossing arms over her chest. "What do you want, Lacy?"

"I'm here to say hello."

"Goodbye."

Lacy reached out for her sister but quickly rethought the gesture. Annie looked as if she might bite her arm off. "Annie," she pleaded, "what about all the letters I wrote you? Why didn't you write back?"

"Because I had nothing to say to you. Still don't."

Crestfallen, Lacy couldn't believe her ears. This wasn't how she'd envisioned their reunion. Rocky, maybe. Thorny, possibly. But absolute rejection? Her sister didn't even want to try? Sliding a hand up her narrow purse strap, Lacy asked, "Can't we catch up on old times? Get back in touch?"

"The old times I remember are you running off with my boyfriend. Sorry, but it's not something I care to catch up on."

"But Jeremiah wasn't really your—" Lacy scrambled for reason. She'd never thought that Annie and Jeremiah were a serious couple. Jeremiah had been with so many others. Could Annie really be that upset she'd moved to Atlanta with him?

"He was my boyfriend," Annie declared, "the one you decided to chase to Atlanta. The fact that he wasn't faithful doesn't change the truth."

Lacy breathed easier. *So she did know.* Then why so mad? "I'm sorry, Annie. I just thought—"

"Thought what? That because he was playing around behind my back, it might as well be you he was playing with?" Disgust rolled through Annie's expression. "You're dead to me."

"Annie Grace!" Lacy cried, punctured by the hateful remark.

"What?" A glimmer of pleasure crept into her sister's gaze. "You don't like hearing the truth?"

Lacy smoothed the ruffled layers of her blouse and searched for onlookers. Eavesdroppers in these parts were as common as oxygen and sure as she was breathing, Lacy knew word would get out about her arrival and this dreadful showdown. But Lacy would not be deterred. "Annie, the truth has more sides than one. I'm sorry you're upset with me about going to Atlanta with Jeremiah, but I thought you two had broken up."

Annie laughed, the sound biting to Lacy's ears. "And I'm supposed to stand here for a lecture on the truth from someone who wouldn't know the truth if it jumped up and smacked her on the head?"

"*Annie.*"

"Don't *Annie*, me. You fibbed as a child and you fibbed as a teenager. I don't expect it to change."

Tears pushed behind her eyes, but Lacy held them in check. She didn't want to break down in front of her sister, the entire salon. It was bad enough people were staring at her from clear across the room. They didn't have to witness her losing it completely.

Lacy pushed back her shoulders and said plainly, "I'm sorry, Annie."

"You're darn right, you are."

Staring into Annie's blue eyes, the black pupils punctuated by white from an overhead drip light, Lacy's heart fell. "This was a mistake," she said quietly. She had hoped to make amends. She had hoped to forgive and forget and move forward with the only family she had left. Daddy was dead, Momma was gone. Annie was it.

Lacy turned to go but stopped. Lifting her chin, she said, "I'm truly sorry about Jeremiah. If I had known you believed he was still your boyfriend, I wouldn't have run off with him. I thought you two were over."

"Save it for the choir boys, will you? Your pouts don't impress me."

Lacy nodded and a heavy tear burst free. "See you around," she said, and plodded toward the door.

"Why don't you go back to Atlanta where you belong," Annie flung at her back.

Because Atlanta isn't home. Lacy pushed out through the front door, the sun bright, the air a blanket of warmth enveloping her body. She breathed in deeply, but expelled the breath in a rush of despair. Annie hated her. Pure and simple. She hated her sister, her own flesh and blood, and would never forgive her. Tears flowed, but Lacy wiped them away. She wouldn't give her sister the satisfaction of hurting her. She wouldn't let Annie know how desperately she had wanted back into her life.

Plodding to a stop, she looked both ways and waited for a slow moving truck to pass. Lacy had been lonely in Atlanta. Not alone, but lonely. Men were always ready and available, but none were interested in her for who she was, what she had to offer as a person. They only wanted what she could do for them, her manager a case in point. He'd chased her, hired her, but the minute she gave in to his advances, he became expectant. Demanding. She had to play by his rules and his rules only. Lacy crossed the street, her calves contracting tightly as she ran across the pavement in heels.

Well, Lacy Owens played by her own rules. She was the boss of her destiny and no man, no how, was going to dictate to her what she was and was not allowed to do—especially when it came to the attention from other men. *How would she ever find Mr. Right if she didn't entertain their flirtations?*

She wouldn't. Besides, she loved men! Men were bold and daring. They were big and strong. Joy sizzled through her veins. Men were smart. Men would help guide her to her destiny, slide over the rainbow with her and share in the treasure of gold waiting at the other end. Pressing the key fob to unlock her car door, she heaved a sigh. Some man would, anyway. Jeremiah had turned out to be a fool, but that didn't mean all men were. Where Annie didn't know he was a two-timing cheat, Lacy did, but she hadn't cared. The day he asked her to join him on his way out of Ladd Springs was the day she'd believed her life would take a turn for the better. They were going to the big city, the land of opportunity.

Unfortunately, opportunity didn't always look the way a girl wanted it to look. Lacy dried her eyes, got into her car and drove to her Aunt Frannie's diner. Time to break the news that her "girls" weren't getting back together.